Daughters of the Promise
Community Tree

Huyards

Abraham (Abe) ⏉ Mary Ellen

Matthew   Luke   Linda (adopted)

Saunders

Kade ⏉ Sadie

Tyler   Marie

Ebersols

Bishop's Grandchildren

Stephen   Hannah   Annie

Millers

Irma Rose (D) ⏉ Jonas — Lizzie

Sarah Jane
|
Lillian

Dronbergers

Josephine — Robert
|
Linda

Barbie Beiler

Bed & Breakfast

Stoltzfuses

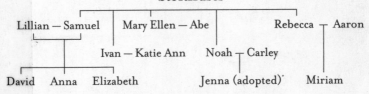

Lillian — Samuel   Mary Ellen — Abe   Rebecca ⏉ Aaron

Ivan — Katie Ann   Noah ⏉ Carley

David   Anna   Elizabeth   Jenna (adopted)   Miriam

Other Novels by Beth Wiseman Include:

Plain Promise

Plain Pursuit

Plain Perfect

Novellas found in:

An Amish Gathering

An Amish Christmas

Plain Paradise

A Daughters of the Promise Novel

BETH WISEMAN

THOMAS NELSON
Since 1798

NASHVILLE   DALLAS   MEXICO CITY   RIO DE JANEIRO

To Barbie Beiler

Published in Nashville, Tennessee, by Thomas Nelson. Thomas Nelson is a registered trademark of Thomas Nelson, Inc.

Thomas Nelson, Inc., titles may be purchased in bulk for educational, business, fund-raising, or sales promotional use. For information, please e-mail SpecialMarkets@ThomasNelson.com.

Library of Congress Cataloging-in-Publication Data

Wiseman, Beth, 1962–
    Plain paradise : a Daughters of the promise novel / Beth Wiseman.
      p. cm.
    ISBN 978-1-59554-823-8 (soft cover)
    1. Amish—Fiction. I. Title.
    PS3623.I83P56 2010
    813'.6—dc22   2009052637

Printed in the United States of America

10 11 12 13 14 RRD 5 4 3 2

Pennsylvania Dutch Glossary

ab im kopp: off in the head
Aamen: Amen
ach: oh
aenti: aunt
boppli: baby or babies
daadi: grandfather
daed: dad
danki: thanks
Die Botschaft: a weekly newspaper serving Old Order Amish
   communities everywhere
dippy eggs: eggs cooked over easy
Englisch: a non-Amish person
es dutt mir leed: I am sorry
fraa: wife
gut: good
gut-n-owed: good evening
hatt: hard
haus: house
kaffi: coffee

kapp: prayer covering or cap

kinner: children or grandchildren

lieb: love

maed or maedel: girl or girls

make wet: rain

mamm: mom

mammi: grandmother

mei: my

mudder: mother

onkel: uncle

Ordnung: the written and unwritten rules of the Amish; the
   understood behavior by which the Amish are expected to live,
   passed down from generation to generation. Most Amish
   know the rules by heart.

Pennsylvania *Deitsch:* Pennsylvania German, the language most
   commonly used by the Amish

rumschpringe: running-around period when a teenager turns
   sixteen-years-old

schtinker: irritable person

scrapple: traditional dish containing leftover pieces of the pig
   mixed with cornmeal and flour

umgwehnlich: unusual

ya: yes

JOSEPHINE DRONBERGER ADJUSTED HER DARK SUNGLASSES as she stared at the faceless dolls on display. She lifted one to eye level then eased her way closer to Linda. Turning the figure about, she pretended to study it even though her eyes were on the seventeen-year-old Amish girl standing with two friends at the neighboring booth.

She inched closer, as if somehow just being near Linda would comfort her. Then she heard one of the girls talking in Pennsylvania *Deitsch*, the dialect most Amish speak and one she regularly heard at the farmer's market. Josie pushed her glasses down on her nose and slowly turned to her left, feeling like the stalker she had become over the past few weeks. She drew in a deep breath and blew it out slowly.

Two of the girls were wearing dark green dresses with black aprons. Linda was clothed in a dress of the same style, but it was deep blue, and Josie instantly wondered if Linda's eyes were still a sapphire color. All of them wore prayer coverings on their heads, as was expected. Not much had changed since the last time Josie had been in Lancaster County.

She watched one of the girls fondling a silver chain hanging on a rack filled with jewelry. Linda reached forward and removed a necklace, then held it up for the other girls to see. Again they spoke to each other in a language Josie didn't understand.

Josie knew she was staring, so she forced herself to swivel forward, and once more she pretended to be interested in the doll with no face, staring hard into the plain white fabric. Until recently, that's how Linda had looked in Josie's mind.

She placed the doll back on the counter alongside the others and then wiped sweaty palms on her blue jeans before taking two steps closer to the girls who were still ogling the necklaces. Jewelry wasn't allowed in the Old Order Amish communities, but Josie knew enough about the Amish to know that girls of their age were in their *rumschpringe*, a running around period that begins at sixteen—a time when certain privileges are allowed up until baptism. Josie watched Linda hand the woman behind the counter the necklace. Then she reached into the pocket of her apron and pulled out her money.

Josie moved over to the rack of necklaces and glanced at the girls. Linda completed her purchase, then turned in Josie's direction so one of her friends could clasp the necklace behind her neck. Josie stared at the small silver cross that hung from a silver chain, then she let her eyes veer upward and gazed at the pretty girl who stood before her now, with blue eyes, light-brown hair tucked beneath her cap, and a gentle smile.

"That's lovely." Josie's words caught in her throat as she pointed to the necklace. Linda looked down at the silver cross and held it out with one hand so she could see it, then looked back up at Josie.

"*Danki*." She quickly turned back toward her friends.

No, wait. Let me look at you a while longer.

But she walked away, and Josie stared at the girls until they rounded the corner. She spun the rack full of necklaces until she found the cross on a silver chain like Linda's.

"I'll take that one," she told the clerk as she pointed to the piece of jewelry. "And no need to put it in a bag."

Josie handed the woman a twenty-dollar bill and waited for her change. She glanced at the Rolex on her left wrist. Then she unhooked the clasp of the necklace she was wearing, an anniversary present from Robert—an exquisite turquoise drop that he'd picked up while traveling in Europe for business. She dropped the necklace into her purse while the woman waited for Josie to accept her purchase.

"Thank you." Josie lifted her shoulder-length hair, dyed a honey-blonde, and she hooked the tiny clasp behind her neck. The silver cross rested lightly against her chest, but it felt as heavy as the regret she'd carried for seventeen years.

Josie straightened the collar on her white blouse. She cradled the small cross in her hand and stared at it. There was a time when such a trinket would have symbolized the strong Catholic upbringing she'd had and her faith in God. But those days were behind her. Now the silver cross symbolized a bond with Linda.

Mary Ellen scurried around the kitchen in a rush to finish supper by five o'clock and wondered why her daughter wasn't home to help prepare the meal. She knew Linda went to market with two friends, but she should have been back well before now. Abe and the boys would be hungry when they finished work for the day. Mary Ellen suspected they were done in the fields and milking the cows about now.

She glanced at the clock. Four thirty. A nice cross-breeze swept through the kitchen as she pulled a ham loaf from the oven, enough to gently blow loose strands of dark-brown-and-gray hair that had fallen from beneath her *kapp*. It was a tad warm for mid-May, but Mary Ellen couldn't complain; she knew the sweltering summer heat would be on them soon enough. She placed the loaf on the table already set for five. Her potatoes were ready for mashing, and the barbequed string beans were keeping warm in the oven.

The clippety-clop of hooves let her know that Linda was home. Her daughter had been driving the buggy for nearly two years on her own, but Mary Ellen still felt a sense of relief each time Linda pulled into the driveway, especially when she was traveling to Bird-In-Hand, a high-traffic town frequented by the tourists.

"Hi, *Mamm*. Sorry I'm late." The screen door slammed behind Linda as she entered the kitchen. Her daughter kicked off her shoes, walked to the refrigerator, and pulled out two jars of jam. "We lost track of the time." Linda placed the glass containers on the table.

"The applesauce is in the bowl on the left." Mary Ellen pointed toward the refrigerator, then began mashing her potatoes.

Linda walked back to the refrigerator to retrieve the applesauce, and Mary Ellen noticed a silver chain around her daughter's neck, tucked beneath the front of her dress. She remembered buying a necklace when she was Linda's age, during her own *rumschpringe*. No harm done.

"I see you purchased a necklace." She stepped in front of Linda and gently pulled a silver cross from its hiding place. "This is very pretty." Mary Ellen smiled before returning to her potatoes. "But I reckon it'd be best if you took it off before supper, no? Your *daed* knows there will be these kinds of purchases during *rumschpringe*, but I see no need to show it off in front of him."

"But it's only a necklace. That's not so bad." Linda reached around to the back of her neck, and within a few moments, she was holding the chain in her hand. "Do you know that Amos Dienner bought a car during his *rumschpringe*?" Linda's brows raised in disbelief. "His folks know he has it, but they make him park it in the woods back behind their house." She giggled. "I wonder what *Daed* would do if I came home with a car and parked it back behind our house?"

"I think you best not push your father that far. He has been real tolerant of the time you've spent with *Englisch* friends, riding in their cars, going to movies, and . . ." Mary Ellen sighed. "I shudder to think what else."

"Want me to tell you what all we do in town?" Linda's voice was mysterious, as if she held many secrets.

Mary Ellen pulled the string beans from the oven. "No. I don't want to know." She shook her head all the way to the table, then placed the casserole dish beside the ham loaf. "Be best I not know what you do with your friends during this time."

"*Ach, Mamm*. We don't do anything bad." Linda walked to her mother and kissed her on the cheek. "I don't even like the taste of beer."

Mary Ellen turned to her daughter and slammed her hands to her hips. "Linda!"

Linda laughed. "*Mamm!* I'm jokin' with you. I've never even *tried* beer." She twisted her face into a momentary scowl, then headed toward the stairs. "I guess I'll go put my new necklace away."

Mary Ellen believed Linda. She trusted her eldest child, and she was thankful for the close relationship they shared. Linda's adventurous spirit bubbled in her laugh and shone in her eyes, but she was respectful of her parents and the rules. If going to the movies and buying a necklace were the worst things her daughter did during this running-around period, she'd thank God for that.

"Something smells mighty *gut* in here." Abe came through the kitchen entrance, kicking his shoes off near Linda's. Mary Ellen could hear her sons padding up the porch steps.

Eyeing the growing pile of shoes, she said, "I don't know why everyone insists on comin' through the kitchen when there is a perfectly *gut* door that goes from the porch to the den." She pointed to the shoes. "I reckon I'd like to have those dirty shoes in my den and not in my kitchen."

Abe closed the space between them, kissed Mary Ellen on the cheek, then whispered in her ear. "But you are always in the kitchen, and it's your face I long to see after a hard day's work." He pulled her close to him.

"Abe . . ." She nodded toward her two sons, who were now adding their shoes to the others, and she gently pushed her husband away. "The children." She tried to hide her reddening cheeks, but she was thankful that her husband of nineteen years could still cause her to blush. He winked at her as he took his seat at the head of the table.

She heard Matthew make a small grunting sound before sitting at one of the wooden benches lining the sides of the oblong table. Mary Ellen glanced at her oldest son, noticing his slight smile. He looked exactly like his father, minus the beard. Dark brown hair, broad shoulders, and a distinctive square jawline that ran in the Huyard family.

She shivered when she thought about how Matthew only had one more year until his running-around phase, and Luke was only a year behind him. Three children all in their *rumschpringe* at the same time. Unless, of course, Stephen Ebersol proposed to Linda soon, as they all suspected would happen any day. Linda would be eighteen in August, and they'd been dating for over a year. Mary Ellen knew there would be enough time to plan a wedding by this November or December—the time designated for weddings, after the fall harvest—but she hoped they would wait until the following year to wed. Another year of dating would be good for them.

"Someone's here," Linda said as she walked back into the kitchen. "I saw a buggy comin' up the drive from my upstairs window."

"It's the supper hour," Abe grumbled.

Mary Ellen wiped her hands on her apron and joined Linda by the screen door. They waited until a face came into view.

"It's Lillian!" Linda darted down the porch steps.

Mary Ellen knew how much Linda loved her aunt. When her brother Samuel had married Lillian several years ago, Lillian became a wonderful stepmother to David, Samuel's son. Then they added two lovely daughters, Anna and Elizabeth, to their family. But Mary Ellen couldn't help but worry why Lillian would show up at suppertime. *I hope Jonas is all right.*

Lillian's grandfather, Jonas Miller, had been battling cancer and Alzheimer's disease for years, but he'd taken a turn for the worse recently. Everyone adored Jonas. He was a pillar of faith in their community and had an unforgettable—if not contrary—charm that drew people to him.

"Is everything okay?" Mary Ellen opened the door and motioned Lillian inside. Linda followed.

"Hello to everyone," Lillian said with a wave of her hand, but it wasn't in her usual chipper manner. "I'm sorry to come callin' at this time of day. I can see you are about to eat. But I was on my way home from work, and this was on my way, so I told Samuel I was going to stop in."

Mary Ellen took a step closer to her sister-in-law. "Is it Jonas?"

"*Ya.*" Lillian hung her head for a moment, then looked back up at Mary Ellen. "*Mamm* had to put him in the hospital this morning. She can't get him to eat, and his blood pressure has been really high."

"Oh, no, Lillian. I'm so sorry to hear that." Mary Ellen shook her head. "I could see this comin'. He looked awful poor last time I saw him." Jonas lived with his daughter, Sarah Jane, and his wife Lizzie, but Mary Ellen knew most of the caregiving fell on his daughter. Lizzie was up in years, and even though she was in much better shape than her husband, she still had medical needs of her own.

Lillian sighed. "As you can imagine, Grandpa was not happy about it." Then she smiled. "He said the *Englisch* will kill him before his time."

Mary Ellen smiled in return. "The *Englisch* will have their hands full with Jonas, I'm sure."

Jonas's offbeat personality wasn't typical of someone in their district. But poor Lizzie. Jonas married Lizzie almost four years ago, after his first wife had passed. Lizzie was going to be lost without Jonas.

Abe stood up. "I'm sorry to hear that Jonas is down, Lillian. Is there anything we can do for your family?"

"No, Abe. But *danki*. Samuel and David take care of things at

Mamm and Grandpa's. I just wanted to let you know. Grandpa is in Lancaster General."

"Can we visit him?" Linda asked.

"*Ya.* He can have visitors." Lillian paused. "I best be gettin' home. I have to stop by Rebecca's and pick up Anna and Elizabeth. And Samuel and David will be hungry."

Matthew stood up from the table, then Luke rose alongside him. "Lillian," Matthew said, "we'll help any way we can."

Luke straightened as if to reach the same height as Matthew, but he was still an inch or so shorter. "Me too, Lillian. I'll help."

Her youngest son sported the Huyard jaw too, but Mary Ellen always thought he looked more like her own father, from what she could remember; he'd died when she was a young girl. Her mother still lived nearby, and they saw her from time to time. But Abe's parents lived in a neighboring district, and they didn't get to see them as often.

Abe shook Lillian's hand, as did both his sons. It warmed Mary Ellen's heart to see the fine young men her boys were turning into. She followed Lillian out the door, Linda by her side.

She hugged her sister-in-law, and Linda did the same.

"We're here for you, Lillian," Linda said. "Tell Sarah Jane and Lizzie, okay?"

Mary Ellen echoed her daughter's sentiments, and they both waved as Lillian drove away. Abe and the boys were waiting patiently when they returned to the kitchen. Mary Ellen took her seat at the opposite end from Abe, and Linda slid onto the wooden bench across from the boys.

"Let us pray," Abe said. They all bowed their heads in silent prayer.

When they were done, Luke picked up the bowl of mashed potatoes and asked, "Is Jonas gonna die?"

"Don't say that!" Linda blasted. "He's just sick, and he's in the hospital until he feels better." She snatched the potatoes from her brother's outstretched hand and cut her eyes at him, mumbling something under her breath.

"Watch your tone, Linda," Abe warned.

Mary Ellen knew Abe didn't like much conversation during the supper hour, and he certainly didn't like any upset. Or visitors for that matter. But he loved Lillian, and Mary Ellen knew that he was glad she stopped by.

Mary Ellen also knew that she would need to prepare her children about Jonas at some point. Jonas was like everyone's grandpa, and Lillian shared him with the community, but it was evident to Mary Ellen that Jonas was on a steady decline.

Luke had taken his first ride on a scooter as a young boy, with Jonas coaching from the sidelines, and Jonas had given Matthew lessons driving the buggy when Abe was busy in the fields. But it was Linda who had spent the most time with Jonas, particularly over the past couple of years. Jonas had taught her to play chess, and Linda took every opportunity to sneak off to challenge him to a game. It was only a matter of time for Jonas, and all the adults knew it. The cancer had been getting worse and worse.

"Jonas could get better." Linda swirled her fork amidst the string beans. "They have chemo—chemo something—that cures cancer."

"It isn't a cure, Linda," Abe said. "It's a treatment. I reckon sometimes it works, but . . ." Her husband's voice trailed off when he saw his daughter's eyes tear up. "We will say extra prayers for Jonas during our devotions each day."

Mary Ellen spooned potatoes onto her plate. She wasn't sure

what to pray for. To pray for an extension of Jonas's life could cause much pain and suffering for him.

"Tomorrow, I have some sewing to do, *Mamm*, but not too much else. I was planning to spend the day with Stephen after that." She paused with her fork full of beans. "Maybe Barbie will take Stephen and me to see Jonas."

Barbie was their *Englisch* friend who ran Beiler's Bed and Breakfast off of Lincoln Highway. She was wonderful about providing rides for people in their district. Barbie's husband grew up Amish, and even though he was no longer Amish, they had strong ties to the community.

"That would be nice," Mary Ellen said. "But doesn't Stephen have to work at the furniture store tomorrow?"

"No, Abner gave him the day off because he worked all last week and then on Saturday too."

"I reckon it would be all right, if you finish your chores around here in the morning."

After they finished supper, Abe retired to the den, and the boys headed outside to tend to the two horses. Linda was helping Mary Ellen clear the table when they heard a car coming up the driveway.

"Are you expecting someone?" Mary Ellen tried to keep the edge from her voice. Linda's *Englisch* friends showed up too often these days. Mary Ellen knew this was normal for someone Linda's age, but it bothered her just the same. When she faced up to the reason why, it was because she had less time with Linda, and she was forced to accept the fact that Linda wasn't the same little girl who had glued herself to Mary Ellen's side since she was young. They'd always been close, and Mary Ellen wanted to selfishly savor the time she had left with Linda before her daughter would go and make a home with Stephen.

"No. I'm not expecting anyone." Linda put two dirty dishes in the sink, then strained to see out the window, past the begonias blooming on the windowsill. "It's a blue car, the kind that's like a truck and a car all in one."

Mary Ellen walked to the kitchen door and watched the blue SUV pull to a stop. Linda walked to her side.

"She's pretty," Linda said as the woman exited her automobile and stepped gingerly onto cobblestone steps that led to the porch, wearing high-heeled silver shoes.

Mary Ellen agreed. The tall *Englisch* woman was thin, yet shapely, dressed in denim pants and a white blouse. Her hair was the color of honey and rested slightly above her shoulders. Her dark sunglasses covered a large portion of her face, but her painted features were most attractive. Mary Ellen didn't recognize her to be any of their non-Amish friends.

Linda let out a small gasp as the woman neared the door, then whispered, "I saw her at market today."

The woman came up the porch steps. "Hello," Mary Ellen said. "Can we help you?" She pushed the screen door open.

"Mary Ellen?"

"*Ya.*"

The woman pulled the dark shades from her face, and Mary Ellen tried to recall where she'd seen the woman before. She was now most familiar looking, but Mary Ellen couldn't place her.

"I—I was hoping to talk to you." The stranger's bottom lip trembled, and she sucked in a deep breath. She glanced at Linda, then back at Mary Ellen. "Alone, if that's okay."

"Is something wrong?" Mary Ellen pushed the screen door wide. "Would you like to come in?"

The woman didn't move but bit her trembling lip for a moment and pushed back her wavy locks with her hand. "You probably don't recognize me. It's been a long time since I've seen you, and—" She took another deep breath, and Mary Ellen struggled to recall where she knew the woman from. "My name is Josie. Josephine Dronberger. I mean—well, it's Dronberger now. It used to be Josephine Wallace."

Mary Ellen's chest grew tight as she remembered where she'd seen the woman before—no longer a scared seventeen-year-old girl but a mature woman, beautiful and fancy. Mary Ellen fought a wave of apprehension that coursed through her. Instinctively, she pushed Linda backward and stepped in front of her.

"*Mamm,*" Linda whispered with irritation, stumbling slightly. "What are you doing?"

Mary Ellen ignored her daughter as her heart thumped at an unhealthy rate. She gazed intently into the woman's eyes, which were now filling with tears.

"I'm sorry to just show up like this, but I—"

"Now is not a good time," Mary Ellen interrupted. She held her head high, fighting her own tears as well. She stepped backward, pushing Linda along with her, until the screen door closed between her and Josephine. "Perhaps another time." She managed a tremulous smile, but she knew Linda would question her about who the woman was the minute Josephine was gone.

Josephine's lip began to tremble even more, and a tear spilled over thick lashes, which she quickly wiped away. "Please. I'll just leave you my number. Maybe you can call me when it's a better time. Please . . ." She reached into the back pocket of her blue jeans and pulled out a card.

Mary Ellen watched with fearful fascination at how Josephine's brows cinched inward, how she slowly closed her eyes, and the way her trembling mouth thinned as she pressed her lips together. The same expression Linda had always had when she was hurting a great deal about something.

"*Mamm?*" Linda edged around her mother, gave Mary Ellen a questioning look, and then stared at the woman. The resemblance was eerie, and Mary Ellen wondered what might be going through Linda's mind.

"*Ya,*" she said to Josephine. "I—I will call you when it's a better time."

Josephine pushed the card in Mary Ellen's direction. "Call me any time. My home phone number and my cell number are both on the card." She sniffed. "I'm sorry."

Mary Ellen took the card, and Josephine smiled slightly, then fixed her eyes on Linda.

"I will call you." Mary Ellen hastily pulled Linda into the kitchen enough where she could push the wooden door between them and Josephine. It closed with a thud, and Mary Ellen's stomach churned with anxiety. Linda was going to have questions, but she needed to talk to Abe first. She needed Abe to tell her that everything would be all right.

Linda ran to the window and watched Josephine get in her car. "*Mamm,* who is that woman? And why was she crying? Why were you acting so strange? Do you know her, or . . ."

Mary Ellen pressed her hands against her chest, still standing and staring at the door, only half hearing Linda's queries, and wondering how the years had gotten away from her without them ever telling Linda that she was adopted.

2

JOSIE SAT ACROSS FROM HER HUSBAND, PICKING AT HER stuffed pork chop and pushing her peas around her plate. Mary Ellen's fearful expression kept flashing through her mind. The last thing she wanted to do was cause Linda and her family any pain, but there just had to be some way for her to share in at least a small part of Linda's life.

"Honey, you're barely touching your food." Robert gazed at her speculatively from his chair on the other side of the dining room table. "Are you feeling all right?"

She scooped some peas onto her fork and forced the bite into her mouth. "I'm eating," she said and began to chew. Maybe her response would convince Robert that her condition hadn't worsened—at least not today. She swallowed, then glanced around the kitchen in their new house, at all the boxes still left to unpack.

"I'm going to hire someone to come unpack these boxes. I don't want you to have to do that." He paused. "Or I can unpack some of them tonight."

"No. I want to do it." She smiled at her husband of twelve years. "But tonight, I just want to cuddle with you on the couch, watch television, and relax. I have all day to unpack these boxes, and I know you're tired from work."

Josie recalled her first trip to Paradise nearly six months earlier, just to verify that Linda still lived with her parents in the Amish community. A woman at the Bird-In-Hand market confirmed that she did. Then, when Robert agreed to relocate to Paradise, Pennsylvania, so that Josie could be near Linda, he'd attained husband-of-the-year status in Josie's eyes. Robert uprooted his law practice, after ten years of working to establish a healthy clientele at the firm he founded. They didn't know anyone in the small town of Paradise, and while geography wasn't an issue for some of his clients, he still lost more than half. Robert had insisted that he was ready to downsize and not work as much, but Josie also knew that he wanted to spend more time with her. Especially now.

"I'm not that tired. Amanda and I finished setting up a filing system today." Robert ate the last of his pork chop, then placed his fork across his plate. "She's a sweet kid. I think she'll work out just fine."

Amanda had answered an ad Robert ran in the local paper for a secretary. He had hired her on the spot, and he was paying her big city wages as opposed to what would be the norm here in Paradise. And Josie knew why. She suspected that Amanda probably had a hard time finding a job, and Robert was always out to help those in need. He took more pro bono cases than he did paying ones.

Robert's new secretary was a petite nineteen-year-old girl who lived nearby in the city of Lancaster, about twenty miles from Paradise. Josie met her on her first day of work over a month ago. Robert had prepared Josie in advance, so she wouldn't be shocked when she saw the girl. Amanda's lips were unnaturally enlarged, almost exuding a duck-like appearance. She'd been born with a cleft palate, which she'd had surgically corrected when she was a young child. However, according to Amanda, it left her lips unusually thin with a scar in the middle of her top lip and impaired her speech. When she turned eighteen, she used the money she'd saved working summer jobs to have her lips enlarged with injections, a new procedure the plastic surgeon promised would enhance her physical appearance and possibly improve her speech.

It didn't work, perhaps because Amanda also had scar tissue on her lip from a childhood bicycle accident. The swelling in Amanda's lips hadn't gone down for the past year, and she didn't have the money to sue the plastic surgeon or get any help for herself. Robert filed suit against the plastic surgeon almost immediately, in an effort to compensate Amanda for her past year of suffering, and offered his services to her for free. There was no guarantee that the plastic surgeon would be held accountable, but Robert met with a local doctor, Dr. Noah Stoltzfus, who was helping him arrange for Amanda to have corrective surgery, regardless of the legal outcome.

When Robert met Noah, who ran a clinic in the heart of Amish Country, he liked the doctor right away. The two had been developing a friendship ever since. Josie wasn't surprised. Everyone loved Robert. No one more so than his wife though.

"Well, I'm a little tired." Josie settled back against her chair and yawned. "But I'm thankful not to have a headache today. That last one I had stayed with me for almost four days."

Josie watched him clear their plates from the table. He was eight years older than her, having just celebrated his forty-second birthday. Josie thought he'd only gotten more handsome with each passing year. He was thirty when they'd married and had a full head of dark hair. Now, his thick mane was a salt-and-pepper

mixture that lent him an air of sophistication. His eyes were shades
of amber and green that changed in different lighting, but they
always brimmed with tenderness and passion. Robert wasn't nearly
as polished as his two partners had been in Chicago, but it was her
husband's ruggedness mixed with a sense of humble power that
attracted her to him in the first place.

She stood up, followed him into the kitchen, then joined him
at the sink. He rinsed, and she loaded the dishwasher.

"Do you think she'll call you?" Robert handed her two spoons.

"I hope so." Josie sighed. "Mary Ellen was having a routine
night with her family until I showed up." She tucked her chin as her
eyes filled with water. "I should have sent a letter first, giving them
all some sort of warning that I was coming. I just thought that if
I spoke to Mary Ellen and Abe in person, it would be harder for
them to say no about me seeing Linda."

Robert turned off the faucet, wiped his hands on a towel, and
turned to her. He clutched her forearms in his strong but gentle
hands. "Josie, I know you don't want to hurt anyone. But I also
know how much you've been looking forward to meeting your
daughter. And I'm afraid you can't have it both ways. I mean, this
will be hard for everyone concerned." He sighed, then gently lifted
her chin. "It's going to take some time for this to soak in for Mary
Ellen and Abe. They'll need time to talk to Linda, and I'm not
sure I'd be expecting a call from them right away. Josie, you're a
good person. I've never known you to intentionally hurt anyone.
Over the years, when we've talked about your daughter, you always
said that someday you wanted to meet her." He shrugged. "Maybe
someday came before you were ready."

"I gave birth to her, Robert. Does that really make her my

daughter? She has a family. A family that I am about to disrupt." She rested her head on his shoulder. "I feel obsessed with knowing her, but I worry about the price of my happiness. Is it really fair to Linda that just because my circumstances have changed, now it's okay to seek her out? Plus, Mary Ellen's expression is etched in my mind, Robert." She looked up at him. "She's so scared. I'm sure she's afraid of losing her daughter and thinks I will try to be a mother to Linda. You and I know that won't happen, but I just need . . ." Robert wiped a tear from her cheek. "I need to know her."

Robert tilted his head slightly and gazed lovingly into her eyes. "Honey, we talked about all this before we made this move. I love you with all my heart, and I know how important this is to you, but you can change your mind at any time."

She ran her finger under her eyes and cleared runny mascara. "I love you so much. And I'm so sorry, Robert. I'm sorry I couldn't give you children. I'm sorry that I'm so obsessed about meeting Linda. You moved your practice for me to be near her. I'm just so—"

Robert gently put a finger to her lip. "Josie, you're my world. I want you to have a peaceful feeling in your heart, and I've loved you since the day I met you. But there's always been something amiss for you. Maybe meeting Linda will fill that void." He smiled. "You certainly can't go on following her around town."

"I know." She shook her head, twisted her mouth to one side. "I've been a stalker."

Robert handed her a bowl. "Okay, my little stalker, let's finish these dishes, and then you can go take a hot bath."

Josie turned toward him again. "What did I ever do to deserve you?"

"Yeah, you're a lucky gal," he teased.

She poked him in the ribs, and he chuckled.

But he was right. She was incredibly lucky to have him in her life. Especially now.

———————

Mary Ellen clutched the sides of her white nightgown and paced the wooden floors in her bedroom, dimly lit by one lantern on her nightstand. *Help me, Dear Lord in heaven, to handle this situation the right way. I need your guidance. Please help me to do Your will without letting my own fears hinder me.*

Abe walked barefoot into their bedroom, his dark hair still wet from his shower and wearing only his black pants. He stroked his beard, which reached the top of a muscular chest covered with wavy brown hair.

"We've made a terrible mistake." His eyes drew together in an agonized expression as he faced Mary Ellen. "We should have known this might happen someday, that the girl's mother—"

"Abe, *I'm* her mother! She's *my* daughter." She walked over to him and fell into his arms. "What does she want after all this time? Why is she doing this to our family?"

"Now, Mary Ellen . . ." He ran his hand the length of her hair. "We must be faithful and trust God to see us through this. Linda is a strong girl, and she—"

"What if she doesn't forgive us for not telling her?" She leaned her head upward and searched his eyes. "Abe, what if she leaves us?"

Abe pushed her gently away and kissed her on the cheek. "She *is* going to leave us soon, Mary Ellen. She's almost eighteen. I reckon she'll marry Stephen and start her own life within the next year or two."

"You know what I mean. What if that Josephine woman has come to claim her, after all these years?"

"*Mei lieb*, it will be up to Linda to decide if she wants to know this woman. You are her *mudder*. You will always be her *mudder*." He sighed, pulled away, and then walked to the other side of the room. In the moonlight, his profile was somber. "But this will be hard for our *maedel*." He shook his head again. "We should have told her."

"Why didn't we?" Mary Ellen walked to the small mirror hung from a silver chain on the wall next to her chest of drawers. She reached up and touched her cheek. "She looks like me. Everyone says so." But then she recalled how much more Linda looked like Josephine, and her heart landed in the pit of her stomach.

"After we asked the community members not to tell her until we felt she was old enough to understand, I reckon the years just got away from us." Abe sat down on the bed. "And now she is a young woman."

Mary Ellen spun around and faced her husband. "I could just not call her back. Maybe she will go away, leave here."

"Mary Ellen, you can't do that." Abe raked a hand through his hair.

"Why not? I don't have to call her." She responded in a tone she'd often scolded her children for using.

Abe patted the side of the bed.

"I can't call her, Abe. I'm afraid," she said while sinking down next to him. She swiped at her eyes and laid her head on his chest. He wrapped an arm around her shoulder.

"I will call her first thing tomorrow morning," he said with authority. "All this guessing about her intentions will do us no *gut*."

Linda sat down on her bed, reached over and flipped on the switch of her battery-operated fan, then leaned her head in front of it to dry her hair a bit. In the evenings, she tried to be the first one in the upstairs bathroom, but tonight both Matt and Luke managed to get their baths before her. Now she'd end up going to sleep with wet hair.

She pulled the comb through tangled strands that ran to her waist and thought about her mother's reaction to the *Englisch* woman who'd shown up earlier. She'd never seen her mother react in such a manner, and Linda couldn't stop speculating about who the woman might be. Although, she had a hunch.

Her parents had celebrated their nineteenth wedding anniversary recently, and Linda knew they were happy, but she'd heard her mother jokingly refer to *Daed's* first girlfriend on occasion—a woman he'd dated before he'd started to date *Mamm*. But Linda thought her name was Naomi, not Josie. And Josie clearly wasn't Amish. *Maybe she was Amish at one time.*

She sat up taller and almost gasped as she recalled what happened to Lena Ann Zook. Lena Ann's husband ran off and left her for another woman, a woman he was seeing behind Lena's back.

No, no, no. Her father would never do that.

Bet that's what Lena Ann's children thought too. She held her head upside down to dry the back of her hair in front of the fan.

She thought about what had happened today, the woman's tearful expression as she pleaded for a return call, and how *Mamm* didn't seem to recognize the woman until she identified herself. When Linda questioned her mother afterward, she had been sharp and told

Linda they would discuss it later. Whoever the woman was, Linda hoped she wouldn't be back. She'd never seen *Mamm* behave in such a way, and one thing was for sure: that woman seemed like trouble.

Abe fastened his suspenders and headed down the stairs, breathing in the aroma of frying bacon and fighting fears about what the day might bring. He'd prayed long and hard last night about this situation that was sure to bring upset to his family, and he'd asked God to guide his words and his actions. He'd prayed for all of them. Josephine too.

He dreaded making the phone call to Josephine, but he knew Mary Ellen didn't have the strength. His wife had tossed and turned most of the night, and there was a sense of desperation surrounding her that Abe could relate to. He hoped his precious daughter could forgive her parents for not sharing the truth with her before the truth came calling unexpectedly.

Mary Ellen was standing at the stove when he entered the kitchen. She flipped the bacon, then turned toward him. Her eyelids were swollen, and Abe wished he could ease her pain. He offered her the best smile he could muster and tried to hide his own fears as he sat down at the kitchen table.

Mathew and Luke waited patiently as Mary Ellen and Linda finished preparing breakfast. Abe didn't have much of an appetite this morning. He gazed at his beautiful daughter who was scurrying around the kitchen, and he wondered how different Linda's life would have been if Josephine had raised her. He thought back seventeen years ago and realized that Josephine was the same age as Linda now, when she showed up on their doorstep.

At the time, Abe and Mary Ellen didn't think it was in the Lord's plan for them to conceive a child since Mary Ellen had been unable to get pregnant. But after they'd adopted Linda, Matthew came two years later, then Luke a year after that. Abe's eyes drifted to Linda's bare feet as she moved toward the refrigerator and pulled out two jars of jam. She had the chubbiest little feet for someone so thin. Adorable feet that she'd loved for Abe to tickle when she was a little girl. Abe swallowed hard as Linda's entire childhood flashed through his mind, and he couldn't seem to take his eyes from his daughter.

"*Daed*, do you need something?" Linda stopped in front of him, holding the jars of jam, her brows raised.

Abe shook his head and fought the unsteadiness in his voice. "No."

Linda shrugged as she walked to the other side of the table.

Matthew and Luke were rambling on about an *Englisch* girl they saw in town who had purple hair, but Abe didn't hear anything else after that. His head was filled with what ifs as he watched Linda place the jars on the table. Mary Ellen would fall to pieces if Linda chose to leave the community to be with her birth mother. Abe filled his lungs with air, then blew out slowly, knowing Mary Ellen would not be the only one to despair if Linda chose a life outside of the community.

But there was one factor largely on their side. Stephen Ebersol. Linda claimed to be madly in love with him, and suddenly Abe found comfort in that thought. For the past few months, he hadn't wanted to hear talk about his daughter and Stephen. He wasn't ready to let her go just yet and hoped that Linda and Stephen would date for another year before mentioning wedding plans.

Now, though, he found himself hoping Stephen would take that next step soon.

"Abe, do you need anything else before I sit down?" Mary Ellen's eyes were heavy with worry, and Abe wished he was able to mask his own emotions better.

"No. *Danki*, though." He forced a smile in Mary Ellen's direction.

Once Mary Ellen and Linda were seated, they bowed their heads in prayer. Luke, Matthew, and Linda filled their plates and, between bites, discussed their plans for the day. Linda was planning to ask Barbie to take her and Stephen to see Jonas after she finished her morning chores, and Luke and Matthew were going to give the barn a fresh coat of white paint, a job that would take them most of the week.

Abe watched his wife trying to keep face in front of her children, smiling when called for, and commenting when appropriate. But he'd been married to Mary Ellen for a long time, and Abe knew it was taking all her effort to keep herself together.

After breakfast, Mary Ellen waited until the children were out of earshot before she spoke of the situation.

"Are you going to call her first thing this morning?" She clutched her apron with both hands. A moment later, she shook her head and paced the wooden floor. "No, no. Maybe I should do it. Maybe I should call her." She stopped walking, then spun to face him. "Abe, let's just don't call her."

Abe got up from the table and walked to his wife. "You know we must call her." He reached for his hat on the rack, placed it on his head, then embraced Mary Ellen. "But I reckon she wouldn't be up this time of morning." Abe eased Mary Ellen out of his arms and nodded toward the window. Only a hint of daylight was visible as the sun began to creep over the horizon. "I have some things to tend to in the barn, and when the daylight is full, I will call her."

Abe was thankful the bishop had started allowing phones in the barns a few years back. Otherwise, he would have to trek over to the Lapp's shanty, and he didn't feel like bumping into anyone right now. He needed time to think.

Mary Ellen folded her hands in front of her and stood a little taller. "I will meet you in the barn after I finish a few things indoors. I should be there when you call her."

Abe nodded. Offering to make the call was the manly thing to do as head of the household, but he'd be glad to have his wife with him when he confronted this woman who threatened to cause much upheaval in their world.

Josie threw her arm across Robert's side of the bed. Empty. She wiped sleep from her eyes, blinked the alarm clock into focus, and forced herself to sit up when she saw that it was almost nine o'clock. She rarely slept that late unless it was a weekend and Robert was by her side. Normally, she got up when Robert left for work during the week, around seven o'clock. Then she recalled the sleeping pill she took the night before, an old prescription that she held on to for nights when she couldn't sleep. She knew sleep wouldn't come, and her doctor had already told her that the pills were compatible with her other medications, if she needed them.

She couldn't help but wonder if Mary Ellen would call today, even though Robert warned her that it might be a couple of days.

She eased her way out of bed and into her robe. It took her

a few moments to recognize the faint beep she was hearing from downstairs. When she realized it was her answering machine, she was suddenly alert and bolted down the stairs. She maneuvered around the maze of boxes in the living room and headed toward the kitchen, her favorite room in the house. She needed its light and cheery atmosphere, with white cabinets and powder blue countertops, lightly-dusted yellow paint on the walls, and a large window that looked out onto freshly tilled soil where Robert had recently planted a garden. Josie had tried to discourage him from the large undertaking, but Robert had always lived in the city, and he wanted to have homegrown vegetables. There was certainly enough room on the five acres that surrounded their new home.

Josie grew up picking peas in her grandparents' garden when she was young. By the time she was ten, she'd made up her mind never to have a garden. Nana and Papa's farm had been right in the middle of Amish Dutch Country in the town of Paradise, where they'd raised their daughters, Josie's mother and her older sister Laura. Every summer, Mom and Dad would drag Josie and her brother, Kenny, to help with Nana and Papa's garden. It was about an hour's drive from where Josie and her family lived in Harrisburg.

Josie loved visiting her grandparents and especially enjoyed playing with the neighboring Amish children. She just didn't care for gardening and always seemed to be the one to stumble into something poisonous or somehow annoy a stinging insect.

Her grandparents had died within a year of each other during Josie's first year of college. Kenny accepted a job in Florida after graduating from college, and he married Stephanie about two years later. When the first grandchild came a few years ago,

Mom and Dad sold the family home in Harrisburg and moved to Florida. Josie hadn't seen her parents in three years.

She recalled her phone conversation with her mother on the night she'd called to tell her that she and Robert would be moving to Lancaster County, to Paradise, to be near Linda.

"You are making a mistake. Why do you want to travel back in time, Josephine?" her mother had asked. "You will only open old wounds. Let the past be the past. Besides, you have far more to worry about than establishing a relationship with that girl."

But for Josie, it was hard to find any peace without facing her past, and she was running out of time. Now, back in Paradise, the past was everywhere.

Josie recalled her trip to the doctor, when he confirmed that she was indeed pregnant at seventeen-years-old.

"Your grandparents are not to know about this," her mother had said on the way home from the appointment, echoed by her father later that evening. "You will go and stay with your Aunt Laura in Chicago until we figure out the best way to handle this."

Mom and Dad told Nana and Papa that Josie was going to Aunt Laura's to finish her last year of high school and then attend college there. But she never saw another day of high school and got her GED instead. College in Chicago did follow but only after Josie was summoned to Paradise to hand her newborn to Mary Ellen and Abraham Huyard just two weeks after she'd given birth. Two glorious weeks during which Josie had called the baby Helen, the name she'd chosen for her daughter.

Josie had begged her aunt and uncle to let her stay with them. She could raise the baby and work. Aunt Laura had said she couldn't go against Mom and Dad's wishes, which were for

Josie to return to Lancaster County and sign adoption papers that had already been drawn up. She remembered the pain of handing over her baby to Mary Ellen on the front porch steps of the farm, where she'd just visited yesterday. Her parents had stood tall behind her. Josie felt like they were forcing a punishment on her by making her give away her baby. Her little Helen.

But it wasn't my fault. I trusted Mr. Kenton.

Larry Kenton was a math teacher at the high school in Harrisburg, and all the girls had a crush on him. But it was Josie he befriended and invited to his house on a cold, December evening, enticing Josie with an offer to help her study for her final exam in trigonometry. She was flattered when he kissed her and told her she was the prettiest girl in the school, but when his hands began to roam, Josie realized that she was in way over her head. She'd kissed boys but never anything beyond that.

Chills ran up her spine as she struggled to push the event from her mind. But at the forefront of her thoughts stayed the hurt and disappointment that her parents wouldn't stand up for her. *He was an adult. A teacher.*

"You were alone with that man in his home, Josephine," her father had said when Josie told her parents what happened three months later, when she was fairly certain she was pregnant. "I'm not sure what you want us to do about this. Larry just doesn't seem like the kind of man who would force himself on someone."

Although her mother was more sympathetic, Josie knew that her parents, pillars of the community, didn't want such a scandal. Their Catholic upbringing prevented them from considering anything but adoption. Mom had met Mary Ellen and Abraham through mutual friends, and Mom knew they'd been trying to have a baby but couldn't conceive. Large families were important to the Amish, and Mom told Josie she was doing God's work by giving her baby to Mary Ellen and Abraham.

She'd hated her parents for a long time after that. Even though she returned to Chicago, her relationship with her aunt was also strained. She went to college during the day and worked nights for three months until she was able to get a small apartment near the campus. Two years later, she had an associate's degree in business management and not much of a relationship with her family. And that was okay.

Over the years, Josie was sure Mom and Dad had run into Linda from time to time before they'd moved to Florida, but Mom swore that she broke contact with Mary Ellen and Abe after the adoption, feeling it was best for everyone. In the beginning, Josie phoned her mother often from Chicago, and with each phone call, Mom had done her best to convince Josie that she would be ruining Linda's life if she caused a ruckus by returning to Lancaster County and seeking claim to her daughter.

Mom and Dad had visited her in Chicago a few times and attended her marriage to Robert, but nothing was ever the same between them. She'd never forgiven them for making a decision that should have been hers to make.

But Linda was seventeen now. And Josie was back in Lancaster County. She didn't care what her parents or anyone else thought about her moving here.

She stared at the number one blinking red on the answering machine, took a deep breath, and then pushed the Play button. At the last second, she wondered if someone other than the Huyards had left a message. Her heart thumped as she waited and hoped to hear Mary Ellen's voice, but instead, a deep, raspy voice came through.

"Hello. This is Abraham Huyard calling for Josephine Dronberger."

3

LINDA TOOK SHALLOW BREATHS AS SHE WALKED DOWN the hallway at Lancaster General. She tried to avoid the odor, which smelled like something *Mamm* used when she cleaned the basement. With each tiny inhalation the stench found its way to her nostrils, igniting memories of the last time she had been in this hospital five years ago. Her Uncle Noah had given her cousin, David, one of his kidneys, but before David was transferred to Philadelphia for the transplant, the family had spent a lot of time here. Both Noah and David were healthy now, but it was a scary time for everyone then. And it made Linda even more fearful about seeing Jonas. She wished Stephen hadn't been called into work at the last minute.

She gently pushed open the door to Jonas's room. Lizzie, Jonas's wife, sat on one side of his bed, and his daughter, Sarah Jane, on the other. Jonas was lying flat on his back with lots of tubes and wires running everywhere, and Linda's chest grew tight for a moment, until Jonas tilted his head toward her and smiled. His cheeks were sunken in and his complexion a grayish-white color—like his hair and beard—but when he smiled in her direction, he was still the same old Jonas she loved.

"Linda, so *gut* to see you." Jonas quickly turned to his daughter who occupied the chair on his right. "Sarah Jane, get up." He raised his brows and lifted his chin.

"No, no," Linda said when she saw Sarah Jane cut her eyes sharply at her father. "I don't need to sit down. I'm just fine standing."

Sarah Jane stood up, shaking her head at Jonas, then turned to Linda and smiled. "You sit and visit with Pop. I need some *kaffi* anyway." She scooted around Linda and coaxed her toward the chair, then faced off with her father. "Pop, I'm not sure it's necessary to speak to me in such a tone. I would have gladly gotten up for Linda, and I could certainly use a break from you."

"*Gut.* Take Lizzie with you and the two of you go do something. All this hovering makes a man nervous. I ain't gonna die in this hospital; I already told you that. And I ain't gonna eat any more of that mush they call food in here either." Jonas swooshed a hand toward Sarah Jane. "Go, now." He turned toward his wife. "The both of ya's."

Lizzie placed her knitting needle in her lap beside a blue roll of yarn. She leaned closer to her husband. "I love you, Huggy Bear. But you are a cranky old man when you are feeling down."

Jonas grunted. "I've told you a hundred times since you locked me up in this place that I don't feel all that bad."

Lizzie stood up, leaned over, and kissed Jonas on the forehead. "We'll be back soon." She pushed a fallen strand of gray hair underneath her *kapp* and walked toward Linda. She smiled and patted Linda on the back. "Enjoy your visit, dear. If we're not back by tomorrow, you'll know we've left him in your hands."

Over the years, Lizzie's sense of humor had begun to mirror Jonas's. Linda suspected that to live with Jonas, a person needed to stay light on their toes and find humor in every circumstance.

"We wouldn't do that to you, Linda. Not to worry," Sarah Jane said to her before turning to Jonas. "Be *gut,* Pop." She playfully pointed a finger in his direction, then she and Lizzie headed out the door.

Jonas rolled his eyes and grumbled. Linda walked toward him and sat down where Sarah Jane had been. "Are you in pain?" It was the one thing that scared her. Pain. She didn't tolerate it well, and she didn't like to see others suffering.

Jonas propped himself up taller in the bed. "Why didn't you bring the chess set? I haven't played chess since the last time you and me played."

"I—I didn't know if you would be well enough to play. But I can bring it next—"

"No, no." He waved his hand in frustration. "There won't be a next time." He leaned closer to Linda. "I reckon they won't be back for a spell, so you got plenty of time to get me out of here."

Linda arched her brows in surprise and stifled a grin. "What?"

He edged upward in the bed even more. "I think they hid my breeches in that closet." Jonas pointed to a cabinet on the far wall. "If you can fetch me those, I'll worry about all these contraptions they have me hooked up to." He paused and twisted his mouth to one side. "Might try to round up my shoes too. And a shirt."

Linda realized that he might be serious. "Jonas, you can't just leave. I reckon that's not how it's done."

He worked his legs to one side of the bed, swung them over, and kicked Linda in the shin. "*Es dutt mir leed,*" he said, apologizing, but planted his feet firmly on the tile floor.

Linda jumped from the chair and put her hands on her hips.

"Jonas, for sure you can't seriously think I'm going to help you to—"

Jonas latched onto her arm. "The *Englisch* will kill me in here. I got a *gut* month or two left, and there ain't no need for them to rush me on to heaven." He released her arm and pointed to his own. "They got me hooked up to all kinds of mind drugs." His brows cinched together in a frown as he shook his head. "There ain't a need for all this. Yesterday, colorful flowers started blooming in the corner over there." Jonas pointed to his right. "They were growing right out of the tile floor." He sighed. "Now, Linda, I'm not a well man, but I reckon there ain't no flower garden growing in that corner."

"Jonas, have you told Sarah Jane and Lizzie all this?" She dropped her arms to her side in frustration. "You can't just pull those tubes out and leave." She shook her head.

Jonas reached for his straw hat on the nightstand and placed it atop his matted hair, then he stroked his beard. "They're keeping me hostage, that daughter and wife of mine."

Linda fought a grin. "Jonas, no one is keeping you hostage. Everyone just wants you to feel better. Don't you want us to be able to play chess when you're feeling up to it?"

Jonas scanned the room with glassy eyes. "Where ya reckon they'd put my suspenders? I've lost so much weight, *mei* breeches will fall plumb down to *mei* ankles."

Linda hoped Sarah Jane and Lizzie would be back soon. "I think you better wait until Sarah Jane and Lizzie get back."

Jonas grunted again. "Those two are the guards in this prison. They ain't gonna help me one bit." He looked up at Linda, his eyes serious. "I'm doing this with or without you. I thought I could count on you."

She sat down and reached for Jonas's hand. It had to be the medications that were making him act like this, a stretch even for him. "Jonas, you know you can count on me, but I'm sure we can't just pull those tubes from you arm. That wouldn't be safe at all. I know you don't like it in here, and I—"

"Hello." Linda immediately recognized the voice and spun around to face Stephen. Relief washed over her.

"I thought you had to work." She released Jonas's hand, stood up, and walked to Stephen, wishing she could fold herself into his arms the way she had last Sunday after the singing. Every time she thought about the kiss they'd shared behind the barn after he brought her home in his courting buggy, she went weak in the knees.

"The *Englisch* worker showed up after all, so Abner told me I could leave if I wanted. I got a ride from Mr. Lauder at the bank next door." Stephen slid past her, but not before winking in her direction, which did cause one knee to buckle. His brown eyes were flecked with gold, like sun-kissed wheat in the field. Stephen's hair changed colors with the seasons, and already his tawny locks were turning a golden shade of blond, which framed his bronzed face in the bobbed haircut Amish men wore. After working long days in the fields, his skin was already tanned, his hard work evident by the way his shoulders filled out his blue shirt. Linda loved everything about him. Stephen Ebersol was as wonderful on the inside, kind and unselfish, and always the first one to volunteer when the community needed someone to take on an extra project. Maybe that was because Stephen was the bishop's grandson, but Linda suspected it could be something else.

Linda felt like Stephen worked harder than most, as if it might make up for the one thing he was particularly self-conscious about. He was born with one leg almost two inches shorter than the other one, and even though he had special shoes to even out his tall stance, he walked with a slight limp and couldn't run very fast, something she knew had bothered him when they were younger.

Over the past year, they'd shared picnics, Sunday singings, and spent all their free time together, but when Linda suggested they go for a swim at the creek, Stephen made up an excuse not to go. She knew it was because he didn't want her to see him without his shoes on, which would make him off-balance. The only thing off-balance was Stephen's way of thinking. She loved him, and to her, he was perfect.

"Hello, Jonas." Stephen extended his hand to Jonas.

"Stephen, you're just in time." Jonas latched onto Stephen's hand. "Linda was just about to break me out of this jail."

Linda tried not to giggle. Jonas was a mess sitting there on the side of the bed wearing nothing but his straw hat and a white hospital gown. She shrugged in Stephen's direction, glad that Jonas was feeling good enough to behave in such a manner.

"Break you out of here?" Stephen smiled benignly. "Jonas, you know we can't break you out of here."

"Well, then—" Jonas reached for the tube running into his arm and Linda gasped. Thankfully, a voice erupted throughout the room.

"Jonas Miller, what in the world do you think you're doin'?" Lizzie marched to his side, slapped her hands to her tiny hips, and leaned her face to his. "This is why we can't leave you for a minute."

Sarah Jane was quickly at her father's bedside. "Pop, you'll be glad to know that we ran into the doctor on the way to get *kaffi*, and they are going to release you, if that's really what you want. But they won't be able to monitor your pain as closely if you aren't in the hospital."

"I'm not in any pain." What little color Jonas had in his face when Linda arrived was quickly draining as he sat on the edge of the bed, and she noticed his hand trembling. Just sitting on the bed seemed to have zapped his energy.

"Pop, you will have to wait until the nurse comes in and unhooks you from everything. Now lie back down." Sarah Jane helped her father back into bed. He grumbled but seemed to be relieved after he was on his back again. "Are you sure this is what you want to do?"

Jonas took a labored breath, then reached for his daughter's hand. He spoke softly. "Take me home, Daughter. I want to watch the sun rise in the mornings and set in the evenings." With glassy eyes, he turned to his wife. "Like I've done my entire life. It's where I want to be."

It was a side of Jonas that Linda had never seen, and she suddenly felt as though she were intruding on a very private moment. Worse, the realization of what Jonas meant punched her in the gut. Stephen's hand brushed against hers, and he discretely looped his pinky finger with hers.

"All right, Huggy Bear," Lizzie said tenderly. "You rest now."

Sarah Jane was still holding her father's hand, and Linda could see her eyes clouding with tears. "I'll go check to see how much longer it will be before you can get released." She blinked back tears, then turned to Linda. "Here, Linda. Come sit. Visit with

Jonas while I go find the nurse." Sarah Jane eased her hand from Jonas's and motioned for Stephen to come closer. "Come over here. I'll be back shortly."

Linda sat down and Stephen stood by her side. "Maybe when you get home, you'll feel like playing chess." She tried to sound hopeful.

"A game of chess will be *gut*." Jonas smiled, but Linda could tell it was forced, and she didn't want him to have to make an effort like that for her sake. His eyes began to close, and after only a few moments, Jonas was snoring lightly.

"It doesn't take much to tucker him out." Lizzie gazed at Jonas, rubbing his forearm with her hand. She looked up at Linda and Stephen. "But I know it means a lot to him that you both stopped by."

"We—we love . . ." Linda swallowed hard and fought to steady her emotions. Stephen put a hand on her shoulder.

"When you get Jonas home, if there is anything you need, anything at all, please get word to me, Lizzie." Stephen's warm smile matched his tone of voice.

Lizzie nodded. "We will have lots of help from everyone, I'm sure. *Danki*, Stephen." Lizzie stared at her husband in a way that caused Linda's heart to ache. *Jonas is going to die.*

"You children should go and enjoy this beautiful weather."

It seemed clear that Lizzie wanted to be alone with her husband, and Linda felt like tears were going to spill over at any minute, so she and Stephen excused themselves. Linda just wanted to get in the hallway before she completely broke down in front of Lizzie.

Once outside the hospital doors, that's exactly what happened. She folded onto one of the benches in the courtyard on the east side of the hospital and buried her face in her hands. Stephen sat down beside her and draped an arm around her shoulder.

"Did you not realize how sick Jonas is?" His voice was comforting, but his words stung.

She pulled her hands away, swiped at tears, and then turned to face him. "I guess not. Jonas has been sick for years, and somehow he always seems to get better." She paused, sniffled. "Remember three years ago, when the doctors told him that he couldn't attend Kade and Sadie's wedding? They said he was too sick and made out like he was going to die any minute." She shook her head and grinned. "But Jonas said he wouldn't miss the wedding for anything, and he insisted Sarah Jane and Lizzie take him. Remember?"

"*Ya*, I remember." Stephen took a deep breath, and with his free hand, he reached for hers and held it tightly. "Jonas is a fighter, but Linda—"

"Don't say it. Just don't say it. Jonas is so special. To everyone."

Stephen nodded, gave her hand a squeeze, and they sat quietly for a few moments.

"How'd you get here? Barbie?"

"*Ya*. She'll probably be here any minute to pick me up. She was going to run some errands."

"I guess I'll catch a ride too. Anything special you want to do the rest of the afternoon?" Linda snuggled closer, but Stephen pulled his arm from around her shoulder and put a tiny bit of space between them when two doctors walked into the courtyard, though he kept hold of her hand. Most men in their community weren't comfortable with much public affection, and Stephen was no exception.

Linda twisted slightly to face him and wished they could just go somewhere, anywhere, so Stephen could take her away from her worries about Jonas. She knew that to worry about such matters was a sin and that Jonas would have a special place in heaven when he arrived, but the thought of not seeing him anymore, playing chess, listening to his wise advice—she just couldn't imagine. Poor Lillian. And Sarah Jane and Lizzie. There would be a huge void in so many lives when Jonas passed.

"Anything with you is fine," Stephen said after the doctors passed by them. Linda could feel her cheeks blush and wondered if Stephen could read her mind, if he knew how much she longed for him to propose. She'd be eighteen in August, on the seventeenth. That wouldn't leave much time to plan a wedding for November or December of this year. Weddings were always scheduled after the fall harvest. Besides, her parents would argue that she was too young to get married, even though *Mamm* and *Daed* were married at seventeen.

"There's Barbie." Stephen pointed to the white minivan, then turned back to Linda, arched one brow, and eased into a smile. "Wanna go to the old oak tree?"

Linda knew what that meant. The old oak tree was a place where couples went to be alone, a huge oak in the middle of a field off of Leaman Road, with arched branches that formed a globe around those who ventured beneath the protective limbs. She felt her face reddening even more, and she nodded.

"We'll get Barbie to just take us to her bed and breakfast, and we can walk to the old oak from there." Stephen stood up, offered Linda a hand, and she rose from the bench along with him, relieved their *Englisch* friend wouldn't know their destination.

Mary Ellen paced the kitchen. She'd sent Matthew and Luke over to Samuel and Lillian's house with two shoofly pies she'd baked that morning, along with a big container of high fiber balls. She knew how much her brother liked the fiber balls filled with peanut butter, honey, raisins, chocolate chips, and coconut. Truth was, she needed to keep busy to keep her mind occupied.

Abe's conversation that morning with Josephine was brief, but they agreed that Linda's birth mother would visit tomorrow morning at ten o'clock. That meant that Mary Ellen and Abe would have to tell Linda the truth this evening, and Mary Ellen's stomach was rolling with anxiety. It was only fair to discuss the matter with Linda first, and privately, so sending Matthew and Luke to Samuel's house worked out perfectly since Linda was due home any minute to help with supper preparation. Mary Ellen dreaded the conversation they would be having with Linda, but waiting could worsen the situation if Linda found out the news some other way. What if Josephine decided not to wait and went to Linda directly? She jumped when the screen door slammed.

"It's just me, Mary Ellen." Abe hung his hat on the rack near the door, then ran a hand through his hair. "It's gonna be all right." He walked to the refrigerator and poured himself a glass of meadow tea, took a few gulps, and then took a seat at the kitchen table.

Mary Ellen brushed flour from her black apron and resumed her pacing.

"Sit down, Mary Ellen. Rest. I know you're nervous, but we will have to trust the Lord to guide us to say the right things."

"There is no *right* way to tell our daughter that we've lied to her for her entire life." Mary Ellen bit down on her lower lip, then eased onto the bench across from Abe. "I've always been close to Linda, and I'm afraid that when she finds out this news, that— that we will lose that."

"We didn't lie, Mary Ellen." Abe raised his shoulders, then dropped them in frustration. "It just didn't come up."

Mary Ellen slammed a hand on the table, something she would normally never do. "Abe! We didn't tell our daughter that she is adopted. Don't you think that should have *come up* at some point?" She regretted the tone she took with her husband, and she could see the anxiety in his expression, the fear in his eyes. But her own worries were overwhelming her as she wiped sweat from her brow. A knot was building in her throat, and the last thing she wanted to do was cry in front of Linda when she arrived. Mary Ellen wanted to calmly tell Linda that it didn't matter one tiny bit who gave birth to her, that she loved Linda as if she'd carried her in her own womb, that she was her daughter, no matter what. And she'd prayed all night that Linda would somehow understand.

"Mary Ellen, where is your faith? It's God's will that things are working out this way. You know that, no?"

To question God's will is a sin, but Mary Ellen had never questioned His will more than at this moment. "Things better work out, Abe." She sat up a little straighter, raised her chin. "We will just explain this to her, and then things will resume the way they were."

"I hope you're right." Abe's tone was doubtful, and doubt was not what she needed from her husband right now. She always relied on Abe's strength, and she needed him to stay strong for her, for them.

Mary Ellen stood from the table, twisted her apron strings, and paced some more, apprehension rippling through her body like a tidal wave that threatened to destroy her. Instead of focusing on her own failure to tell Linda the truth, she wanted to lash out at someone, and she knew Abe wasn't any more at fault than she was.

"I just don't know why she would want to ruin all these lives like this, that Josephine woman." She shook her head, then stopped pacing and turned to Abe. "I reckon she's not a *gut* Christian woman, or she wouldn't be doing this."

"Mary Ellen, you don't know that. I'm sure this is hard on her too."

She clenched her lips tight and bit back words that the Lord would surely not approve of.

Abe turned toward the door when he heard the clippety-clop of hooves, then stood up and walked to the threshold. Mary Ellen followed him and together they peered through the screen. They watched Linda walk up the driveway, then hop barefoot across the cobblestone steps that crossed the yard. When she reached the porch steps, she closed the distance between her and her parents and smiled. A smile that quickly faded. She stopped on the other side of the screen, facing them. No one moved or said anything for a few seconds.

"What's wrong?" Linda's brows narrowed, and she glanced back and forth between Mary Ellen and Abe.

Mary Ellen pushed the screen door open and motioned Linda inside. "Linda, we need to talk to you."

4

LINDA SCOOTED PAST HER PARENTS AND INTO THE kitchen and wondered if she'd done something wrong. She was a little late to help prepare supper, but it didn't even look like *Mamm* had started yet. Her time with Stephen at the old oak tree had helped to ease her worry about Jonas. It wasn't just the few kisses they shared, although those would keep her up at night, but the deep conversation. Stephen's faith seemed stronger than Linda's, and he had a way of making her understand about God's will, something that the *Ordnung* taught was not to be questioned. But when something bad happened, Linda tended to question the event just the same. She suspected that Stephen would follow in his grandfather's footsteps someday and become the bishop. And hopefully, she'd be by his side as the bishop's wife.

"What's wrong?" she asked again when both her parents just stood off to one side of the kitchen, her mother's face drawn into an expression of dread. Her father's brows furrowed as he stroked his beard.

"Let's go into the den." *Daed* led the way, and Linda glanced at her mother as they followed him into the den, but *Mamm* just took a deep breath and kept her head down.

Linda sat down on the couch, and each of her parents took a

seat in the rocking chairs across the coffee table from her. That
was usually where they sat when they were reprimanding her or
one of her brothers. Again, she tried to recall something she might
have done to upset them.

"We have something to tell you, *mei maedel*, but first I want you
to know how much your *mamm* and I love you. You are our daughter always." *Daed* swallowed hard, and Linda's chest tightened.
Could something have happened to Jonas since she and Stephen
left the hospital? She sat quietly and waited, but she noticed that
her mother wouldn't look at her.

"Your *mamm* and I tried to have *kinner* for almost two years before
we—before you were born," her father began. "We went to the
natural doctor who sent us to an *Englisch* doctor in Lancaster. But I
reckon no one could figure out why we couldn't have a child."

This seemed an inappropriate conversation, and Linda's anxiety heightened as she wondered where her father was going with
this. She sat up straight on the edge of the couch and folded her
hands in her lap. Her mother had never talked with her about
where babies came from; it just wasn't a conversation that a mother
would have with her daughter. These things were learned when a
girl got married. But Linda's *Englisch* girlfriends had educated her
about the matter early on in her *rumschpringe*.

"We wanted a child so badly," her mother chimed in. "A little
one to love." *Mamm's* eyes filled with tears, and Linda tilted her
head to one side and gazed at her forlorn expression. Then it hit
her, and her embarrassment reddened her cheeks as she gasped.

"Do you think Stephen and I are—" She didn't even know how
to speak the words. "We would never. I kissed him, but that's all."
Linda tucked her chin. "Maybe I shouldn't have, but I know that

won't make a baby." She looked up to see both her parents' jaws simultaneously dropping.

"No, no," her mother said as her cheeks took on their own rosy shade of red. "That's not what we were thinking."

"Then what is it? You're scaring me."

Her mother left the rocker and joined Linda on the couch. She grasped Linda's hand tightly within hers, then looked intensely into Linda's eyes as her own eyes clouded even more with tears. *Mamm* opened her mouth to speak but sighed heavily instead and turned to *Daed*.

Her father leaned forward, put his elbows on his knees, and rested his chin on his hands. Linda's heart was thumping so hard it was making her chest hurt. "When we couldn't have a baby of our own, we were given another woman's baby to raise. We signed papers that a lawyer wrote up."

She didn't understand. "What woman gave you a baby?" She glanced around the room. "And where is this baby?"

Mamm cupped Linda's face with both hands. "*You* are that baby, *mei maedel*. I did not carry you in my womb. Another woman did. You're adopted. The pretty woman that came to the house. She is your—your mother."

Linda eased out of her mother's grasp. "This can't be so." She turned to her father. "*Daed*, tell me this isn't true."

Her father left the rocker and bent on one knee in front of Linda. "You are our daughter. You will always be our daughter. Just because you do not carry our genes, it makes you no less our child. We love you, and that will never change. Do you understand?"

"No. I don't." She edged further away from both of them as her chest rose and fell with labored breaths. Tears threatened to spill, but she blinked them back. Too many unanswered questions. "Are you saying that the *Englisch* woman didn't want me, so she gave me to you?"

"Linda, she was only seventeen years old at the time. Your age. She didn't know how to care for a baby. And there was no father around or in the picture to help her." Her mother reached out to her, but she jerked away.

A father. The sting continued to worsen. "Where is my father then?" She glanced up at the person she'd believed to be her father her entire life, and indeed her tears did spill over.

"I—I am your father, Linda. I will always be your father." *Daed* swiped at his eyes, something Linda had never seen him do before. "As for the man whose genes you share, we do not know about him."

Linda jumped from the couch and put her hands over her face. "Why are you telling me this now?" Her voice was elevated and cracked as she spoke. "Isn't this something I should have known before now?"

"*Ya.*" Her mother stood up and walked to her. "Linda, please, try to understand. We made a mistake. We should have told you when you were younger, but it just didn't matter to us. You have always been our daughter, and nothing was going to change that."

Luke and Matthew. "Do Luke and Matthew know about this? I reckon they should be told too."

Her father was now beside her mother on the couch, both of them with teary eyes. "We thought you should know first." *Daed* sighed, his voice filled with anguish.

Linda swallowed hard and knew this would be difficult for Luke and Matthew. She looked at her parents. *Parents?* She'd never felt more lost than at this moment. Her thoughts momentarily trailed to the *Englisch* woman. No wonder *Mamm* was so upset. But she would need to be strong for her brothers, despite this complete lack of responsibility by her parents.

"I reckon Matt and Luke might not understand this either. When you tell them that they were adopted, they are going to take it even harder. How could you do this? How could you not tell us—"

Her father grabbed her arm gently. "No, no, Linda." He shook his head. "*Mei maedel*, your brothers were not adopted."

She wanted to run into her mother's arms and beg her to say this wasn't true, but *Mamm* only nodded in agreement, muttering how sorry they were.

Sobs of grief began to rack Linda, and she was having trouble breathing. "You mean, I don't have any brothers either?" *Dear Lord in heaven, do something. Please. This can't be true.* "But you said you couldn't have any *kinner* of your own."

"We didn't think we could, Linda, but we were able to have Luke and Matthew. We don't know why, but the Lord graced us with the boys, and—"

"I'm not your daughter! I have no parents. I have no brothers." Her sense of loss was suddenly beyond tears, quickly being replaced by anger. She backed away from her parents. "I have no one."

"Linda, my beloved daughter. I am your mother. We are your parents. It will always be that way. We love you, Linda. Please forgive us for not telling you this sooner. Please, Linda . . ." *Mamm* reached for Linda again, and this time Linda stepped even further away from them.

"We know this is hard, Linda, but over time you will realize that we are still your parents, no matter what." Her father continued to fight a buildup of tears in his eyes, and there was a part of her that wanted to run to him, to them both, to comfort them, ease their pain. But she felt suffocated by her own grief.

"Why are you telling me this now?"

Her parents looked at each other, and then her father spoke. "The *Englisch* woman, she wants to see you. She wants to meet you tomorrow morning and spend some time with you."

"But you don't have to go." *Mamm* stepped forward. "We will just tell her that you are not interested in meeting her, and—"

"I want to meet her. *She* is my *mother*." Linda kept her voice steady and cut her eyes at Mary Ellen. *Mary Ellen*—the person who raised her. She should have felt remorse at the way her cutting words sent tears streaming down Mary Ellen's face. But instead, she twisted the dagger. "What am I supposed to call you both now? *Mary Ellen* and *Abe*?"

"Watch your tone, Linda," her father said as he wrapped a protective arm around his wife.

Linda grunted, stood taller. *They can't tell me what to do. They aren't even related to me.*

"We know that you're hurt, dear, but nothing has to change, and—"

"Stop it! Everything has changed." Linda wrapped her arms around herself, never needing a hug from her mother more than at this moment. The woman she thought was her mother. From someone. Someone who loved her.

"Please, Linda . . ." her mother cried as she reached out to her. "Please, my darling baby . . ."

"I'm going to Stephen's. He'll be my family someday! Then I'll have a family!"

She ran out the door, down the porch steps, and didn't stop running until she got to Black Horse Road, where she collapsed onto the gravel shoulder and sobbed. It took a few moments for her to realize her toe was bleeding and only another minute or so before a buggy came along. She wiped her eyes, then blocked the sun's glare with her hand until the buggy came into view.

Her cousin David. She waited while he pulled to a stop beside her.

"You okay?"

David was two years older than Linda, and he'd been through a kidney transplant, so she wasn't sure he'd have much sympathy for her throbbing toe, but her bloody foot was the least of her worries. David jumped from his topless courting buggy and ran to her side. He knelt beside her and put a hand on her shoulder.

"Here, let me see." He lifted up her dirty bare foot covered in blood. "Ouch," he said as he crinkled his nose. "That's a nasty cut, but I reckon it doesn't look like you need any stitches. I'm on my way to *Onkel* Noah's clinic. You wanna go and have him clean it up?"

Linda stood up, wiped her eyes, and shook her head. "No. Can you just take me to Stephen's *haus*? Please, if you don't mind."

"Sure." David helped her into the buggy, then went around and got in beside her. He'd barely settled into a steady trot when the tears started again. She just couldn't seem to stop. "Does it hurt that bad?"

She heard the concern in David's voice, much like that of a protective brother. "It's not my toe. It's—it's . . ." Linda covered her face with her hands. "David, I'm adopted. My parents aren't my parents."

"What?" He twisted in the seat to face her, a confused expression on his face.

"I just found out. *Mamm* and *Daed* . . ." she paused as she sniffled. "I mean *Mary Ellen* and *Abe* told me that I have a birth mother, someone who gave me to them when I was a baby. And I'm so upset, and . . ." She lowered her head, then looked David's way. He was staring straight ahead, keeping the horse at slow pace. After a few moments, he turned her way.

"Linda, I'm sure that news was a shock." He glanced back and forth between her and the road, then steadied his gaze on her. "But . . ." He gave her a small smile. "I think I'd like to thank your folks for raising such a wonderful cousin for me."

Linda tried to manage a smile through her tears, but the news was too raw for her to pretend for more than a moment that she was anything but destroyed.

David slowed the buggy before he reached Stephen's house and eventually came to a stop. He turned to face her in the seat again, then wrapped his arms around her, which only caused her to cry more.

"Linda," he finally said in a soothing tone. "Mary Ellen and Abe are your parents, no matter what." David gently eased her away. "You know how much they love you."

In her heart, Linda knew it to be true, but the reality of the situation was overwhelming her. "Why didn't they tell me? Why would they keep something like this from me?" Then she had a horrible thought. She took a deep breath. "David, did you know about this? Since *mei mudder*, I mean Mary Ellen, is your *daed's* sister."

"She's still your mother, Linda, and no, I didn't have any idea about this." David pulled his straw hat off and ran his forearm over a sweaty forehead. "I think of Lillian just like *mei mamm*, and I know Lillian loves me just like her own son. I reckon you don't have to be born into a family to be a part of it."

Linda knew that when Lillian married Samuel, she'd raised David as her own son, but somehow her situation seemed much different. "It's the betrayal. The fact that no one told me."

They sat quietly for a few minutes. "So, what now? What are you going to do?"

Linda recalled the looks on her parents' faces. *On Mary Ellen's and Abe's faces.* Every time she mentally corrected herself, the pain she felt was even worse. She shrugged. "I don't know. I'm supposed to meet *her* tomorrow."

"Still want to go to Stephen's? I reckon you look a mess." David grinned, poked her in the arm. They'd grown up together, and David had always been like the older brother she didn't have. Again, she thought about Matt and Luke.

Linda sniffled. "*Ya.* I need to see Stephen."

David nodded, then flicked the horse into motion. "Linda, everything's gonna be all right. Mary Ellen and Abe love you, and that's what matters. It was just God's will that the other woman helped them out."

Linda shrugged. "I guess. I'm just not sure how I feel about all this." However, the look on her parents' faces was enough for her to know that, despite her own hurt, they were suffering too.

Stephen pushed back his hat, looped his thumbs beneath his suspenders, and walked across his front yard toward David's buggy, wondering what would bring Linda to his house so near the supper hour. He watched Linda hug her cousin before she stepped out of the buggy and shut the door. David waved, and Stephen returned the gesture, but he couldn't take his eyes from Linda as she ran barefoot across the yard.

"What's wrong?" She was a few feet from him when he noticed blood on the top of her bare foot and tears rolling down her cheeks. "What happened?"

She threw her arms around his neck. "My life is ruined."

"What?" He held her for a few moments, then gently eased her away and looked down at the blood on her foot. "Do you need a doctor?"

She swiped at swollen eyes and shook her head. "No. My foot is fine."

Stephen raised his brows and gazed into her eyes. "Then what is it?"

"I'm adopted!" She took a step backward and clinched her fists at her sides. "Abe and Mary Ellen aren't my parents, Stephen! A woman named Josephine is my mother. I don't even think I really have a father. Luke and Matthew aren't my brothers." She squeezed her eyes shut as tears rolled down her cheeks. "I'm adopted! And no one bothered to tell me until my *mother* showed up at our house yesterday."

Stephen swallowed hard and searched for something to say. He stepped toward her and touched her arm. "Are you sure?"

Her eyes flew open in a rage. "*Ya*, I'm sure. They—Mary Ellen and Abe—just told me." She covered her face with her hands and mumbled something Stephen couldn't understand, then she moved forward and buried her face in his chest. "Tell me it isn't true."

He wrapped one arm around her back and cradled the back

of her neck with his other hand. "I'm sorry, Linda. What can I do?"

"Just hold me." She pressed her body closer to his, and Stephen struggled to stay focused on the issue at hand.

After a while, she pulled from the embrace and gazed into his eyes. "It hurts, Stephen. Make it stop."

"I—I . . ." He raised his shoulders and dropped them. "I don't know what to say, Linda." How could he ease her pain if this was really true?

She tried to blink back more tears, but they spilled down her cheeks as she continued to wait for him to say something. He knew he was failing miserably, so he stepped forward and cupped her cheeks in his hands, then kissed her softly on the lips. He couldn't stand to see her hurting like this, but he wasn't sure what he could say to make her feel better. She returned the kiss, then eased away, and her eyes begged him to say something more to comfort her.

He took a deep breath. *Please, God. Let me say the right thing.*

"Linda, I don't think Mary Ellen and Abe could love you any more than they already do, and I reckon they are your parents no matter what." He paused as she sniffled and wiped her eyes, seeming to wait for more from him. "I've seen you and your *mamm* together, and I don't think anything is going to change between the two of you."

"Everything has changed." She tucked her head and sniffled again.

Stephen gently lifted her chin. "Linda, Mary Ellen is your *mudder*. Talk to her." He kissed her on the forehead. "Let me take you home."

She nodded as she bit her bottom lip.

"It'll just take me a minute to ready the horse and buggy. Wait here. We can talk more on the way to your house."

Stephen ran toward the barn, moving as quickly as he could. His grandfather was due for supper any minute, and the last thing Linda needed was for Bishop Ebersol to question her tears right now. Stephen knew his grandfather would find out soon enough. *Daadi* always found out everything.

Linda listened to Stephen do most of the talking on the way home. He was sweet for trying to make her feel better, insisting that not much would change for her. But he was wrong. Everything was going to change.

When a crisis had presented itself in the past, she always went to her mother. *This is a crisis* . . . Right now, she wanted to go inside, and have her parents reassure her that she was, indeed, loved. She told Stephen good-bye, and they shared a brief kiss in the driveway.

"It's going to be fine, Linda," he said one last time as she exited the buggy.

She crossed the yard, then stepped on the cobblestones that led to the porch steps. She thought about how Matt and Luke were not her true brothers, and she began to cry again.

Linda looked up when she heard the porch screen slam and saw her mother standing on the porch with her arms stretched wide. Her mother, not Mary Ellen. *This woman is my mother, no matter what.*

Linda ran to her as fast as she could, and *Mamm* wrapped her arms around her tightly.

"I'm sorry, *Mamm*," Linda cried.

"No, my precious daughter. I'm sorry."

At breakfast the next morning, no one said much. Mary Ellen served scrapple and some dippy eggs, along with some flapjacks, because they were Linda's favorite. They decided the night before that Abe would talk to Matt and Luke when they went to market later in the morning while Linda was spending some time with Josephine.

Mary Ellen recalled her conversation with Linda late last night. When she'd heard her daughter crying, she went to her room, and they'd spent the next two hours talking. She prayed that she had convinced Linda that everything was truly going to be all right and how very much she loved her. That nothing had to change.

Mary Ellen glanced at the clock. Straight up ten o'clock. Abe and the boys had left nearly two hours ago, and Linda had busied herself cleaning the upstairs. Mary Ellen hadn't seen her or heard any movement from upstairs in about an hour. She finished running a damp mop across the wood floor in the den and headed toward the stairs. When she got to Linda's room, she knocked.

"Come in."

Mary Ellen slowly pushed the door open, and Linda was sitting on her bed in her newest dress, a purple one the color of a ripe plum, the one Mary Ellen had made for her just last week. Her black apron was a newer one, bold in color and not faded by multiple trips through the wringer. Linda was twisting one of the ties on her *kapp*, but not one brown hair was out of place, each strand tucked neatly beneath the prayer covering. Her black leather shoes shone as if Linda had run a wet cloth across the top, and her ankle-high black socks were neatly folded to the rim of her shoes.

When Mary Ellen sat down on the bed beside Linda, her

daughter stopped twisting the tie of her *kapp*, folded her hands in her lap, and took a deep breath. Mary Ellen patted her leg. "She will be here any minute. It's ten o'clock." She paused and waited for Linda to say something, but Linda merely bit her bottom lip and stared at the floor. "You can change your mind," she said softly, wondering if the hopefulness in her comment had shown through.

Linda shook her head but didn't look up. "No. I'm going."

Mary Ellen had prayed last night, and again this morning, for the Lord to lift the worry from her heavy heart. But that was only the beginning of a long list of prayers that weren't normally included during her devotions. At Abe's insistence, she'd prayed for Josephine, although she wasn't sure what to pray for. If things went well between Josephine and Linda, would she lose her daughter? She tried to banish the selfish thoughts, since apparently Linda hadn't changed her mind about the visit. Mary Ellen couldn't stop thinking about what Linda and Josephine might do together, what places they might visit, conversations they might have.

"*Mamm?*" Linda twisted her neck and looked into Mary Ellen's eyes.

"*Ya?*"

"What do you think she wants?" Linda paused and chewed on her lip again for a moment. "I mean, will she want to be my mother? Because I already have a mother."

Mary Ellen felt better than she'd felt since Josephine came calling. She smiled at Linda, reached for her hand, and squeezed. "I'm glad to hear that." She thought for a moment. "I reckon she wants to know you. That's all. Maybe have a place in your life."

"What kind of place?" Linda's confused expression, paired with her questioning eyes and fidgety feet, took Mary Ellen back to a time when Linda was five-years-old and being reprimanded for picking all the strawberries in the garden before they were ripe and giving them to their dog Buddy.

Tires churning up loose gravel on the driveway diverted both their attention, and Linda suddenly turned pale. Mary Ellen knew that she must be strong for her daughter.

"Linda, you go and have a *gut* time." Mary Ellen cupped Linda's cheek and smiled. "You are very pretty, like her."

"I'm nervous, *Mamm*."

"I know. Me too."

Linda threw her arms around Mary Ellen. "I'm sorry for how I behaved yesterday." Mary Ellen gently nudged her away and pointed a finger in her direction.

"Do not apologize to me, Linda. I should be apologizing to you. I hope that you can forgive your father and I for not—"

"*Mamm*, I already have forgiven you." Linda sighed. "I thought a lot about this last night, and I know you and *Daed* are hurting and worried. But you will always be my parents."

"*Danki* for saying so. We love you very much."

Then they heard a knock at the door.

5

JOSIE CHECKED HER LIPSTICK IN THE REARVIEW MIRROR, ran a hand through her hair, and wondered if she should have worn something different. After several outfit changes, she'd chosen a pair of capri jeans, a tan T-shirt with no imprint, and flat brown sandals. She'd toned down her jewelry also—only her wedding ring and small silver hoop earrings. It was a far cry from what she knew Linda would be wearing, but she didn't want to come across as flashy, so she'd ditched spiked heels for sandals, left the Rolex at home, and even gone light on her makeup today.

She took a deep breath before she stepped out of the car and wondered if she should have taken Robert up on his offer to come with her. She took in her surroundings and saw that she'd parked near two buggies. One was the familiar box-shaped buggy Lancaster County was known for, and the other one Josie recognized to be a spring buggy, without a top, room for four, with a storage area in the back. In this warm weather, she'd seen lots of spring buggies on the roads.

Josie glanced around the property as she made her way across cobblestone steps that led to a long wooden porch with two entryways. It seemed to Josie that the Amish must get on hands and knees to trim their grass so perfectly around every flower bed, cobblestone, and planter that occupied the space between the gravel driveway and the front porch. Every tree in the spacious yard was encased by a pristine flower bed sporting red, pink, and white blooms. The white clapboard house appeared to have a fresh coat of paint, and in grand contrast, the home had a green tin roof that matched the roofs of two barns nearby.

A horse whinnied from the barn to Josie's left, and she turned to see the animal poke his head out opened shutters, as if voicing a hello in her direction. It was picturesque, and under different circumstances, Josie knew it would be a calming, peaceful place. But as she headed up the porch steps, Josie's heart was pounding against her chest and beads of sweat were accumulating on her forehead.

Two doors led into the house, and Josie headed to the one directly in front of the porch steps, which appeared to be the main entrance. As she drew near, she could see through the screen door and into a den, then she heard footsteps, and the door swung open.

"Hello," Mary Ellen said softly. She motioned for Josie to come in. "Linda will be down in a few minutes. Please, have a seat. Can I get you some tea or *kaffi*?"

Josie hesitantly sat down on the tan couch, folded her hands in her lap. "No, thank you. I'm fine."

Mary Ellen's home was tastefully decorated with more décor than other Amish homes Josie had been in when she was younger. She'd heard that the bishop was more lenient about allowing a few ornamental trinkets here and there, as well as conservative wall hangings. As she glanced around, Josie thought this could have been any number of non-Amish homes in the area. Two oak rockers faced the couch with a matching coffee table in between, and a colorful rug rested beneath the setup. A large leafy ivy was in a planter in the far corner next to a bookshelf that went almost to the ceiling, filled with books, cards, and various games. A large framed picture of a cottage nestled among colorful foliage resembling a Thomas Kinkade painting hung above the fireplace, and on each side of the mantel were large glass lanterns filled with a yellowish liquid.

Spying the lanterns was a reminder that this was indeed an Amish household, and Josie glanced around to see no electrical outlets, overhead light fixtures, and of course, no television or radio. But it was still much more ornate than what she remembered. One thing still stood true; the Amish didn't believe in photographs, taking them or posing for them, so there were no pictures of family scattered about the home. Josie instantly realized that there would be no pictures for her to see of Linda growing up. What did she look like when she was two-years-old? Five? Thirteen?

Mary Ellen sat down in the rocker facing Josie on the couch, but it was only a few moments later when they both heard footsteps coming down the stairs. Both women stood up. Josie watched as Linda descended the last few steps, then paused before she slowly entered the den.

"Hello," Josie said tenderly to the girl in the deep purple dress who stood before her. *My daughter*. She held her position and waited for Linda to come a little closer.

"Hi." Linda's eyes locked with Josie's, but only for a moment. "What time would you like me to be home, *Mamm*?"

Mary Ellen smiled, but Josie could still see fear etched into her expression. "Take as long as you like," she said bravely. Then she walked to Linda, whispered something in her ear, and pulled her into a gentle hug. After a moment, she eased away and turned to Josie.

"Katie's Kitchen is a nice place for lunch. They haven't been open long, and we try to support them, since they are Amish-owned and operated." She paused, then shrugged. "Linda likes it there, but I'm sure anywhere will be fine."

"I think Katie's Kitchen sounds nice for lunch." Josie glanced at her wrist and remembered she hadn't worn her watch. "Probably a little early for lunch." She turned to Linda. "I thought I would take you to my home, if you'd like. We could talk there, maybe have some tea or coffee. Then we can head to Katie's Kitchen later. If that's okay? I'm open to anything really. It doesn't matter. Is there something else you'd like to do? Or maybe . . ." Josie stopped when she realized she was rambling. Then she had a thought, an idea that perhaps would make the entire day easier on everyone. She turned to Mary Ellen.

"Mary Ellen, would you like to come with us?"

Mary Ellen's eyes widened, and she glanced at Linda, but ultimately shook her head. "No, I think it'd be best if you two spent some time alone."

"But *Mamm*, she said you can come, and—" Linda's pleading voice made Josie realize just how nervous Linda was. *I'm nervous, too, sweetheart.*

"No, Linda. I have much to do around here." Mary Ellen took a step backward, waved, and said, "Now, go and have a *gut* time." Mary Ellen continued to ease backward until she had almost rounded the corner into the other room. "Have fun," she hoarsely whispered, and Josie could see Mary Ellen's eyes clouding with tears.

"Are you sure you don't want to join us?" Josie's heart ached for Mary Ellen.

"It's okay. Let's go," Linda said to Josie when her mother shook her head again. "*Mamm*, I'll be home this afternoon." Then Linda said something in Pennsylvania *Deitsch* to Mary Ellen—something Josie didn't understand—but Mary Ellen smiled, then she left the room. Linda followed Josie out to the car.

"Does this car have air-conditioning?" Linda climbed into the passenger seat up front and strapped on her seatbelt.

"Yes, it does." Josie turned on the air-conditioner as soon as she started the engine.

"Some of the *Englisch* don't use their air-conditioning, or they don't have it in their cars. I don't know which." Linda looked out of the window as they drove down the driveway.

"I can't imagine not having air-conditioning. Even though it's only May, it's already really warm." Josie glanced at Linda, who was staring at her. "I mean, I know you're used to not having air, but I guess it's just hard for me to imagine."

Linda finally pulled her gaze from Josie and looked straight ahead. "It's not so bad."

A few awkward moments of silence ensued. "So, would you like to see my home?"

Linda shrugged. "Sure."

"It has air-conditioning too," Josie said with a grin, trying to lighten the mood. Linda didn't say anything and kept her eyes on the open road ahead of them. Josie turned off of Black Horse Road and turned left onto Lincoln Highway.

"That's Barbie Beiler's place." Linda pointed to a bed and breakfast on the right. "Do you know her?"

"Uh, no. I haven't met very many people since I've—since I've been back." The questions were sure to come, and Josie hoped she could explain things in a way that Linda could understand. And forgive her.

"She's a *gut* friend. She gives us rides and helps us with things." She turned toward Josie, twisted her mouth to one side, and then asked, "Are you married?"

Wow. That came without much warning. "Uh, yes, I am." Josie pushed a strand of hair from her face. "His name is Robert."

"Is he . . . ?"

Josie turned her head to face Linda.

"Is he . . . my father?"

"No, oh no. He's a wonderful man, but he isn't your father. We've been married for twelve years."

"Do you have other . . ." Linda drew in a deep breath. "Do you have children?"

"No, we weren't able to have any. I mean, I wasn't able to have any more children after you were born."

"I have a lot of questions." Linda's voice was soft as she spoke, void of much emotion, and Josie worried what must be going through her head.

"And I will answer them all, as best I can." She pulled into her driveway.

Josephine's house was a big brick mansion and looked a lot like Barbie's bed and breakfast. "Just you and your husband live here?"

"Yes." Josephine turned off the car and opened her car door. Linda did the same, then walked alongside Josephine on the way up the sidewalk. She smelled good, sweet like honeysuckle. "Are you wearing perfume?"

"Yes, I am. Do you like it?" Josie turned the key in the front door. Linda nodded and tried to see through the fancy glass, but Josephine pushed the door open before Linda could preview what she was walking into. A whoosh of cool air hit her in the face, and she could hear soft music playing. Josephine pushed the door wide and motioned for Linda to walk in ahead of her.

Linda was barely inside the door, but she knew for sure that this was the fanciest house she'd ever been in. Her eyes drifted upward to a light that hung high in the entryway with lots of twinkling bulbs and dangling crystals that shone onto a white tiled floor. Farther in front of her, she could see wooden floors spreading throughout a large den area, but these floors were glossy and bright, unlike those at home. Josephine's furniture was rich-looking, and her blue couch spread in a half-circle around the room.

"Come on into the kitchen, and I'll pour us some tea." Josephine walked ahead of her, and Linda followed, walking slow, taking it all in.

When she entered the kitchen, she immediately felt more comfortable and was glad Josephine had suggested talking in here. The yellow walls and blue countertops made this room seem warmer, not so fancy. She saw familiar electric gadgets on the counter. Nothing out of the ordinary. She'd been in plenty of *Englisch* homes. Then her eyes rested on something new.

"What's that?" She pointed to a silver-shaped box with some sort of metal pipe coming out of it.

Josephine was pouring two glasses of tea but looked up. "Oh, that's an espresso machine. Robert and I often have a cup of cappuccino at night."

Linda stepped closer to the appliance to have a better look. "Is it like *kaffi*?"

Josephine placed two glasses of tea on a kitchen table that didn't look like any table Linda had seen before. It was all glass and had six high-back chairs with thick blue cushions. In the center, a pretty glass vase held a mixture of flowers and greenery, although the flowers weren't like anything Linda had seen in Amish gardens either.

"It's coffee, Italian coffee. It has milk foam on top." Josephine raised her brows. "Want me to make us each a cup?"

Linda stepped back from the elaborate coffeemaker. "Oh, no. That's all right. You've already prepared us tea." She nodded toward the two tall glasses of iced tea on the table but glanced back at the coffee machine on the counter.

Josephine ran her hand through hair that was the color of wheat, not brown like Linda's, and then she smiled. "You know, I think a cappuccino is just what we need. It sure sounds good to me. Why don't I make us some?"

"Okay." She liked coffee, although *Mamm* didn't encourage drinking too much of it. But she was anxious to see the machine work and to see coffee with foam on top.

Josephine began a process that captured Linda's attention, especially when Josephine poured milk into a small pitcher, then placed it under the pipe that made all sorts of odd sounds.

"We're steaming the milk now." She smiled at Linda. "I like to sprinkle nutmeg and cinnamon on mine. Do you want me to do that to yours too?"

"Sure." Linda watched her add white foam on top of two cups

of steaming coffee, then sprinkle the spices on top. "Josephine . . ." She stopped and realized she had yet to call this woman by name. "What do I call you? I mean, I have a mother and all."

Josephine carted the two cups of coffee to the table, pushed the two glasses of tea to the side, and pulled out a chair for Linda. "Here, sit down," she said.

Linda sat down and waited for her answer.

"My name is Josephine, but my friends and family call me Josie." Her face shone with kindness, and Linda took a deep breath and tried to settle her nerves. "Linda . . ." She paused, placed an elbow on the table, then rested her chin atop it. "I would never expect you to call me mother. Of course, you have a mother. I am just hoping to be your friend, in whatever capacity you will allow me. I just want to get to know you." She smiled. "Taste the cappuccino."

Linda brought the porcelain cup to her mouth and blew. "Hot," she whispered, then took a sip. "It's *gut*." She took another swig. "It's very *gut*." It was the best coffee she'd ever had.

"I'm glad you like it. Robert and I became fans of cappuccino about six years ago. Now it's our thing to curl up on the couch and have a cup in the evenings. Some people can't do that because the caffeine will keep them up at night, but it doesn't bother us."

Linda took another sip and thought about how she'd like to drink this kind of coffee every day.

"Josie? It's okay if I call you that?" Linda set the cup down and Josie nodded.

"Of course. Josie is just fine."

Linda's stomach churned with anxiety, but she had to know. "Why did you give me away? What would make a mother not want her baby?"

Josie's eyes instantly clouded with tears, but Linda knew she needed this question answered first, before she and Josie could even move forward as friends. Josie stirred uneasily in her chair and tried to blink back tears.

"I wanted you very much," she said as a tear rolled down her cheek. She quickly wiped it away. "But my parents didn't want me to raise a baby. I was only seventeen at the time. Your age." She smiled at Linda, even though another tear trickled down her cheek. "But I wanted you very much. Handing you over to your parents two weeks after you were born was the hardest thing I have ever done. I prayed each day that you would be cared for and grow up to live a good life. My parents said that I was doing what God would want me to do, since Mary Ellen and Abe couldn't have children. Or, they didn't think they could at the time."

Linda was relieved to know that Josie had wanted to keep her, but equally as relieved to hear her speak of God. "I only found out about all this yesterday. My parents never told me that I was given to them."

"I know. Your father told me that on the phone when we arranged this meeting. I'm sorry, Linda. I know this must have been a shock to you." Josie took a sip of her coffee, then leaned back against the blue cushion. "But not a day has gone by that I haven't thought about you. I wanted you to be old enough to understand why I did what I did and to know that I loved you from the moment I laid eyes on you." Long black lashes blinked feverishly to keep more tears from falling. "I have a whole box full of pictures that I took that first two weeks after you were born."

"You do?" Since photos were not allowed, Linda had no idea what she looked like as a baby.

"Do you want to see them? Do you think your parents would mind?"

"They won't mind. *Ya*, I'd like to see them." Linda thought for a moment. "Do you have other pictures? Of you?"

Josie's eyes lit up. "I have lots of photo albums of me as well, but do you really want to see those?"

Of course I do! "*Ya*, I do, but . . ." Something was still looming over them.

"What is it, sweetie?"

Maybe it was the way Josie called her "sweetie," but Linda felt warm inside and comfortable enough to ask, "What about my father? What happened to him? Why did the two of you not get married?"

Josie rubbed her forehead with her hand, the one with the big ring on her finger. "We didn't love each other. He was older than me . . . and I didn't want to do what he wanted to do, but he forced me to, and . . ." She paused. "Linda, are you following what I'm saying?"

Linda shook her head. "No."

"Linda, he forced me to have sex with him, and that's how I got pregnant. He was not a very good man. He died a long time ago. I'm sorry to tell you this."

Linda could feel the flush in her cheeks. "Oh," she said softly, unsure how she felt about this news. They were quiet for a few moments. "Did he hurt you? This man who is my father."

Josie reached over and placed her hand on top of Linda's, and it felt strange, but nice. "My biggest hurt was losing you. And all that matters at this point is that we are becoming friends, and that you know that I always loved you, and never wanted to be away from you. Each year on your birthday, I'd have a cake, and I'd light candles for however many years old you were, and I'd sing to you."

"Really?"

Josie nodded. "Do you want to look at pictures now, while we have time before we go to lunch?"

"*Ya*, I would."

Linda had helped Josie lug several photo albums from her bedroom to the kitchen. Josie looked at them, scattered all over the kitchen table, most of them she hadn't opened in years. She'd tried not to bring the albums with pictures she wouldn't want Linda to see, like the one of her with her girlfriends at a bachelorette party when she was in her twenties, the time when a male dancer showed up. It was innocent, but Linda might not understand. Then there was the one when she and Robert were in Mexico, and Josie remembered the skimpy bikini she'd bought for that trip. Her mind was racing when Linda reached for one of the photo albums and opened it.

"Is that me?" She pointed to a baby in a pink T-shirt that said, *Mommy loves me.* Linda's eyes were glowing and hopeful.

"No, sweetheart. I'm afraid that's me." Josie remembered putting her two weeks' worth of photos in a little blue album, only big enough to hold single shots of Linda. She picked it up and handed it to Linda. "These are pictures of you."

"But the name on the front says Helen." Linda looked up at Josie with big blue, questioning eyes.

"That's what I called you. For two weeks anyway. I named you Helen."

Linda smiled. "Can I look at them?"

"Of course." Josie scooted her chair close to Linda. She wanted to put her arm around her, to hold her close. But just sitting next to her daughter, in her home, would be enough for now.

Linda giggled, and Josie's insides warmed like that of a proud mother. "That's me?" her daughter asked. "I look like a frog!" She laughed again.

Josie playfully poked her in the arm, smiling ear to ear. "Don't you dare say that about my beautiful baby! You did not look like a frog. You were beautiful, still are." She took a chance and put her arm around Linda, and instantly she felt Linda stiffen up and edge forward in the chair. Josie eased her arm back down to her side and refused to let that small thing derail the wonderful time they were having.

"Look at you there." Josie pointed to a picture of herself holding Linda on her aunt's couch, with her arm stretched wide. "I held the camera out and took that picture of us, that's why it looks kinda odd."

"You're so young." Linda turned toward Josie, frowning.

Josie stared at the picture. She remembered buying the disposable camera and hiding it from her aunt. Aunt Laura had thought it best for Josie not to keep any pictures of the baby, but Josie took pictures of Linda every chance she could. "I was your age. Seventeen. Almost eighteen."

"I'll be eighteen in August."

Josie smiled. "I know." She choked back tears as she thought that perhaps this year she would light candles and sing to her baby in person. To Helen. To Linda.

"I like the name Helen."

"I like the name Linda too." Josie watched her flip through the photos, slowly, as if memorizing each and every one.

When she looked at the last picture, she turned to Josie, her expression serious. "Did it hurt? To have a baby?"

"They say you forget about the pain, and I guess that's true, but I do remember it being rather painful." Josie handed Linda another photo album. "This one is pictures of me, before you were born. It was my sixteenth birthday."

Josie watched in awe as Linda smiled and studied the photos. "I look like you, no?"

"Yes, you do." She covered her mouth with her hand and fought the knot building in her throat.

Josie watched Linda scan each and every photo album and answered all her questions about those in the pictures. It took over an hour for her to go through them all.

"*Danki,*" she said when she closed the last album.

"You're very welcome. Do you want to go to Katie's Kitchen now?"

"*Ya.*"

Josie left the albums on the table, found her purse, and they headed out the door. "Do you have a boyfriend?"

"*Ya.*" Linda smiled as her cheeks turned a rosy shade of pink. "His name is Stephen Ebersol."

"Oh, I'd like to hear all about him at lunch, if you'd like to tell me."

"*Ya,* I would."

Linda was glowing, and Josie knew that this was the happiest day of her life. And since the doctors had told her to enjoy each and every day she still had, that is exactly what she planned to do.

6

MARY ELLEN PACKED A BASKET WITH A LOAF OF ZUCCHINI bread, two loaves of regular homemade bread, and a generous supply of raisin puffs. Her nephew, David, loved the fluffy cookies rolled in cinnamon and sugar. She knew Lillian was racing back and forth between her own home and her *maam's* so she could help take care of Jonas and Lizzie. It was a small offering, but if Mary Ellen were honest with herself, she also needed the distraction to keep her thoughts from venturing to Linda and Josephine.

She hitched up the spring buggy, loaded the basket in the back, and headed to Lillian and Samuel's. On the way, though, she barely noticed the gentle breeze and colorful foliage. Every time she thought about Linda and Josephine spending the day together, her stomach twisted in knots. And she wondered how Abe's conversation was going with Matt and Luke. Would their boys be just as upset by the news of Linda's adoption as Linda? *I should have gone with Abe to tell them.*

"Whoa." She pulled the buggy to a stop next to the family buggy parked at Lillian and Samuel's, picked up her basket, and headed to the house. Lillian met her on the porch.

"How are you holding up?"

"What?" Mary Ellen offered her the basket. "What do you mean?"

Lillian pushed back a strand of loose hair, tucked it beneath her *kapp*, then stepped closer and accepted the basket. She put her free hand on Mary Ellen's forearm. "David told us. About Linda. About her being adopted. I honestly didn't know."

Mary Ellen wasn't surprised that Linda had confided in her cousin; they'd always been close. "It happened so long ago, way before you married Samuel. We just don't speak of it, so I'm not surprised that Samuel didn't tell you."

"When I asked Samuel about it, he said he just never thought to tell me, that Linda is just as much a part of this family as anyone." Lillian opened the screen door and motioned Mary Ellen into the kitchen. "Here, sit down. Samuel and David are working in the barn, and Anna and Elizabeth are down for their naps. This is a perfect time for us to talk."

Mary Ellen took a seat on one of the wooden benches in Lillian's kitchen. "They're together now. Linda and her mother."

"*You're* her mother, Mary Ellen. Nothing is going to change that."

"And Abe is telling Matt and Luke this morning." Mary Ellen covered her face with both hands and shook her head. "We made such a mistake, Lillian." She pulled her hands away and rubbed tired eyes. "We should have told Linda and the boys about this a long time ago, way before Josephine came callin'."

"Maybe so. But, Mary Ellen, love runs much deeper than a bloodline. You know that. No one is ever going to replace you as Linda's mother."

Mary Ellen was quiet for a few moments. "I know nothing about this woman Josephine. Is she a good Christian woman? Will she be a *gut* influence on our Linda?"

"Linda might not even want to have a relationship with this woman. They might just spend the day together and that will be it. Linda might just be curious now that she's been told, and she might not want to see this woman again."

Mary Ellen sighed. "Lillian, I know it's wrong of me to want that, but that's exactly what I want. God help me, but I don't want that woman in our lives. I'm praying about it constantly, and I know my thoughts aren't Christian, but I can't help it."

"Did she seem nice?"

"*Ya*, she did. She even invited me to go with her and Linda."

Lillian sat up taller. "Why didn't you?"

Mary Ellen shrugged. "I reckon we've made a mess of things up to this point, and I felt like Linda should have this time with Josephine by herself." She paused. "She's very pretty, the *Englisch* woman."

Lillian smiled. "So are you."

Mary Ellen forced a smile. "*Danki*, Lillian." But these days when Mary Ellen looked in the mirror, she no longer saw the person she remembered herself to be. Instead, the face that stared back at her had tiny lines feathering from the corners of each eye, and depending on the hours of sleep she'd had, often dark circles underneath eyes that seemed smaller somehow, less vibrant. And her hair, once a silky dark brown, was now speckled with gray. She thought about Josephine's honey-blonde hair, her perfectly made-up face, and the way her clothes complemented her shapely figure. Mary Ellen knew that vanity is a sin, but as her thirty-eighth birthday approached, it was hard not to see the physical changes taking place. She glanced at hands worn by years of hard work, and she suspected Josephine used fancy lotions to keep her hands smooth and young-looking.

"How is Jonas?" Mary Ellen was ready to talk about something else.

Lillian blew out an exasperated breath and rolled her eyes. "Demanding." She smiled. "It's a *gut* thing we all love Grandpa so much, because some days he is just a *schtinker*." Lillian shook her head. "*Mei mamm* and Lizzie have their hands full. I go by there every day and try to help, but it's hard because I have *mei* own family to take care of too."

"Is there anything I can do?"

Lillian pointed to the basket. "I don't have to bake any bread tomorrow morning since you brought us that basket. *Danki*, Mary Ellen. That's a big help."

"I'll do whatever I can." Mary Ellen reached over and placed her hand on Lillian's.

"*Danki*. We're all getting by just fine, but when Grandpa gets in one of his nasty moods, it's just terrible. I know he feels badly and all, but yesterday he demanded that someone shave his beard off. We didn't know what to do."

Mary Ellen let out a slight gasp. "Why? That would be unheard of."

"*Mamm* tried to calmly remind him that when a man gets married, he never shaves his beard." Lillian stifled a grin. "Do you know what he told her?"

Mary Ellen arched her brows. "No tellin'."

"He told *Mamm* that there are tiny little people living in his beard and that they talk all the time, keeping him up at night. Then he talked ugly to *Mamm* and told her he'd shave it himself."

Mary Ellen chuckled, but quickly bit her bottom lip. "I'm sorry, Lillian. I know it's not funny."

"It's okay. It's hard not to laugh at something so out of character for Grandpa."

"What did Sarah Jane do?"

Lillian smiled. "*Mamm* told the little people in his beard to be quiet, then pretended to give them one of Grandpa's sleeping pills."

"Did that work?"

Lillian shrugged. "Seemed to."

Mary Ellen thought for a moment. "Does Jonas understand what's happening?"

"*Ya*. He does. When his mind is *gut*, he says he is ready to go be with the Lord."

They sat quietly for a minute.

"How is Lizzie handlin' things?"

"Pretty *gut* on most days, but I heard her crying in the bathroom the other day. She won't show much emotion in front of anyone, especially Grandpa, but I know she's hurting."

"Of course she is." Mary Ellen paused. "The world won't be the same without your grandpa in it."

"No. It won't." Lillian's eyes filled with water. "But how blessed we all are to know him and have him in our lives."

Mary Ellen nodded as she blinked back her own tears.

Abe loaded the last of the tools he'd purchased at the farmer's market, while Matt and Luke stowed several bags of groceries in the buggy, items from Mary Ellen's list. His wife had offered to be with Abe when he told Matt and Luke about Linda's adoption, but Abe feared his wife's current state of mind might only make things worse. Matt and Luke were young men, and Abe reckoned he should be the one to talk to them. He waited until they were clear of the city and moving down Black Horse Road toward home.

Matthew was in the front seat with Abe, and Luke sat beside the groceries and tools in the backseat. Abe slowed the horse to a trot and took a deep breath.

"Boys, there is something I need to talk with you about." He held the reins with one hand as he tipped his hat back with the other, wiping sweat from his brow.

Neither boy said anything. Matt seemed preoccupied with a flyer he was reading, something about an upcoming Mud Sale in nearby Strasburg.

"It's about Linda," Abe continued.

"What's she done?" Matt didn't look up, but snickered.

Abe sighed as he stifled his irritation at Matt's comment. "She didn't do anything."

Matt closed the brochure. "Then what is it?"

Abe stared straight ahead and wondered why he hadn't planned out this conversation. He'd prayed that it would just come to him. "Your sister is adopted. Your *mamm* and I adopted her when she was two-weeks-old. We should have told you before now, but as we speak, Linda is spending time with the woman who gave birth to her." Abe glanced to his right. Matt's eyes were wide, his jaw dropped. "I'm sorry we didn't tell you before now."

"Are you serious?" Matt raised his brows at his father.

"*Ya.* I'm serious."

Matt looped his thumbs beneath his suspenders and sat taller. "I knew there was something different about her. That explains it." Then he chuckled.

"Shut up, Matt! Just shut up! You're just stupid, and . . ." Luke slammed both hands on the top of the seat in front of him.

"No, you're stupid!" Matt twisted in his seat, his eyes blazing with anger.

"Whoa!" Abe quickly pulled the horse and buggy to the side of the road. "Both of you, stop it this minute!"

"*Daed*, is it true?" Luke leaned forward into the front seat. "Is Linda really not our sister?"

Abe twisted in the seat to face his youngest son, whose eyes were filled with tears. "Linda will always be your sister. No matter what."

"I don't understand then." Luke's bottom lip trembled.

Abe looked at Matt, who was staring straight ahead, his lips pressed firmly together. Matt always hid his feelings with anger, so Abe wasn't surprised at his reaction. He focused on Luke as he spoke.

"Your *mamm* and I tried to have children for quite a while. When the Lord didn't bless us with any, we began to think that perhaps we just weren't able to have any *kinner*. Linda's birth mother was seventeen and pregnant at the time, and a lawyer made an arrangement for us to raise Linda as our own."

Matt kept staring straight ahead, but grunted. "*Ya*, I reckon someone should have mentioned this before now."

"Does Linda know yet?" Luke's voice trembled as he spoke.

Matt spun around. "Aren't you listening? *Daed* said she's with that woman now."

"Matthew, that is enough. You watch that tone of voice. Do you hear me?" Abe leaned forward toward his son.

Matt turned back around and stared straight ahead. "Yes, sir."

"Linda's my sister." Luke held his head up high. "No matter what."

Abe smiled. "That's right. Nothing is going to change."

"Everything has changed." Matthew shook his head, and Abe knew that his oldest son was taking this harder than he let on. When Abe saw Matt's bottom lip quiver, he reached over and laid a hand on Matt's shoulder.

"I know you boys are hurting right now. Your *mamm* and I are hurting too. But this will take a toll on Linda more than anyone, and I need you boys to be strong for her. She is still your sister."

Abe faced forward, grabbed the reins, and flicked the horse into motion. He looked forward, but he saw Matt swipe at his eyes.

He knew his boys were strong young men. It was just going to take them a little time. That's all. Time.

We should have told them all sooner.

But for now, there was nothing else to say. Abe raised his chin and kept his eyes straight ahead.

Josie pulled the car to a stop in front of Linda's home, sad that their time together was coming to an end.

"*Danki* for showing me all the pictures and for buying *mei* lunch at Katie's Kitchen." Linda reached for the handle on the passenger door, but first turned to Josie and smiled. "And for letting me put on some of your perfume."

"You're welcome." Josie's mind was spinning. There hadn't been enough time. Linda pushed the car door open. "Linda?"

"*Ya?*"

Josie couldn't say anything for a moment; it was like looking

into a mirror seventeen years ago, except that Josie would have been
wearing blue jeans, a T-shirt, and her hair in a ponytail, but Josie
recognized herself in Linda's face for sure. "Would you like to do
something on Saturday? I don't really know what's allowed, and I
wouldn't want to do anything to upset your parents. I guess movies
aren't something you can do, or—"

"I can." Linda's face brightened. "I'm in *mei rumschpringe*, so I
can go to movies and do things in the *Englisch* world."

"Want me to pick you up around noon?"

Linda tapped her finger to her chin. "Would you mind if
we made it around three, so I'll have time to finish my Saturday
chores?"

"Sure."

Linda smiled, then pushed the door open and stepped out of
the car. Josie watched her walk up to the house, unfamiliar feelings
rising to the surface and filling her with a love she didn't think
she'd ever known.

As Linda tiptoed into the house, an overwhelming feeling of guilt
overtook her. She'd had a good time with Josie and found her to
be kind, generous, and fun to be around. Linda liked the way she
smiled, too, the way she looked. She was pretty, and Linda couldn't
help but wonder if people thought she was pretty too, like Josie.
She sniffed her wrist, the spot where Josie had sprayed the sweet-
smelling perfume.

"Hello."

Linda jumped when she heard her mother speak to her from
the bottom step of the stairs. She was holding a broom, and more

guilt consumed Linda as she realized that her chores fell on her mother today. Linda crossed the den and reached for the broom.

"I'll finish up. I'm sorry I was gone so long. I didn't know—"

Mamm pulled the broom back. "No, no. I'm done, and no harm done. Let's sit. I want to hear all about your day with . . ." She paused. "What is that sweet smell?"

Linda could feel her cheeks reddening. "Josie let me try a little of her perfume." She held her wrist up, just in case her mother wanted to get a better whiff. She didn't. Linda followed her to the couch and took a seat beside her.

"Did you go to Katie's Kitchen?"

"*Ya*, we did. Anna Marie was our waitress." Anna Marie was Ben and Martha King's daughter, and Linda had grown up with her.

"Did you tell Anna Marie who—who you were dining with?"

Linda shook her head. "No, *Mamm*."

Her mother let out air she'd seemed to be holding. "What else did you do?" *Mamm* clenched her lips tight, and Linda wasn't sure how much to say.

"Not much." She shrugged.

Mamm twisted on the couch to face Linda. "Linda, you don't have to be afraid to share with me." She looked down. "Or, if you're not comfortable, I understand."

Linda didn't say anything for a moment as she tucked her chin. Then she looked up to see her mother waiting for some sort of response. "She's nice."

"*Gut.*"

This was the first time Linda had ever felt awkward talking to her mother, yet it was the one time when she felt like she needed her the most. "She has the fanciest house I've ever seen, *Mamm*.

And it's big." She paused and checked her mother's expression. *Mamm* smiled, but not a full smile. "She's married too. But they don't have any other—I mean any children."

Her mother nodded, then her eyes warmed, and Linda's stomach settled a little bit. "You're very pretty, like she is." *Mamm* pushed back a strand of hair that had fallen from beneath Linda's *kapp*.

"I always thought I looked like you," Linda said sheepishly. "That's what everyone always said."

"*Ya*, people have always said that. They say you have my cute little pug nose." She playfully poked Linda's nose. Linda smiled.

"*Mamm*." Linda reached for her mother's hand. "You should have told me a long time ago about Josie."

Her mother twisted her head and stared at the wall to their left. "I know."

"But nothing is going to change. I love you. You are my mother and will always be my mother."

Mamm kept her head turned toward the wall but reached up and swiped at her eye. When she turned to face Linda, all Linda wanted to do was crawl in her lap like she'd done when she was a little girl and have her mother stroke her head, the loving way only a mother can. When *Mamm* opened her arms, Linda folded into them, and they both held each other for several minutes.

"She wants to see me again on Saturday afternoon," Linda said after a while. She felt her mother instantly stiffen, and she wondered if perhaps she'd forbid her to go.

"I suspected that she would want to spend more time with you." *Mamm* eased out of the hug, cupped her hand under Linda's chin, and said, "And that is all right."

Linda felt relief, but there was something about the way her mother spoke that made Linda suspect that it wasn't as all right as *Mamm* let on.

Josie had a spring in her step that she didn't remember having for years, and it had been a long time since she'd used her fine china and set the table in the formal dining room, complete with candles and fresh flowers. She stepped back to inspect her work. *Perfect.* She heard the front door open, glad that Robert was on time. She had so much to tell him. The timer on the oven dinged, and she headed back to the kitchen. She pulled the pan from the oven just as Robert entered the kitchen. She looked up in time to see him glance into the formal dining room.

"I take it things must have gone well today." He placed his briefcase on the kitchen counter, waited for her to put the pan down, then wrapped his arms around her.

"Oh, Robert. It was a perfect day." She buried her head in his chest and squeezed him tightly.

He gently eased her away. "Josie, I'm so glad, and I want to hear all about it, but I have some news for you."

She arched her brows. What could possibly be more important than her news?

"Remember Dr. Noah Stoltzfus, the doctor who put me in touch with some people at Lancaster General regarding Amanda?"

She nodded.

"Well, Noah also knows someone whose specialization is the type of inoperable tumor that you have."

No, no. Don't ruin this day. She pulled away, turned her back toward him, and combed a hand through her hair. "Robert, I don't want to see any more doctors. I've seen plenty, and they all say the same thing."

Robert gently spun her around, cupped her cheek, and gazed lovingly into her eyes. "Just one more, Josie. Please. Do it for me."

Josie twisted her mouth to one side, then the other. "I thought Dr. Stoltzfus ran a small clinic and catered mostly to the Amish community."

"He does. But he used to work at Lancaster General, and he has friends there. You know how hard it can be to get an appointment with a really good specialist. It can take months." They both looked at each other, and there was no need to verbalize what was on both their minds—how many months? "Please," he said again, his eyes begging her. He kissed her on the cheek. "I invited him and his wife for dinner. Can we set two more place settings?"

Josie pushed away from him. "Robert, why didn't you give me any warning?" She thrust her hands on her hips. "And I have so much to tell you about my day with Linda, and . . ."

"I know, baby. I tried to call all the way home and kept getting 'call failed' . . . And I want to hear every little detail about your day with Linda. I'm so happy for you. But I think it's important for you to meet Noah. I've met his wife several times when I've been at his clinic. I think you'll like her."

Josie let out a heavy sigh. "I guess I don't have much choice. Let me go get two more place settings."

Robert gently grabbed her arm. "Hey, come here, you." He pulled her close again, cupped the nape of her neck, and whispered, "I'm not giving up. Do you hear me?"

Josie eased away and looked him in the eyes. "This was such a good day for me, Robert. I just want to share it all with you, and I'm so tired of talking about medical stuff."

"Tonight, over a glass of wine, after our guests are gone, I want to hear every little detail of your day with Linda." He paused with pleading eyes. "But let's hear about Noah's specialist. Please."

Josie forced a smile for Robert's sake. She'd accepted her fate years ago. It terrified her, but she'd accepted it. Robert hadn't. "I hope they like beef parmesan and fettuccini," she said in a pouty voice.

"They will love whatever you made. They will love you." He kissed her on the lips, then pulled away when they heard a knock at the door.

"They're here."

7

JOSIE HAD BARELY ADDED THE EXTRA PLACE SETTINGS when Robert opened the door.

"Carley, Noah, so nice to see you." Robert stepped aside so the couple could enter. Josie joined them in the foyer, and she tried to mask her disappointment by forcing a smile. Good thing she'd chosen her good china.

"This is my wife, Josie."

Josie extended her hand to Carley, then to Noah. "So nice to meet you both."

Robert motioned everyone toward the living room, and he wound his way around the wet bar in the corner. "Can I get anyone a drink before dinner?"

"No, we're fine," Noah said as his eyes scanned the room. "This is a beautiful home you have."

"It really is." Carley smiled at Josie.

"I'm still unpacking boxes. I should already be done." Josie waved her arm around the room where a few boxes were still pushed up against the walls.

"It takes time." Carley smiled warmly. "But you've done an amazing job so far. It's really pretty."

I want our home to be perfect for Robert after I'm gone. "Thank you."

She paused. "Robert said you have a daughter?" Josie walked toward the couch, sat down, and motioned for Carley to do the same. Robert and Noah sat down in high-back chairs facing the couch. "I thought he said her name is Jenna? How old is she?"

Carley's face lit up at the mention of her daughter, and Josie could certainly understand that. "Jenna is nine, and we've had her for four glorious years. We adopted her when she was five."

"Really?" Josie crossed her legs and leaned forward. "From an agency?"

"No. Actually, Jenna's parents died and her older sister, Dana, had been raising her, but when Dana went off to college, she asked Noah and I if we would like to adopt Jenna. Noah was a good friend of their family before he and I got married." Carley paused. "I couldn't have any children, so we felt very blessed to be able to adopt Jenna."

"Josie recently reconnected with her daughter that she gave up for adoption," Robert said, much to her horror. How could he possibly bring up something so personal to these people she didn't even know? She cut her eyes at him in a way that told Robert he'd messed up. "She was very young," he added, as if that would make up for his blunder.

"Well, we are big advocates of adoption," Noah said. "I think it's a wonderful thing you did. You said you recently reconnected?"

Even though Noah directed the question to Josie, Robert stepped in once more. "The main reason we moved here is so that Josie could find her daughter. She's seventeen now. This is where Josie used to live, in Lancaster County."

"It was an open adoption," Josie added. This was not how she had envisioned her night at all, sharing something so personal with total strangers. She'd looked forward to a quiet dinner with Robert and an opportunity to share everything with him about her day with Linda. To make things even worse, a knot was building in her throat, and she choked back tears. She could feel Carley's eyes on her.

"Josie, I'd love to see your house." Carley stood up, and Josie stood up beside her.

"Sure."

"You girls go ahead," Robert said. "Okay with you, Noah? I'll show you around later."

Noah nodded, and Carley followed Josie around the corner and down a hallway lined with four bedrooms. "This is our bedroom," Josie said as her emotions about everything continued to build.

Carley didn't seem too interested in the bedroom, but instead stood staring at Josie, and then did the most unexpected thing. She walked toward her, grabbed her hand, and said, "You looked like you were about to lose it in there. Are you all right?"

Josie clutched this stranger's hand. Shallow gasps escaped, she bit her lip, and shook her head. As a tear fell, she let go of Carley's hand and wiped it away. "I'm so sorry. I've just had a very emotional day, and I just didn't expect Robert to bring up the subject of Linda."

Carley's eyes were kind and sympathetic. "Yes, I could tell that it bothered you. You don't even know us. Is that your daughter's name? Linda?"

"Yes. I spent the day with her today for the first time since I gave her up for adoption seventeen years ago."

"Oh my gosh. We shouldn't even be here." Carley shook her

head. "I'm sure you want to spend time with your husband and tell him all about it." She smiled. "Instead, Robert drags in dinner guests."

"No, no. It's fine, really." Josie was starting to feel somewhat comfortable around this woman. "It's just very—very personal."

"Of course it is. We don't have to talk about it at all. I just thought you might want to get away from the men for a few minutes. Men. They're so insensitive sometimes."

"Yes, they can be." Josie appreciated Carley's attempt at light-hearted humor.

"When we adopted Jenna, I worried about so many things. I know that I was on the other end of the spectrum, but if you ever want to talk, please call me. I know that tonight, Noah wants to talk with Robert and you about a specialist at Lancaster General who deals with the kind of tumor you have." Carley took a deep breath. "Wow. You have a lot going on, huh?"

Josie smiled. "You could say that. But I know everything is going to work out fine."

"I will pray for you, Josie. For you. For Linda. And for good news from this new doctor."

Josie smiled and thanked her, even though she knew prayers would go unanswered. Why would God possibly help someone who'd turned away from Him a long time ago? Josie could recall a time when she had a closer relationship with God, before she married Robert. But Robert didn't believe in God, and slowly over time, Josie's own beliefs had veered to questioning whether or not such an entity existed.

But with little time on her side, she couldn't help but speculate about God. And the possibility of heaven. Or hell.

After dinner, Josie served everyone coffee in the living room. Noah said Dr. Phillips had agreed to meet with Josie on the following Thursday at Lancaster General to evaluate the tumor growing inside her brain stem.

"Thank you for setting up this appointment." Robert took a sip of his coffee. "We really appreciate it."

"Yes, we do," Josie echoed to be polite. She'd enjoyed meeting Noah and Carley. Dinner conversation had been light and engaging, but she was ready to spend some quiet time with Robert, fill him in about her day with Linda.

"We'd like to put you on our prayer list at church," Noah said. "There's nothing like the power of prayer."

"That would be great." Josie glanced at Robert, who merely smiled. "We'd appreciate that."

"I don't know if it's ever come up, but I grew up Amish." Noah pushed back dark wavy locks, and Josie tried to envision the doctor with a bobbed haircut and sporting suspenders and a straw hat.

"Really?" Josie's eyes grew wide. "What happened?"

Noah set his coffee cup down on a coaster on the coffee table. "I had a strong calling to become a doctor." He paused. "If I'd made that decision before I was baptized, things would have been a lot easier. Instead, I was baptized into the faith, then chose to leave, and I was shunned by my family."

"Oh, no." Josie said. "I remember when I was growing up here, I heard of a man getting shunned. I didn't know him very well, but I just remember that he couldn't have anything to do with his family, not even sit down and have a meal with them."

"I had a terrible time understanding the whole shunning process," Carley chimed in. "But, luckily for Noah, his family eventually came around, and the bishop has pretty much looked the other way and allowed members of the community to visit his clinic."

"So, you have a good relationship with your family now?" Josie took a sip from her own cup of coffee.

"Yes, I do. But it took a while. My brother, Samuel, had a really hard time accepting me back into the family. It's a long story. I ended up giving my nephew one of my kidneys, and I think everyone had to take a good long look at the whole issue of shunning."

"Wow. That's amazing," Josie said. "How is your nephew now?"

"David is great. He's had no trouble since the transplant." Noah paused, glancing at his wife. "We've all been very blessed. My other brother, Ivan, and both my sisters eventually came around, and we don't flaunt it in front of the bishop, but we all spend time together. My sister, Mary Ellen, was sort of the cheerleader, pushing everyone to play nice." He chuckled. "And my niece, Linda, even worked for me for a couple of weeks a year or two ago, doing some filing for us. So, we've all come a long way."

Josie's heart began to thud against her chest. She glanced at Robert who had begun to squirm in his chair, then Robert stood up, and offered to pick up everyone's coffee cup, almost a rude gesture that the night should come to an end. Josie knew he didn't mean it that way, and she could tell by her husband's worrisome expression that he was fearful Josie had heard Noah loud and clear.

"Linda is your niece, and Mary Ellen is your sister?" Josie stood up when Carley and Noah did.

Robert set all the dishes haphazardly down on the coffee table, spilling coffee out of one. "We'll have to do this another time," he said smiling. "This has been great getting together like this."

Carley and Noah began to move toward the door. "It really has been fun." Then Carley turned to Josie. "Oh, and yes, Linda is the name of Noah's niece and Mary Ellen is his sister."

The two women locked eyes, and Josie knew her own eyes were big as golf balls. As if connecting to Josie's thoughts, Carley's bulged too. "Linda . . ." she whispered. "*Your* Linda?"

Josie nodded to Carley.

Friday morning, Mary Ellen was busy deep cleaning the downstairs in preparation for worship service at their home on Sunday. Abe and the boys were at her brother Ivan's house, helping him paint his fence, and Linda had gone along to visit with Katie Ann. Mary Ellen knew that Katie Ann was lonely, no children to take care of. No one was quite sure why they hadn't been able to have children. Once, Mary Ellen mentioned the possibility of adoption to Katie Ann, but Katie Ann wouldn't hear of it. "The Lord will bless us when He's ready," she'd said. Ivan and Katie Ann certainly knew that Linda was adopted, so she didn't understand why they wouldn't mull over the possibility, but it was not her business.

Her thoughts drifted back to Linda and Josephine as she finished up dusting, giving the mantel a final swipe, when she heard a knock at the door.

She saw Noah at the screen door. "I needed a break." She pushed open the door to the den. "Come in, *mei bruder*." She narrowed her brows. "What are you doing here? Shouldn't you be at the clinic?"

Noah blew out a heavy sigh and scratched his forehead. "Yeah, but I need to talk to you about something."

Mary Ellen stuffed her cleaning rag in the pocket of her black apron. "You look so serious. Everything is all right, no? Jenna, she is okay? Carley?"

"Yes. Everyone is okay." Noah sat down on the couch. "Do you remember when I told you that I'd recently met an attorney that I was helping find a doctor for his receptionist?"

Mary Ellen sat down on the couch beside Noah and thought for a moment. "No, I don't think so . . . *Ach*, wait, the girl with the disfigured lip?" Mary Ellen recalled a conversation she'd had with Noah a few weeks ago at his office. She'd taken Matt to see his uncle for a deep cut he'd gotten while working out in the barn. As Noah stitched up Matt's arm, he'd told her about the lawyer he'd met who offered to help his receptionist. "I remember, you said you thought a lot of this man."

"Yes, I do. He seems to go out of his way to help others, often without taking any money for his services. I admire his work ethics." Noah sighed. "Carley and I dined with him and his wife last night."

"That's nice," she said hesitantly. She knew Noah well enough to know that he was trying to get to a point, and it must be an important point to cause him to leave the clinic on a Friday morning to come talk to her.

Noah blew out a long breath. "Samuel told me about Linda, about her being adopted. He didn't want me to find out from someone else, since her birth mother has come looking for her."

I should have known what he was coming to talk about. "It has been a *hatt* situation." Mary Ellen rubbed her forehead. "We just never spoke of it, and of course, we took Linda in when you were away."

Noah stood up from the couch. He didn't look like a doctor in his blue jeans, loafers, and a bright yellow shirt—a "golf shirt" is what he'd called it in the past, which didn't make much sense since Noah didn't play golf. Noah always dressed that way when he worked at the clinic. Seemed to make people in the community more at ease when they saw him wearing it, as opposed to what doctors usually wore, either starched white shirts or those blue pants and shirts that looked like pajamas.

He tucked his hands deep into the pockets of his pants and paced for a moment. "Robert is the name of my friend." He glanced at Mary Ellen. "His wife gave up a baby for adoption."

Mary Ellen rose from the couch and walked toward him. "Why would they, Robert and his wife, do such a thing if they are married?"

"No, no. *They* didn't give up a baby; *she* did. A long time ago."

Mary Ellen tilted her head to one side and waited for Noah to go on.

"His—his wife's name is Josephine."

Mary Ellen put her hand to her chest and hoped that Noah wouldn't confirm what she knew to be true.

"Yes, Linda's mo—I mean the person who gave birth to her."

"And you are friends with these people?" Mary Ellen's brows leaned into a frown, and she knew that she had no right to feel betrayed, yet she did.

"I've been friends with Robert for weeks, but I only met Josephine last night when Carley and I ate dinner with them. I've been trying to help them—"

"I don't want to hear." Mary Ellen held one hand in the air, then turned her back to Noah. "I have to hear about Josephine from Linda, and it's hard for me." She covered her mouth with her hand, as if that would prevent her from spewing the vicious thoughts in her mind where Josephine was concerned. She'd given her baby away, and she should have respected that decision. Mary Ellen turned slowly around to face her brother. "Do you understand, Noah? Do you understand that her being here is a complete upset to our household? Not only was Linda upset, but Matt and Luke began to question whether or not I'd actually given birth to them, even after Abe talked with them. It's just all been terrible, and I'm afraid . . ." She choked back tears.

"Afraid that Linda will leave to go be with Josephine and live in the *Englisch* world?" Noah put a hand on her shoulder. "That's not going to happen."

"How can you be so sure?"

Noah stared long and hard into Mary Ellen's eyes. "Josie is sick."

"What do you mean, sick?" Mary Ellen folded her hands in front of her.

"That's what I was trying to tell you. I'm helping them get in to see a specialist at Lancaster General. It usually takes months to get an appointment to see Dr. Phillips, but I knew him well when I worked with him at the hospital, and he is doing this as a special favor. When Robert told me about Josie, I wanted to help, to make sure they'd utilized all their options."

"What do you mean, this utilizing of options? What does that mean?" *And what is wrong with her?*

"Mary Ellen . . ." He paused as his eyes saddened in such a way that Mary Ellen feared what he would say. "Josie is going to die within six months because she has an inoperable tumor on her brain. I want Dr. Phillips to have a look at her. He could be their last hope, and Dr. Phillips is a brilliant surgeon."

Mary Ellen folded at the waist and grasped her knees. "Oh, no." Her insides twisted in agony as a stab of guilt bore into her heart.

Noah wrapped his arm around her shoulder. "Mary Ellen, are you all right? I didn't realize that you knew Josie that well, or at all. I mean, I know Linda will be upset." He paused. "She just wants to know Linda while she has a chance. They moved here just for that reason."

"Oh, no," Mary Ellen said again. "Dear Lord, forgive me. Oh, Heavenly Father, forgive me."

Noah latched onto her shoulders and forced her to a standing position. He faced her and said, "Mary Ellen, what is it? Tell me what's wrong."

"Oh, Noah," she cried. "I've done a horrible thing. I've sinned a far greater sin than I could have imagined myself to do. Oh, Noah." She leaned into his arms. "This is my fault. It's my fault she's dying."

Noah pushed her away. "What? What are you talking about?"

"I prayed, Noah. I prayed to God to make her go away, to leave here, and—"

"Mary Ellen, listen to me. This is not your fault. Josie has been sick for a long time. Do you hear me? You didn't have anything to do with her brain tumor."

Mary Ellen sniffled and felt her guilt subsiding a little, but then she thought about the beautiful *Englisch* woman only a few years younger than her and how her life might be tragically cut short. Only moments earlier, she was wishing and praying for Josephine to go away, but never like this. Then she remembered the specialist and hoped her guilt would be even more relieved. "Will your friend, this Dr. Phillips, be able to save her?"

Noah sighed. "I don't think so. But I want him to review her test results, just to be sure."

They were quiet for a minute. Mary Ellen sat down on the couch, propped her elbows on her knees, and put her chin in her hands. "Linda finds out that she has a mother, only to have her taken away."

"You're her mother, Mary Ellen." Noah sat down beside her.

Mary Ellen rubbed her tired eyes and sat quietly, thinking. Then she turned to Noah. "You will let me know about this meeting with Dr. Phillips, if he can help her or not?"

"Yes. I will."

"Maybe we shouldn't say anything to Linda until we know for sure."

"I agree." Noah paused. "Mary Ellen, do you think maybe it's Josie's place to tell Linda?"

Mary Ellen swallowed hard. "*Ya*, I reckon so."

"I need to get back to the clinic." Noah stood up and walked toward the door. Mary Ellen got up and followed him. "I just wanted you to know what's going on. Linda might need you more than ever in the near future, especially if she gets close to Josie."

Mary Ellen nodded, then thanked Noah for stopping by. After the door closed between them, she stood where she was and bowed her head.

Forgive me, Lord.

8

Stephen helped Linda's father and two brothers set up benches in the family's den in preparation for worship service the following day. When Stephen's family hosted worship, they removed a wall partition that separated a small den from a larger living area, but the Huyard's den was exceptionally large and all the benches fit nicely after moving the couch and two rockers into another room.

As was tradition, they lined several rows of benches for the men facing one way and more benches for the women facing toward them, leaving room in the middle for Stephen's grandfather, the ministers, and deacons.

Stephen poked his head into the kitchen and saw Linda pulling a loaf of bread from the oven. Someday, she'd be baking bread in a home they would share together, just as soon as Stephen could build up enough courage to ask Linda to marry him. He loved her plenty, that was for sure, and they were both planning to be baptized in the fall, but being married to Linda would mean that she'd see him without his elevated shoe on, hobbling around the house off-balance. She'd told him over and over that it didn't matter to her one bit.

He smiled when he recalled Linda pulling her dress up slightly above her knee to reveal a birthmark she'd had since birth, an oblong circle of red that ran a good four inches up her leg. "See, I'm not perfect either," she'd said.

But she was perfect. Warm, loving, beautiful, and a great cook. He'd eaten plenty of meals with the Huyards since he and Linda had started dating a year ago, and many of those meals Linda had prepared. She was going to make a wonderful wife, and Stephen knew he needed to just go ahead and do it, ask her to be his *fraa*. They would publish their announcement in the paper and most likely wait until the following November or December to get married, when they were both almost nineteen and after they'd both been baptized into the faith.

Stephen helped Luke shift the last bench into place just as Linda rounded the corner into the den.

"Looks *gut*." She folded her arms across her chest. "And I finished all my chores."

Good. Stephen was ready to have some alone time with Linda. He playfully raised one brow in her direction and waited until Luke was out of earshot. "Let's get out of here." His eyes met with hers, and he couldn't wait to hold her in his arms, kiss her again.

"I can't. Josie is picking me up at three. Didn't I tell you?"

Linda had filled him in about her time with Josie, but he couldn't recall her saying that she was spending Saturday afternoon with her. He was pretty sure she hadn't or he would have remembered, but he tried to mask his disappointment since he knew all this was hard on Linda.

"I'm sorry." She reached up and touched his arm. "But we'll see each other here at worship tomorrow."

"*Ya.* It's all right. I know it's important for you to get to know this woman."

She kicked at the wood floor with her toe and tucked her chin. "I guess. It's just all strange." Linda lifted her face to his, gazed into his eyes, and pressed her lips firmly together for a moment. "I just don't know what she wants from me. I mean, she's nice enough and all, but I have a mother."

"Maybe she just wants to be your friend."

"That's what she says." Linda tilted her head slightly to one side. "Do you think it's okay to be friends with her?"

"*Ya,* I reckon so."

"I think we're gonna go eat and go to a movie." She shrugged. "Which I guess is all right since I'm at the age to do these things."

Stephen nodded, disappointed he wouldn't be spending the afternoon with Linda, but glad that she seemed to be handling this news about her mother much better than she had in the beginning. He thought back to her uncontrollable sobs when she'd first told him.

"Want to walk me to my buggy?"

She smiled, and he hoped there would be a good-bye kiss in store for him, but when they got out to the buggy, Linda's aunt and uncle, Katie Ann and Ivan, were just pulling in.

"It wonders me what brings them out here." Linda brought a hand to her forehead and blocked the descending sun as they pulled in. "We see *Onkel* Samuel and *Aenti* Rebecca, and even *Onkel* Noah and their families all the time, but we only see *Onkel* Ivan and *Aenti* Katie Ann at worship usually."

"Why do you think that is?" Stephen whispered as Katie Ann was climbing out of the buggy.

Linda shrugged. "I don't know." She waved her hand. "Hi *Aenti* Katie Ann and *Onkel* Ivan."

Katie Ann lifted a brief hand in Linda's direction, but kept her head down as she walked toward the house. Ivan trailed behind her and smiled briefly.

"*Mamm* said she thinks they're sad because they don't have no *kinner*," Linda said after her mother let them into the house. "They're old not to have a family."

"Hmm." Stephen zoomed in on Linda's lips again. Then he gently pulled her toward him. "I guess I'll see you tomorrow." He quickly brushed his lips against hers, and the feeling sent the pit of his stomach into a wild swirl. He couldn't wait to make Linda Huyard his wife.

Josie was anxious to see Linda, and she'd spent way more time than probably necessary planning out their afternoon. She reached up and fondled the cross necklace and wondered if Linda would be wearing hers too.

Linda was waiting in the yard when she pulled in, and Josie was glad to see a smile on her face as she crawled into the front seat.

"I have that same necklace." Linda pulled her necklace from beneath the collar of her dark blue dress.

Josie smiled and waited for her to buckle her seat belt before she pulled out. "I know. I bought mine that day at the market in Bird-In-Hand when I saw you purchase one just like it." She glanced briefly in Linda's direction. "I hope that's okay." She shrugged. "I guess I just wanted us to have something—something the same."

Linda smiled. "It's fine. I'm glad we both have one."

Josie was happy to see Linda relaxed, and she had high hopes for the afternoon. "I thought we could go see a movie, and then, if it's all right with you, I'd like for you to meet Robert." Josie couldn't wait to introduce Linda to her husband. After Carley and Noah had left the other night, Josie and Robert stayed up late talking about Linda and what a wonderful day Josie had with her daughter. And Robert had apologized for bringing up the subject of adoption in front of Noah and Carley, although they both agreed that it was best to know that Noah was related to Mary Ellen and Linda, especially in light of the friendships that were forming.

While Josie thought Carley was nice enough, she had no plans to get close to anyone. Only Linda. What was the point anyway?

"I'd like to meet your husband." She raised her eyebrows. "What movie?"

"There're several playing." Josie reached into the backseat and handed Linda the newspaper. "Here. You pick."

"Hmm." Linda scanned the movie section. "How about this one?"

Josie slowed the car down as she approached a buggy in front of her, then carefully sped up and made her way around it. She leaned over to see which movie Linda was pointing to. "It's rated R. How will your parents feel about that?"

"*Ach*, it'll be fine."

Linda spoke with such confidence that Josie immediately suspected it would not be fine. "Have you ever seen an R-rated movie?"

Linda sighed. "No."

"I just don't want your parents upset with me. I know that at your age you're given some freedoms, but that movie is going to be . . . *steamy*, I guess is the word."

Linda grinned. "It's a love story." She paused. "Please."

Josie couldn't say no. Under different circumstances, she might have told her they'd do it another time, but time wasn't on Josie's side. "Okay." She hoped the movie was a mild R.

Only twenty minutes into the movie, Linda whispered to Josie that she had to go to the ladies' room. Josie suspected that her hurried departure had something to do with the content on the screen. The movie was anything but mild, and more than once, Josie saw Linda's eyes widen with disbelief. No violence or language to speak of, but there was enough bare skin to make up for it, and Josie felt terrible for taking Linda to see the movie. Even though she was of age, it was quite clear that she was shocked by what she saw. Josie was glad that Linda was in the bathroom when things began to really heat up on the screen.

"We probably should have seen something else," Josie said when she found Linda standing outside the bathroom, her hands folded in front of her, her eyes cast down. Josie wondered if she was praying.

"I'm sorry, Josie." Linda looked up at Josie. "I reckon that movie is not for me. I kept thinking what *Mamm* would think, and . . ."

"No, don't apologize." Josie touched her arm and motioned her to walk alongside her and toward the exit of the theater. "I should have known you wouldn't like the movie." Josie silently blasted herself for agreeing to that particular movie. A good mother would have insisted they see something different.

They walked quietly for a few moments, and Linda waited until they were in the parking lot before she commented again.

"It wasn't that I didn't like it." Linda tucked her chin as Josie unlocked the passenger door. "It just—it embarrassed me."

Josie nodded, opened Linda's door, then walked to her side of the car and climbed in. "I shouldn't have agreed to that movie." *Mary Ellen wouldn't have.* Josie started the engine and backed out of the parking space.

"Josie?" Linda twisted beneath her seatbelt until she was facing Josie.

"Yeah?"

"Is that really how a man and woman are together when they're in *lieb*?" Her cheeks reddened, but her eyes pleaded with Josie for an answer.

Josie thought about Robert, their relationship, and how very much she loved him. "Yes, it is." She turned toward Linda, whose expression was drawn into a frown. "Linda, what is it?"

"I don't understand."

Josie drew in a breath, quite sure it was not her place to explain about sex to Linda. "Which part do you not understand?" *Oh dear.*

Linda avoided looking at Josie. "*Mei Englisch* friends told me how—how babies are made." She paused, glanced briefly at Josie, then looked away. "*Mamm* said I would learn when I get married, but I'm curious about one thing."

"Okay." Josie fearfully waited for Linda to get to the part that she didn't understand.

Linda shifted her weight, folded her hands in her lap, and stared straight ahead. Josie wondered if she was just going to drop it.

"It's just that—" Linda turned to face Josie, but then turned quickly forward again and shook her head. "I reckon I don't know how to ask . . ."

Josie pulled onto the main highway then briefly glanced at Linda. "I know we don't know each other well at all, Linda, but if you want to ask me something, anything at all, you can."

Linda shook her head. "Such matters should not be talked about."

"Okay." Josie waited since Linda's mouth was open, as if she was going to keep talking anyway.

Linda arched one brow. "They didn't show everything in the movie, did they?"

"No, they didn't. Most of what they showed leads up to intercourse."

Linda's face drew a blank. "Leads up to what?"

Surely in this day and time, Amish or otherwise, a seventeen-year-old girl would know what intercourse is. "Intercourse. You know what that is, right?"

"Of course." She sounded a bit irritated that Josie even had to ask. "It's a neighboring town," Linda finished confidently.

Josie stifled a grin. Lancaster County was known for the odd names of towns. Towns like Bird-In-Hand and Intercourse. She remembered questioning the unusual names when she'd lived here as a kid. Surely Linda knew that Intercourse referred to more than just the name of a town?

"Linda, you do know that intercourse means something else, besides just the name of a town, you know that, right?"

Linda faced her, widened her eyes. "What does it mean?"

It seemed too soon for Josie to be having this talk with Linda and way too late for Linda to just now be discovering this word or learning about the act itself. Josie sighed and feared she was stepping on Mary Ellen's toes in a big way. But as delicately as she could, she explained lovemaking to Linda. She watched Linda's eyes grow big as golf balls.

"But the couple in the movie weren't married." Linda sat up taller as she twisted to face Josie.

"No, they weren't."

"But that's wrong, then, no?"

Josie let out an uncomfortable sigh. "I suppose it is."

Linda tapped her finger to her chin. "I have one question," she said in a determined voice.

"What's that?" Josie pulled into her driveway.

"Does it hurt?"

Josie thought for a moment. "Well, I suppose the first time it can . . ."

Josie barely had the car in Park when Linda reached for the car door and jumped out. Josie grabbed her purse and also exited the car. She saw Linda standing on the other side. Josie stared at her across the hood. "Linda, it's just—"

But Linda waved her hand as if she didn't want to hear. "It doesn't matter. I'm not doing it. Ever!"

Josie hid her smile with her hand. "Linda, I'm sure that you will change your mind about that." She walked to the other side of the car, and together they began to walk up the sidewalk.

"Please, don't speak of this in front of your husband." Linda's eyes grew fearful and her expression serious.

"I won't," Josie assured her as she put the key in the door, but she hadn't even twisted the knob when the door flew open.

"Hello. This must be Linda." Robert extended his hand to Linda, and Josie felt an unfamiliar sense of pride. *Yes, this is my daughter.*

Linda tucked her chin, something Josie noticed she did when

she was feeling uncomfortable. She wanted Linda to feel comfortable around Robert. Her husband promised to look after Linda, financially or otherwise, after Josie was gone, and Josie hoped the two of them would be close. Then a pain surged through her head, and she reached for her temple. *No. Not now.*

Her head began to throb the way it did before she had an episode, and she could feel her mouth going dry. Robert's eyes met with hers as she and Linda walked through the doorway. He knew right away what was happening; he'd seen it plenty of times.

"I'll get your pills," he whispered. He put a hand on her shoulder. "Is it a bad one?"

Linda walked into the living room while Josie and Robert lingered by the door. "I don't know yet," Josie said. She squeezed her eyes closed.

"Are you all right?" Linda was walking back toward them.

"I just have a headache. I'll be right back." Josie moved past Linda and headed toward her bedroom, her legs shaky, her balance off, and vivid colors flashing around the room. Her doctor said the symptoms were similar to a migraine, but Josie knew what it was, and just knowing that a tumor was pushing on her brain stem often caused her to have a panic attack, wondering if this was it. Her doctor said he thought she had several months left, but he also told her he wasn't God, so there were no guarantees.

Josie sat down on the bed, reached for the pill bottle on her nightstand, and popped two of the pills, knowing they would make her sleepy. She'd fight to stay awake and spend time with Linda. She took a deep breath, closed her eyes, and hoped the pills would take effect soon without completely knocking her out.

God. She thought about Him a lot lately. It was hard not to.

She'd grown up in a religious household, and even though her parents stopped going to church when she was in junior high, Josie had continued on for a couple more years. Then Robert came along. Such a good man, but he had lots of valid arguments against the entire concept of God, life after death, and the teachings of the Bible. But now, more than ever, she found herself recollecting her time at church, the fellowship, the prayer, and the relationship she thought she'd had with God. *Illusions. Not real.* Must have been, if she was so easily swayed away. *Is there a heaven? Did Jesus really die on the cross to save us? Is there a hell?*

As the pain began to subside, Josie did something she hadn't done in many years. "If You are there, please take care of my daughter when I'm gone," she whispered, then thought for a moment. "Maybe you could even give me a little sign that you're there."

She knew the headache wouldn't completely go away for a while, and she wanted to spend time with Linda, so she picked herself up off the bed and made her way downstairs. Linda was sitting on the couch watching television. She didn't see Robert anywhere.

"Did Robert abandon you?" Josie sat down beside Linda, who smiled.

"He's getting us all a piece of pie."

Josie kicked off her brown flip-flops, crossed her legs, and brushed a piece of fuzz from her blue jeans. "First a steamy movie and now TV. Your mom would kill me."

Linda pointed to the television. "Look, Josie! It's the man in the movie we just saw."

Yes, with clothes on. "It sure is." She turned her head from the television and gazed at Linda. She'll marry her boyfriend next year and go on to have babies. She has her whole life in front of her, a life that she will share with Mary Ellen and the rest of her family. As it should be. What Josie wouldn't do to stand on the sidelines and watch her grow and become a wife and mother. She swallowed hard.

"I watch television with my *Englisch* friends at their homes. *Mamm* knows. But once I'm baptized into the faith, I won't do those things."

"You're close to your mom, I can tell."

"*Ya*, I am." Linda turned back to the television, but then Robert entered the room balancing three pieces of key lime pie.

"Here you go, ladies." He handed the first piece to Linda, then passed a plate to Josie.

Linda took a bite of pie and swallowed. "This pie is very *gut*, did you make it?"

"No. Robert brought it home the other night. Honey, didn't you pick it up at that bakery on Lincoln Highway?"

Robert had a mouthful, but nodded.

Josie wasn't hungry, and she was afraid the pie wouldn't stay down, but she took a small bite just the same.

"Linda, did Josie tell you that I have to go out of town for two weeks?"

"No, I haven't had a chance to," Josie cut in.

"I have a trial that's been going on for years, and it looks like it is finally going to wrap up, but I have to go to China." Robert took another bite of pie, then went on. "Anyway, maybe you could stay here with Josie while I'm gone."

"Robert, no." Josie's tone was sharp. She couldn't believe he would ask Linda this. "I'll be fine."

"I just thought that it might be a nice way for you two to have some girl time together, that's all." Robert's expression grew solemn.

Robert had done everything humanly possible to get out of the business trip, but Josie kept urging him to go. She knew it was important to him, but he didn't want to leave her alone. Much to her horror, he'd even called and asked her mother to come stay with her, starting next week when he had to leave. Josie had quickly called her mother and squelched that plan. One day with her mother would be too much for Josie, even though Mom was ready and willing to come be with her. Josie had two friends back home that she stayed in touch with, and she was sure that Kathy or Paula would come and stay with her, but she refused to disrupt their lives for this. She'd look forward to a visit from her friends when it was convenient for them. Robert's parents, sweet as they were, could barely take care of each other.

"No, Robert. Linda can't just give up her life to come stay with me for two weeks, I'm sure." Although, there was nothing Josie would like more.

Linda glanced back and forth between the two of them. "No, I couldn't," she said sheepishly. "I have many chores to tend to at the farm." She paused and smiled. "But maybe I can come visit some."

"Anytime." Josie set her pie on the coffee table after taking only one bite. "I guess I ate too much popcorn at the movies," she lied. Her head was splitting, and she needed to lie down.

Robert sat up taller in his chair. "Baby, are you okay?"

Don't alarm Linda. They'd discussed this. Josie didn't want Linda to know about the tumor. Not yet. She didn't want Linda to feel sorry for her.

"I'm fine, Robert."

Linda placed her clean plate on the coffee table. "*Danki*, Mr. Robert. This was so *gut*."

"You're very welcome, Linda. And just call me Robert."

Linda nodded. Robert looked older than Josie, but he sure seemed to love her very much. He looked at her the way Stephen often looked at Linda and also like the man in the movie looked at that woman. Linda cringed and wondered how she'd ever have a baby if making one would hurt. She knew that actually having the baby hurt; Aunt Lillian had said it hurt bad. But Linda always figured that once she was in a family way, the baby was coming out no matter what. It never occurred to her that the making part would be painful.

She glanced around the room at all the paintings on the walls as she enjoyed the cool air-conditioning. She thought about what it would be like to stay here for two weeks. Linda had seen Josie's bathroom on her first visit, and she couldn't imagine what it would be like to take a bath in a tub twice as big as the one at home. She envisioned herself taking a long soak in bubbles up to her neck.

"Maybe I could spend one night?" She smiled at Josie.

"That would be great!" Josie reached over and squeezed her hand. This was all very confusing, but Linda couldn't help but like her birth mother. She and her husband both seemed very kind. "Any night you want," Josie added.

"Josie, I'm going to try one more time to get out of this trip. I'm just not comfortable leaving you alone, and—"

"No, Robert. I already told you that I'll be fine. Really." Josie glared at her husband, and Linda didn't understand why he didn't want to leave her. *Daed* had left *Mamm* several times for a few days to go purchase farm equipment in another town. Of course, *Mamm* had her *kinner* around, and Josie didn't have anyone.

Linda faced Robert. "What day do you leave, Mr. Robert? I mean—Robert." Linda couldn't help but wonder if Josie had fancy lotions and bubble baths in her bathroom too.

"I leave on Tuesday morning."

"Monday is wash day, but Tuesday is a slower day. Maybe I can spend the night with you on Tuesday night, if it's all right with you. And with *mei* parents."

"I would love that." Josie slapped her hands to her knees. "I'll cook us something. Anything you'd like. Do you have a favorite?"

"I like meatloaf and potatoes." *Mamm* made the best meatloaf, but for some reason, she hadn't made it in a while.

Linda watched Josie and Robert glance at each other and smile, even though Linda wasn't sure why.

"Then meatloaf and potatoes it is." Josie was smiling, and Linda wanted her to be happy. But she wanted *Mamm* to be happy, too, and she wasn't sure if this news would make her mother very happy, or if *Mamm* would even allow her to stay overnight with Josie. But the thought of bathing in that warm bathtub, with the air-conditioning running, and maybe even the television on, told Linda she was going to ask for permission.

But she couldn't help but be leery as to exactly what Josie wanted from her and how much she had to give in return.

9

MARY ELLEN ALWAYS ENJOYED HAVING WORSHIP SERVICE at their home, and her family hosted about every nine months. Much preparation went into readying the house. On this Sunday morning, she was pleased at how well things had come together. Her house was clean, benches were in place, food was prepared and ready to serve, and Linda had stayed unusually close to her throughout the morning.

Her daughter didn't say too much about her visit with Josephine, just that she'd had a good time and that they'd gone to the movies. And she mentioned meeting Josephine's husband, commenting that he seemed like a good fellow. Mary Ellen still wasn't comfortable with the situation or pleased that Josephine had disrupted their lives in such a way, but Noah's information certainly shed new light on the circumstances. It stood to reason that Josephine would want to know her daughter. Mary Ellen's heart ached when she thought about Josephine's short future, but she also wanted to make sure that Linda was grounded in her faith and would stay on course with her studies of the *Ordnung* in preparation for baptism. Mary Ellen and Abe had worked with all the children from the time they were young to make sure they had a good understanding of the code of conduct by which they lived, so that each one would know the *Ordnung* well and be able to choose baptism into the community.

Mary Ellen glanced at the clock as time for worship service drew near, then looked out the window to see a line of buggies coming up the driveway. Her yard was green and plush, her flowers in full bloom, and Abe had even cleaned up the inside of the barn, knowing the men would gather there in the afternoon to tell jokes and possibly sneak a few cigars, or even a glass of homemade wine. Everything was ready.

"Stephen's here." Linda bounced across the living room and out the front door. Mary Ellen watched through the window as the two met in the front yard, showing no affection, but Mary Ellen could see the looks in both their eyes. She was quite content knowing that Stephen would someday be her son-in-law. They were both still young, but Mary Ellen hoped he would ask her to wed soon. Somehow, in her mind, that would solidify Linda's staying in the community and dissolve the threat that Josephine brought into their world. Even though Linda was of age to experience her running-around period, Mary Ellen knew that her exposure was heightened when she was in Josephine's fancy house and doing things Mary Ellen certainly wouldn't approve of.

At eight o'clock everyone was seated, and the service began with thirty minutes of song in High German, followed by the opening sermon which always lasted about twenty minutes. After the sermon, there was a short silent prayer before the deacon read a Scripture verse. Mary Ellen caught Linda and Stephen winking at each other from across the room. However inappropriate, Mary Ellen couldn't help but smile.

Two hours into the service, they listened to the minister give the main sermon, and today he seemed to be speaking directly to Mary Ellen. "We don't always understand the circumstances that we find ourselves in, but we must remember that to question His will is a sin and often leads us down a path that is not of His choosing."

Mary Ellen knew she'd been guilty of questioning God's will from the moment Josephine showed up on the doorstep. However, she tried to recall that day Josephine arrived at Mary Ellen and Abe's house seventeen years ago. She suspected it was just as hard on Josephine then, if not more so. Mary Ellen cringed when she thought about the way Josephine's mother spoke to Josephine all those years ago, and it had been clear at the time that Josephine was being forced to give away her child. Perhaps Mary Ellen and Abe should have backed out of the adoption because of that.

Her thoughts were interrupted when the congregation began to sing, and she regretted allowing her mind to drift and missing the end of the sermon. She sang with conviction her praises to the Lord for the next fifteen minutes of the service, and then worship came to a close. She hurried to the kitchen to start getting things ready for the meal.

She bumped into her friend, Sadie Saunders, who was with her husband, Kade, and their two children. They chatted for a moment, then Mary Ellen excused herself.

"I'm going to put the meal out so everyone can get started."

Sadie handed Kade their daughter, Marie. "I'm coming to help."

By the time Mary Ellen and Sadie worked their way through the crowd to the kitchen, several of the ladies were already putting the food on the counter. Every two weeks after worship service, the noon meal consisted of the same thing. Mary Ellen had wondered for years if that would ever change, but it didn't appear so. Ten loaves of homemade bread sat next to large containers of peanut butter and cheese spreads. Sandwiches were made by swiping both spreads onto the bread. The tastes complemented each other, and they'd all been raised on it. Occasionally, an *Englisch* person was invited to worship service, and they were always interested in the consistency of the peanut butter spread, which was made using traditional peanut butter, but with added ingredients that made it sweeter and thinner.

Pickled beets, seasoned pretzels, pickles, and snitz pie were always served as well. On this late morning Mary Ellen's stomach was growling, and she was wishing for more than the usual offerings.

"I notice that none of Lillian's family is here. Not her, Samuel, or the children. And neither are Jonas, Lizzie, and Sarah Jane." Sadie twisted the lid from a jar of pickles and placed them on the table. "It wonders me if everything is all right."

"I haven't heard anything." Mary Ellen poured the homemade pretzels from a plastic bag into a large bowl as speculations about the family's absence began to stir worry. "I reckon maybe Linda can pay them a visit this afternoon, see if everyone is all right. She enjoys visiting with Jonas."

"Did I hear my name?"

Mary Ellen turned to see Linda snatching a pickle from the jar on the table. "We're just concerned that Samuel, Lillian, and the children aren't here, and neither is Jonas, Lizzie, or Sarah Jane. I was wondering if maybe you'd like to go check on them in a while."

Linda nodded with a mouthful, then swallowed. "*Ya.* I noticed they weren't here. I hope Jonas is all right, but don't you think Barbie or someone would have gotten word if—if something bad happened?" Linda paused, bit her bottom lip, and waited.

"I think so." Mary Ellen comforted herself with that thought.

"*Mamm* . . ."

"*Ya?*"

"Do you think I could drop off a piece of snitz pie for Josie and her husband on the way? I mean, if there's any left." Linda tucked her chin, then raised her eyes to Mary Ellen. "They seem to like pie," she said sheepishly.

"I reckon that would be all right." Mary Ellen recalled her conversation with Noah and she offered another silent prayer for Josephine.

Linda shared a kiss with Stephen back behind the far barn after almost everyone had gone home later that afternoon. His touch sent a tingle up her spine and caused her body to react in ways she didn't exactly understand. She immediately thought about the movie she'd watched with Josie, and she edged away a bit.

"Have you told your *mamm* that you want to spend the night at Josie's house on Tuesday?" Stephen pulled his arms from around her waist and sat down on a nearby stump.

"Not yet. I'll talk to her tonight." Linda was dreading having to ask permission. She could see the tension in her mother's expression anytime Josie was mentioned.

"Linda . . ." Stephen pulled his straw hat off and swiped his forearm against beads of sweat building on his forehead. "I reckon you gotta be careful 'bout what you're doing."

She sat down on a stump facing him, rested her elbows on her knees, and cupped her cheeks. "What do you mean?"

"Gotta be careful 'bout getting unequally yoked with outsiders. We hear about it at worship and in our studies of the *Ordnung.*" He twisted his mouth to one side. "That's all I'm saying."

Linda sat up straight. "I know that."

"*Daadi* says that lots of them are *gut* Christians, but we don't know for sure, so it's best to stick with our own, not be tempted by their ways."

Just because your grandfather is the bishop . . . "I'm just enjoying my freedom during my *rumschpringe*, that's all." She paused, feeling defensive. "It wouldn't hurt you to do a few things in the *Englisch* world, while you can. We'll be baptized soon enough, and you'll never be able to experience some of those things."

Stephen shrugged. "I reckon I don't care to experience that stuff. I'm happy here. With you." He reached over and latched onto her hand.

"I'm happy here, too, with you." Linda blew air upward to clear a strand of hair that had fallen from beneath her *kapp*. Stephen pulled his hand from hers and was gently brushing the hair from her face when they heard footsteps coming around the corner of the barn.

"*Daadi.*" Stephen rose from the stump as his grandfather approached. Linda stood up also.

"Hello, Bishop Ebersol. Lovely worship service today." Linda forced a smile. Bishop Ebersol made her nervous, always had. His gray beard stretched the length of his chest, and his bushy brows jetted inward, giving him the appearance that he was always angry. He was tall, slightly bent over, but with an air of authority and the appearance of someone who demanded instant obedience. Stephen said he just looked scary but really wasn't.

"Linda, I came to speak with you about this woman, Josephine." Bishop Ebersol looked briefly in Stephen's direction, as if he wasn't sure whether to continue talking to her in front of his grandson.

"*Ya.*" Linda waited as she twisted the strings on her apron.

"This is an *umgwehnlich* situation." The bishop paused, then narrowed his eyes, which only made him look even scarier. "My door is always open if you would like to talk about this."

Linda nodded, but knew she'd never approach the bishop about anything if she didn't have to. She recalled a time when she was about ten years old, when the bishop came to her house to speak with her parents. She could still recall the scared look on both her parents' faces when Bishop Ebersol pulled into the driveway that Saturday afternoon. Linda never did find out what happened, but just his presence still sent her knees to shaking.

"*Danki*, Bishop Ebersol," she finally said. Although if she needed to talk to anyone, she knew exactly who it would be, and she'd be seeing him later. Jonas.

The bishop glanced back and forth between her and Stephen, and Linda could feel her cheeks reddening. Bishop Ebersol just seemed to know things, and Linda wondered if he knew she and Stephen had been kissing behind the barn.

"Stephen, I think your parents are preparing to leave." The bishop raised his brows, as if waiting for Stephen to walk back to the house with him.

"*Ya, Daadi.*" Stephen gave Linda a quick wave good-bye, followed by a wink when his grandfather wasn't looking, and Linda watched them both walk back to the house.

About fifteen minutes later everyone was gone, and Linda loaded up two pieces of snitz pie in a basket, prepared to stop by Josie's house before going to see Jonas to make sure everything was all right. It made sense that Jonas, Lizzie, and Sarah Jane couldn't make it to worship, but it seemed odd that *Onkel* Samuel's family wasn't there either, unless Jonas was in a real bad way. She decided to go by and see Jonas first.

When she pulled in, she saw several buggies out front, and her heart began to pound against her chest. She parked alongside a buggy she thought she recognized to be Lillian's, and when she took a peek inside the buggy, she saw the car seat her aunt and uncle used to cart baby Elizabeth around in. She hurried to the front door and knocked.

Linda could tell her aunt had been crying when she looked at Lillian's face. A knot rose in her throat as she fought the tremble in her bottom lip.

"Hello, Linda." Lillian pushed the screen door open and motioned for her to come in.

"*Mamm* wanted me to come and check on everyone, since no one was at worship today." She wanted to just go home. David's eyes met with hers when she walked into the den, and she could tell her cousin had been crying as well. Her knees began to tremble.

"Jonas has had a hard day." Sarah Jane placed a hand on Linda's shoulder. "But I know he would want to see you."

"Is he in pain?" Linda cringed and drew in a deep breath and held it.

"He is feeling better than he was earlier today." Sarah Jane motioned her toward the stairs. "Go on up, dear. Lizzie is upstairs with him."

Linda didn't move. "I can come back another time."

Sarah Jane smiled, but her eyes welled with water. "I think you should go see him now."

Oh, no. Dear God, don't take Jonas. Not yet.

Linda's feet were rooted to the floor, and she glanced at David. He nodded toward the stairs. "He'll want to see you," her cousin said.

Linda left them all, and the sound of sniffling echoed behind her as she made her way up the stairs. She didn't turn around and silently prayed that Jonas was not in any pain. When she pushed open the door to Jonas's bedroom, she wanted to pinch her nostrils as the smell of sickness hit her in the face, but even worse was the way Jonas was propped up in the bed, his hands folded across his stomach. Like he was dead.

"Hello, Linda." Lizzie cupped her hand to her husband's cheek. "*Mei lieb*, Linda is here."

Linda stood in the doorway not moving as she watched Jonas's eyes slowly open. He licked parched lips as white as the rest of his face, and Linda closed her eyes for a moment.

"Linda," he whispered. "I'm glad you came. I've been . . ." Jonas took a deep, labored breath. "I've been wanting to talk to you."

Lizzie stood up from the chair beside Jonas's bed. *Don't leave me in here with him, Lizzie.*

"I'll be back in a bit." Lizzie clutched the footboard on the bed as she eased toward Linda. "Go sit. Talk with Jonas, dear."

Linda nodded, but didn't move. Then Jonas's lips parted into a slight smile.

"Don't look so scared." Jonas licked his lips again. "Could you pour me a glass of water?" He pointed to his nightstand where a pink plastic pitcher was surrounded by pill bottles, a box of tissues, several small white cups, and a pair of reading glasses.

"*Ya, ya.*" Linda moved quickly to the pitcher, filled the glass, and hurriedly handed it to Jonas. She waited for him to finish sipping the water. "Are you in pain?"

Jonas raised his brows. "I'm dying. I reckon so."

"*Ach,* no. How bad? How much pain?" She sat down in the chair, reached over, and touched his arm. "What can I do?"

"Tell me about meeting your birth mother."

Linda wiped clammy hands on her black apron. "Right now?"

"Unless I die while you're talking. Then be best to stop and go get Lizzie."

"Jonas!" Linda wished he was teasing, but his expression was pained and it seemed to take effort to keep his eyes open. Then he smiled.

"I ain't gonna die this very minute. Tell me about meeting Josephine."

Jonas's voice took on the tender tone Linda loved, and she watched his eyes widen with concern.

"I reckon it's all right. Meeting her, I mean." She paused, pulled her eyes from Jonas's, and tucked her chin. "I wish someone would have told me." She looked back up at him. "You knew, didn't you?"

"We all knew. And then we didn't know." He slowly raised his hand to his beard and stroked it slowly. "We forgot, Linda."

"What?"

"We forgot," he repeated as he gave a slight shrug. "You were as much a part of this family as if our blood ran in your veins. We simply forgot."

Linda pulled her eyes away again, not sure how to respond, but feeling like she wanted to crawl in the bed beside Jonas and have him wrap his arms around her. She blinked back tears.

"Dear Linda, from the time your mother held you in her arms, you were Mary Ellen and Abe's child. There is no love like that which a parent has for a child. It's a different kind of love. I reckon I'd lay myself out on a train track for Sarah Jane." He chuckled. "Don't know if I'd do that for Lizzie or not."

Linda smiled.

"You won't understand what I'm tellin' ya until you have *kinner* of your own."

"*Mamm* and *Daed* will always be *mei* parents. That will never change."

"Of course not. And I reckon they'd lay themselves on the train track for you and both your brothers." Jonas raked his hand through his beard again. "But here's where it gets tricky." He squinted in her direction and then pointed a finger at her. "I reckon Josephine would lie down on a train track for ya too, give her life willingly for you. That puts you in a unique position. All these people that love you. Do you have room in your heart for all of them?"

She thought about what Jonas was saying for a few moments.

"I don't really know Josie, though. I don't know how I feel." It was true. Linda liked Josephine, but . . . "I can't love her just because—because she is the one who gave birth to me."

"True." Jonas smiled slightly. "But I reckon she already loves you an awful lot."

Linda sat quietly for a moment. "I don't think *Mamm* likes this, me spending time with Josie. And I don't want to hurt her."

"Every wise woman buildeth her house: but the foolish plucketh it down with her hands."

Linda recognized the verse from Proverbs.

"Your *mamm* is a wise woman. This might be *hatt* for her, but she will make *gut* choices. Which you must do also." Jonas smiled, and his eyes clung to hers. "Keep your love for one another at full strength, because love covers a multitude of sins."

"The Book of Peter," she whispered, then smiled.

"*Ya.*" Jonas reached for her hand. "I will miss you, *mei* dear sweet Linda. And I will miss our games of chess."

Linda squeezed his hand as a tear rolled down her cheek. "Are you scared, Jonas?"

"No." He answered quickly. "I feel the presence of Jesus around me, Linda. I'm not afraid. Be strong in faith, Linda. Always."

"But—but, are you afraid it will hurt, that there will be pain?"

"When I go to be with my Father, there will be no pain. Only love."

Linda felt another tear run down her cheek. "Oh, Jonas . . ."

Jonas squeezed her hand as his own eyes clouded with tears, then the door creaked open.

Linda saw her uncle's face peer into the room. "Hi, *Onkel* Noah." She brushed away tears, sniffed, and sat up taller in the chair.

Noah walked to the other side of Jonas's bed and touched his arm. "I have some news."

"Just tell me." Jonas shook his head. "How long do I have? Weeks, days, or hours?"

Linda choked back tears and pressed her eyes tightly closed, not wanting to know.

"Actually . . ." Noah said slowly. "I think you're going to be around a lot longer than that."

Jonas's eyes opened wide. "I know you're the doctor and all,

Noah, but with all due respect, I feel like I could go at any minute. Downright awful is how I feel."

"I know. I just got back from the lab. You're having a reaction to one of your medications. Once we take you off that medication, you are going to feel better." Noah patted Jonas's arm.

Linda brought her hands to her mouth and stifled a gasp.

"You hear that, Linda?" Jonas's lips parted into a smile.

"*Ya*, I did!"

"I reckon you better go get my Lizzie and tell her I won't be heading to heaven just yet." He chuckled, and Linda realized by his reaction to the news that Jonas could say whatever he wanted—that he was ready and not afraid to die—but Linda could see that he was relieved to have more time. Maybe God knew that he just wasn't ready yet. "And next time you come, you bring the chess board."

"I will, Jonas. I will." She kissed him on the cheek, said her good-byes to Noah and those downstairs, and then headed to Josie's to deliver the slices of pie.

10

JOSIE WISHED ROBERT WAS HOME TO GET HER PILLS from upstairs. Clearly, one pain reliever hadn't been enough when her headache had started up again. She lay back against two blue throw cushions on her couch. Robert had left over an hour ago to visit an Amish man named Kade Saunders, someone he'd met through Noah. Mr. Saunders needed an attorney to handle some routine business for him, and although he refused to talk business on a Sunday, he'd invited Robert to his home for tea this afternoon.

Josie picked up the *Forbes* magazine Robert had left on the coffee table with Mr. Saunders's picture on the front. The magazine was dated ten years ago, and Josie couldn't understand how a man of Kade Saunders's wealth and power could give all that up to be Amish. She shook her head, which only made the pain worse. She tossed the magazine back on the table, then closed her eyes, and draped her forearm across her forehead. She fought the tears building. Crying would only make her head hurt more.

As the pain beat against her temple like a steel drum, the pain in her heart was equally fierce. She had the most wonderful husband on the planet. She had a daughter she was just getting to know. A beautiful home. And a tumor that would eventually kill her. When? Her stomach was constantly churning with fear and apprehension. Void of hope, Josie wondered why she was even bothering with any of this—getting to know Linda, unpacking the boxes in their home, or even getting dressed in the morning. She'd be gone soon, and with each passing day, routine things were beginning to seem pointless.

Her lids rose slowly when she heard a knock at the door. She let out a heavy sigh, and pulled herself to a sitting position, her head throbbing to the point she felt like she might vomit. *Please, make it stop. Please.* She wasn't sure who the thought was intended for, but if there was anyone out there—God, a supreme being, or anyone to offer aid—she was willing to try.

Josie stumbled to the door as strobe lights flashed in her head and caused her vision to blur. She glanced at herself in the mirror by the front door, and she knew that she should care how she looked. No makeup, slept-on hair, and a raggedy T-shirt and blue jeans. But the pain in her head was overriding everything else. Robert had offered to stay home, and she should have let him. She wasn't up to seeing anyone. Josie pulled the door open and attempted a smile when she saw Linda.

"Hi." She tried to sound as chipper as she could.

"I brought you and Robert a piece of snitz pie. I made it." Linda pushed a small basket, almost like a miniature picnic basket, toward Josie, and a smile lit her daughter's face in a way that made Josie just want to drop to her knees and beg to live.

When the doctor first diagnosed her, Josie went through all the emotions, even had counseling. She thought she'd been handling her fate with a sense of bravery, mostly for Robert's sake, but as Linda stood there in the doorway, smiling and offering her pie, every valiant bone in Josie's body crumbled, and her loneliness and hopelessness welded together in an upsurge of fear. Her lip began to quiver. She latched onto the basket.

"Thank you." Josie bit her bottom lip and tried to calm the rest of her body, although the pounding in her head was causing her to feel faint.

Linda's eyes narrowed with concern. "Josie? Are you all right?"

"Oh. Yeah." Josie drew in a deep breath and blew it out slowly. "I just have a really bad headache, that's all." *I want to invite you in, but I feel so awful.*

Linda stood there, her bright blue eyes confused as she tilted her head slightly to one side. "Is there anything I can do?"

Josie's thoughts churned inside a splitting head that couldn't seem to decipher much of anything, but one worry bounced ahead of all the others. *What if this is it? What if I never see Linda again?* She stepped aside and motioned for Linda to come in. "Visit with me for a while."

"Sure." Linda hesitated as she stepped through the door, and Josie caught another glance of herself in the mirror.

"Sorry, I know I look a mess. My head is just really hurting." She sat down on the couch, and Linda took a seat right beside her, then surprised Josie by reaching for her hand.

"Let's pray." Linda squeezed Josie's hand, closed her eyes, and bowed her head. Josie waited for her to say something, but Linda just kept her chin tucked and her eyes closed tightly. She knew how devout the Amish were in their faith. Maybe Linda had some sort of inside track to God, if He existed.

"Okay," Josie said, hoping Linda would open her eyes and say a prayer on Josie's behalf. At this point, she was willing to try anything.

Linda opened her eyes and looked at Josie. "Oh, we usually pray silently. Do you want me to offer a prayer aloud?"

Josie was so touched by her offer, along with the fact that she was even here, that she nodded. "Please."

Linda bowed her head again and closed her eyes as she kept a tight hold on Josie's hand. "Dear Blessed Father, please cure Josie's headache if it is Your will. Help her to not feel pain. Be with her on this day, and . . ."

Josie pulled her hand from Linda's, brought both hands to her face, and began to sob. Even for Linda's sake, she couldn't hold it together when something so powerful seemed to be latching on inside of her and threatening to deny her the resolve to be strong, to accept what was happening to her. She didn't want to be strong.

"I'm so incredibly unworthy." Josie cried harder, knowing that if a God existed, He'd never help her. She had been gone far too long, and to come to Him in a time of need when she'd never graciously thanked Him for all He'd given her . . . it seemed a futile attempt at the eleventh hour to reach out to someone she wasn't even sure she believed in.

Josie felt Linda's hand on her shoulder, a gesture which caused her to cry even harder, only elevating the pain in her head.

"We are all unworthy." Linda's voice was calm, nurturing, like a mother. Josie pulled her hands from her face and gazed into her daughter's eyes. "But God is good. He knows we are all unworthy, and He loves us just the same, and He wants to help us. Please, Josie. Don't cry."

Josie swiped at her eyes, sniffed, and smiled at Linda. "Thank you." *But the prayers won't do any good; my fate is sealed.* Josie stared at

Linda and wondered how she'd given birth to someone who possessed such goodness.

"Would you feel better if you lie down? I'll go so that you can rest." Linda stood up, and Josie wanted to hug her more than anything in the world. Josie stood up alongside her.

"I want you to stay, but I'm so sorry that my head hurts so much." She brushed a strand of hair out of her face.

"No worries." Linda smiled. "We have Tuesday night."

Josie walked with Linda to the door. "Yes, we do. And I'm looking forward to that." When they got to the door, Linda pulled it open, scooted over the threshold, and turned to face Josie.

"I hope you feel better." She smiled, and Josie wanted to cry again.

"Thank you so much for stopping by and bringing us the pie. Do you want your basket back?" Josie twisted around, ready to go get the basket.

"I'll get it Tuesday." Linda stared at Josie with concern in her expression. "Where is Robert?"

"He is visiting a friend, but he'll be back soon."

"All right." Linda gave a little wave. "See you Tuesday."

Josie smiled, closed the door, and leaned her head against it. She felt the tears building again, and she fought the urge to cry, to feel sorry for herself. Instead, she raised her head, ran a hand through her tangled hair, and headed back to the couch to lie down. Then the strangest feeling came over her. All her thoughts quieted, and a sense of peace flowed over her. She reached up and touched her forehead.

Then she realized she felt no pain at all. Her headache had vanished. Gone.

Linda gave her horse a flick of the reins and pulled out of Josie's driveway. She'd never seen anyone in such pain from a headache, and that kind of pain scared her more than anything else. Hopefully, Josie would be feeling better by Tuesday. And maybe she'd offer up that big bathroom. Linda smiled as she pictured herself lathered up in sweet-smelling bubble bath, soaking in the big tub while watching television. Maybe she'd even call her *Englisch* friend, Danielle, while she was bathing. She wondered what such luxury would feel like. Then she recalled Stephen's warning, to watch out for those unequally yoked. They'd been taught that their entire lives, and she didn't need him to remind her of it. She knew what she was doing. But she didn't understand Josie getting so upset during prayer. It must have been the pain that caused her to act in such a way.

She glanced to her left as she came over a hill and passed a buggy coming from the other way, no one she recognized, but she nodded in the woman's direction. No other buggies or automobiles shared the street with her for as far as she could see beneath a cloudless blue sky, just the open road winding between fields of freshly planted soil that filled her senses with hope for a plentiful harvest. She leaned her head back as the warm breeze blew against her face, and she thanked God for the beautiful land, the cows mooing in the distance, and the sense of calm that she felt at this moment. Then she prayed for Josie again.

As she neared the bridge at Ronks, she recalled her first kiss with Stephen. Late at night, they'd traveled on foot scooters and secretly met underneath the bridge after everyone was sleeping. She could still remember the feel of his lips meeting with hers for the first time. They'd met several more times since then, always late at night after their families were asleep. Linda knew her father would tan her hide if he knew she snuck out that late and scooted all the way to the bridge at Ronks, but it had become their special place.

She guided her buggy underneath the crimson structure with openings at both ends and smiled when she thought about how much the tourists loved the covered bridges. Sometimes they would gather off the side of the road and take pictures. But not today; all was quiet. She glanced to her left as she made her way under the bridge to the spot where Stephen had first kissed her. A white piece of paper was stuffed between two pieces of wood with a pink ribbon tied around it. She passed by it, but then pulled her horse to a stop and eased him slowly backward. Pink was her favorite color, and even though she wasn't allowed to dress in it, she'd told Stephen repeatedly it was her favorite. She squinted at the rolled up piece of paper bound by a thin strip of pink. *Surely not.*

Smiling, she stepped down from the buggy and walked toward it. She pulled it from its resting place and unrolled it. Her heart began to flutter as she read:

> Sunshine is smiling upon you, like a wave of happiness; never to diminish or fade, like the love in my heart.

She brought the letter to her chest and closed her eyes. *Stephen.* More than once, he'd said, "The sunshine is smiling on you." It was just something he said, and it always made her smile. She crawled back into the buggy, checked to make sure no one was coming in either direction, then she reached for a pen in the buggy's storage compartment.

You are my sunshine, that wave of happiness that I carry with me
when we are apart; like the love also in my heart.

They'd never told each other that they loved each other face-to-
face. This was the closest Stephen had come to doing so, and she
wanted to make sure he knew how she felt as well. She rolled the
note back up, tied the pink ribbon around it, and walked over to a
slightly different spot from where it was before.

As hooves echoed beneath the tunneled bridge, Linda visualized
her marriage to Stephen, the exchanging of vows in front of their
family and friends. She'd envisioned the event so many times that
she could even see her mother and father smiling to her right, her
brothers standing to her left, and her cousin, Rachel, as her maid
of honor. Bishop Ebersol always seemed less scary in the daydream,
almost smiling as he said, "We are gathered here today to bless the
marriage of Linda and Stephen . . ." It would be a perfect day.

Josie. Her vision clouded. Where would Josie be? She would
have to be there. Where would she be sitting or standing? Would
Mamm still be smiling? Would Josie bring her husband, Robert?
The daydream vanished completely as she thought about Josie's
place at her wedding—and in her life.

———

Mary Ellen handed Abe a piece of rhubarb pie, then joined him
at the kitchen table with her own piece.

"Where's Linda? I haven't seen her since right after worship service." Abe glanced at the clock on the wall. "Be time to start supper
soon, no?"

"*Ya.* Probably shouldn't be having this pie; it's going to spoil our appetites." Mary Ellen tapped her fork gently on the plate. "She went to go check on Jonas." She took a deep breath. "And to drop off two pieces of pie for Josephine and her husband."

"You say that like it irritates you." Abe took a bite of pie and swallowed. "Now that we know that she's . . . ill, I hope you won't prevent Linda from seeing her."

Mary Ellen plunked her fork down on the plate, louder than she'd intended. "Of course I'm not going to keep Linda from seeing her. I'm not some kind of monster, Abe."

"I never said you were, Mary Ellen. You're a *gut* woman. I also know that you feel real threatened by Josephine, but Linda is our daughter. That ain't gonna change." He shook his head. "We better just count ourselves blessed that Linda forgave us for not telling her that she was adopted. This whole thing could have gone another way, and we were in the wrong about not telling her a long time ago."

"I know all that, Abe."

"Maybe we oughta have Josephine and her husband to supper sometime. Might be *gut* for Linda if we are friendly with them, and—"

"I will not." Mary Ellen sat taller. "It's fine for Linda to get to know her birth mother, I suppose, but I just can't do that."

"Why?" Abe raised his brows, and she didn't like his tone.

"Because—because I just don't think . . ." She picked up her plate and got up from the table. After she placed the uneaten piece of pie on the counter, she spun around to face him. "It would just be too awkward, Abe."

"Doesn't have to be." Abe scooped up the last of his pie and closed his mouth around the fork.

Mary Ellen folded her arms across her chest. "Why are you pushing me on this? Linda can visit Josephine, but I don't have to entertain her in my home, Abe." She shook her head. "I just don't want to do that."

Abe shrugged. "All right."

"This is dangerous, Abe. But you just don't see it."

Abe chuckled, and Mary Ellen took two steps toward him. "You think this is funny? It's dangerous enough that Linda spends all that time with her *Englisch* girlfriends, but it's her *rumschpringe*, so not much we can do about that. But, not only is Josephine unequally yoked, she is the girl's kin. Linda could choose a life with her, and . . ."

"Are you listening to yourself? Josephine doesn't have much *life* left, Mary Ellen."

"What if she exposes Linda to her fancy life so much that Linda decides to leave?"

"She ain't goin' anywhere. She's gonna marry Stephen, and our *maedel* is grounded in her faith. You are worrying about something that ain't ever going to happen."

Mary Ellen picked up Abe's empty plate and placed it in the sink. "I hope you're right."

"There's our girl now." Abe pointed to the window, and Mary Ellen saw Linda turning the buggy into the driveway. "I hope everything is all right with Jonas. That poor fella has been fighting this cancer for years, and every time I think it's come his time, that old coot pulls through again." Abe followed Mary Ellen to the window and wrapped his arms around her waist. "Everything is going to be fine, Mary Ellen."

They watched Linda move the horse toward the barn, then they sat down on the couch in the den for their usual reading time.

Mary Ellen looked up from her Bible when Linda walked in a few minutes later. Abe had his head in a book that had a man on a motorcycle on the cover.

"How is Jonas?" Mary Ellen marked her place with her finger.

Linda fell into one of the rockers and crossed her legs. "He looked bad when I got there, *Mamm*. I thought he was going to heaven any second. The worst I've ever seen him." Linda shook her head, and then her face brightened. "But then *Onkel* Noah showed up and said that Jonas's medications were making him sick, and he said he'll start feeling better now that they know to take him off some of his pills."

"What did I tell you?" Abe looked above his gold-rimmed reading glasses at Mary Ellen.

"*Ya*, Jonas always seems to overcome and surprise everyone, but Linda . . ." Mary Ellen paused. "You do know that Jonas is still on a downward spiral. He's eaten up with the cancer. It is just a matter of time."

Linda smiled. "Miracles happen sometimes."

Mary Ellen was proud of her daughter's faith, and she silently reprimanded herself for questioning the choices she'd feared Linda might make. "*Ya*, they do." She smiled back at her beautiful girl, even though Mary Ellen didn't think God granted the type of miracle Linda was searching for. Jonas had beaten the odds for a long time, and Mary Ellen feared his time was near.

"*Mamm? Daed?*"

Mary Ellen waited for Linda to speak, but she tucked her chin the way she did so often. "*Ya?*" she finally asked when Linda looked up at her. "What is it?"

Linda avoided eye contact. "Josie wants me to spend the night at her house Tuesday night. Tomorrow is wash day, and I think if I work late tomorrow, I can get some of Tuesday's chores done. Do you think that would be all right? Her husband is going out of town for two weeks." Linda pulled her eyes away from Mary Ellen's. "Actually, he asked me to stay with her for two weeks, but—"

"Two weeks!" Mary Ellen slammed the Bible shut. "That's impossible. How could she even ask you such a thing?"

"She didn't ask me, her husband did. But *Mamm*, I told her I couldn't, of course."

Linda's eyes started to fill with tears, and Mary Ellen instantly regretted her reaction. Once again, she hadn't trusted her daughter's judgment.

"I think one overnight visit would be fine." Abe said and glanced at Mary Ellen before turning to Linda. "As long as you can get your chores done." He looked back at Mary Ellen. "Don't you think, Mary Ellen?"

"*Ya*, I reckon so." She took a deep breath and blew it out slowly. "I'm sorry I snapped at you, Linda. It's just that the *Englisch* often don't have an understanding about how busy our day is, and I just wasn't expecting you to say two weeks." The nerve of her husband to even ask Linda such a thing. Then Mary Ellen felt her heart sink into the pit of her stomach. The woman is sick. Of course he doesn't want to leave her alone. *I am a mean, selfish woman. Forgive me, dear Lord.* "Does Josephine have any kin here in town?"

"No, she doesn't." Linda scowled, a confused expression on her face. "And her husband doesn't seem to want to leave her alone." She glanced at her father. "But you've left *Mamm* for days when you've had to go out of town. Maybe it's different since *Mamm* has us with her." She shrugged. "I don't know."

Mary Ellen silently prayed. Somehow she needed to try to make up for doubting Linda, questioning the Lord's will, for not telling Linda she was adopted, and mostly for the ugly thoughts she'd had about Josephine since she'd come into their lives—a woman with little time to live and who'd given birth to their beloved Linda.

Mary Ellen raised her chin and folded her hands in her lap. "It is your *rumschpringe*, and Josephine is your birth mother. Maybe you should go and spend the two weeks with her."

Abe's mouth dropped open, and Mary Ellen held her breath as she waited for Linda to answer. And, again, she prayed—that this wouldn't backfire on her.

11

STEPHEN BROUGHT HIS FOOT SCOOTER TO A HALT AND pulled the note from the bridge, his pulse racing as he wondered whether or not Linda had found the note and responded. He uncoiled the paper and exhaled a long sigh of contentment as he read.

You are my sunshine, that wave of happiness that I carry with me when we are apart; like the love also in my heart.

He pulled his pen from within his front shirt pocket.

My dearest Linda, There is much to be discovered in an ocean. It can be shallow. It can be deep. Life it can give. Life it can take. Never to be taken for granted. Found all around us, making the world smaller. My love for you is like an ocean.

Stephen shook his head. *If my buddies knew I wrote this stuff* . . . But Linda loved his poems, and that's all that mattered. He continued.

I love you. Will you marry me?

Always, Stephen

Every time he'd tried to ask Linda to marry him, he froze up with worry about things he needn't be worrying about. *Hopefully, she will think this is romantic and not dumb.* He quickly stuffed the note back in between the wood slats, then scooted off as the clouds became shaded with orange and the sun settled on the horizon in front of him.

Linda could hardly believe she was going to go stay with Josie for two weeks. She'd never had a vacation, and even though Josie's house was only a few minutes from home, this would certainly seem like a holiday. She pinned the last towel on the line, after getting up early to start the wash this sunny Monday morning.

She still didn't understand why *Mamm* was allowing this. A tiny part of her was hurt that her mother suggested she go stay with Josie for two weeks. Had something changed for *Mamm*? Did she no longer feel like Linda's mother? Linda didn't ever want *Mamm* to feel that way, but she wouldn't turn down the offer. Again, she thought about the luxuries in Josie's house. Air-conditioning, for starters. And that bathtub. She smiled to herself.

"Almost done?"

Linda twisted her neck to see her mother approaching. "*Ya.* Last load." She picked up the laundry basket to head back inside, but *Mamm* inched closer to her, then put her arms around Linda's neck and pulled her close.

"Do you know how very much I love you?"

Linda eased away from her. "*Mamm*, I won't go tomorrow if you don't want me to."

Her mother kept hold of Linda's arms and gently ran her hands up and down. "No. I think you should go."

Linda tucked her chin, but *Mamm* gently eased her face back up, then locked eyes with her. "I'm so sorry, *mei maedel*, for not telling you about your adoption." She smiled, gazed into Linda's eyes, and then spoke softly, with such tenderness that Linda considered not going. "Everyone always says how much you look like me, and I think we just really started to forget."

"That's what Jonas said." Linda smiled back. "Are you sure that it's okay with you if I go, *Mamm*? I don't want this to hurt you." She shrugged. "I probably won't like it there." Linda cringed inside as she told the tiny lie.

"Josephine gave you life. She gave you to us to love and raise. I think she is deserving of a chance to know what a lovely young woman you have grown into. But Linda . . ."

Linda waited. *Mamm* frowned a bit and just stared at her for a moment.

"There will be much temptation in Josie's world. All the things that are forbidden to us. Televisions, radios, electricity, and everything modern that we don't agree with. I know this will be like a vacation for you, away from all the hard work, but I will pray constantly that you remember the *Ordnung* and stay steady in your faith. I know it's your *rumpschpringe*, and to worry is a sin. I'm going to work hard to keep worry and fear from my heart." She paused. "Your *daed* and I love you very much."

Linda threw her arms around her mother's neck. "I love you too, *Mamm*. And you will always be my mother. Always." She eased away. "And no worries. My life is here, with all of you, and with Stephen. Please don't worry."

"Things are *gut* with Stephen?" Her mother's eyes brightened.

"*Ya*. I love him very much."

"I think he is much in *lieb* with you as well." *Mamm* playfully arched her brows a couple of times. "Perhaps a proposal will be in order soon, no?"

Linda giggled. "I hope so!"

They started toward the house with Linda carrying the empty laundry basket. She wanted to assure her mother what she knew in her heart to be true. "I won't be tempted, *Mamm*. I know things will be different at Josie's house, but it's only for a couple of weeks so I can get to know her better—as a new friend."

"I know, dear. I trust you to make wise decisions."

It was after dark when Stephen came calling Monday evening. They were just finishing up family devotion time when Linda heard a buggy pulling up.

Daed scowled from his seat on the couch. "A little late for that boy to be showing up here."

"Linda will be busy the next couple of weeks, Abe. I'm sure they want to spend a little time together." Mary Ellen winked in Linda's direction.

"Don't seem fair that Linda gets to go stay with that woman for two weeks." Matthew shook his head. "I reckon we are supposed to take care of her chores while she's gone on her little vacation?"

Daed closed the Bible and peered over his reading glasses. "Watch yourself, Matt."

"I tried to do as much as I could before I leave tomorrow." Linda stood up from the rocker so she could let Stephen in.

"Well, it ain't enough to make up for two weeks," Matthew grumbled as he walked out of the den.

Luke didn't say anything, but Linda suspected by the scowl on his face that his thoughts matched Matthew's. Maybe this whole thing was a bad idea.

"It's late, Linda. Keep your visit short." *Daed* set the Bible on the coffee table next to one of two lanterns that illuminated the den, then stood up. "I'm heading to bed. Outten all the lights when you come in."

"*Ya, Daed.* Good night." Linda picked up the flashlight by the door, opened the screen door to the den before Stephen had a chance to knock, and met him coming up the porch steps.

"I'm glad you came. I have something to tell you." She latched onto his hand and pulled him down the steps toward the garden.

"I'm happy to see you too." He chuckled as Linda pulled him toward the entrance to the garden surrounded by a white picket fence. She shined the light on the latch, flipped it open, and wound her way to a white bench on the far side of the garden and sat down. Stephen took a seat beside her.

"You are never gonna believe this." She turned off the flashlight and blinked her eyes into focus in the dark until Stephen's handsome face was illuminated by the full moon above them, a spark of mischief in his eyes. "I'm leaving tomorrow to go stay with Josie for two weeks."

Stephen's expression soured instantly. "What?"

"Josie's husband is going out of town for two weeks. At first, I was only going to spend one night, but *Mamm* and *Daed* said I can go stay with her for two weeks, to get to know her."

"Why?"

"What do you mean, why?"

Stephen shrugged, and even in the darkness, she could see his mouth take on an unpleasant twist. "I don't know. Seems odd."

"It's not odd." Linda pulled her hand from his. "Why do you say that?"

"Why would you even want to stay with her for two weeks, in the *Englisch* world?"

"I told you. To get to know her."

Stephen eyed her with a critical squint. "And your parents are allowing this?"

"*Ya.* They are."

Linda didn't want to squabble with Stephen about this or put a damper on his visit. "Did you get my note?" She broke into a wide open smile, hoping to lift his mood.

"*Ya,* I did. And I left you another one."

"*Ach, gut!* I'll go by and get it on the way to Josie's tomorrow." She reached for his hand again. "I really do love your poems, Stephen."

"I think you'll really like this one." He leaned in and kissed her gently on the lips. "I'll be anxious to hear what you think." Then he pulled away hastily. "Am I going to see you during these two weeks?"

"Of course. Josie isn't going to keep me under lock and key. She'll probably even drive me places, if need be."

"Okay. Thursday, I get off work early. We could go to the creek and swim?"

Linda couldn't believe it. Stephen never wanted to go swim at the river. "Sure. That'd be great. What time?"

"I'll pick you up at four o'clock." He leaned in and kissed her again, longer this time, as he cupped the nape of her neck. "I want to know what you think about the poem I left you."

"I will love it, I'm sure."

"I really hope so."

Stephen kissed her again, and Linda was certain that everything in her life was going to turn out perfectly. *Mamm* was coming around about Josie, she and Stephen were growing closer, and Linda was about to embark on a two-week adventure filled with fancy bubble baths and air-conditioning.

―――⋅●●⋅―――

Tuesday afternoon, Josie was anxious for Linda to arrive, and thankful to be having a headache-free day. She had meatloaf in the oven and potatoes were peeled and ready for boiling. Robert had called her from the airport before his plane left for China, and she'd assured him that she would be fine while he was away.

"I shouldn't be going," he'd told her again. "I don't want to leave you alone."

Josie promised to call if there was a problem and told him he could catch the first plane back home, though there usually was nothing to do except take the Vicodin and steroids. Each episode just had to take its course. Josie reached down and rubbed the top of her right hand with her other hand. Still no feeling. It had been that way since yesterday morning, but she knew if she told Robert, he would cancel this important business trip.

She lit two candles in the living room and put on some soft music and hoped Linda would enjoy her overnight stay. Josie had her room all ready. She couldn't remember a night this important in a very long time. She wanted everything to go perfectly and for

Linda to like her, to know her, to have a tiny bit of Josie's heritage to carry with her in life.

No tears today. Only happy thoughts. She recalled how her headache had gone away on Sunday after Linda prayed with her and how she'd followed up with her own prayer. It didn't mean there was a God, but perhaps she could allow the possibility to give her a tiny bit of hope. She'd told Robert what had happened, but he'd firmly said that the medicine had just kicked in. He was adamant that God had nothing to do with anything. "I wish there were such a being, Josie," he'd said. "I wish that more than anything on this earth, but you know I just don't believe that. But, Josie, you need to believe what's right for you. Don't let my beliefs interfere."

Josie found that interesting, since Robert had always given up a hundred arguments to any point she'd made about God early in their relationship. Eventually, she'd had to admit that Robert's point of view made much more sense than hers. But with her own mortality hanging in the balance, she wished there was something to believe in. She needed hope. As she felt the knot forming in her throat, she shook her head. "No, not today," she said aloud.

A loud knock interrupted her thoughts, and she hurried to the door and pulled it open.

"Wow. That's a lot of luggage for one night." She smiled at Linda who was standing on the doorstep with two fairly large suitcases. Mary Ellen was turning the buggy around, and Josie waved, but Mary Ellen didn't see her.

Linda awkwardly cleared her throat. "Actually, *Mamm* and *Daed* said I can stay for the whole two weeks." Linda tucked her chin. "I probably should have asked you first."

"Oh my gosh! No! Are you kidding? Get in here, you!" Josie

grabbed one of the suitcases and motioned Linda in. "I'm so excited. This is going to be great."

Linda's face lit up, and she scooted in the door. "I smell meatloaf."

"Yep! Just for you." Josie thought she might burst. *Two whole weeks with my daughter. Thank you, God!* The thought came out of nowhere, but it seemed fitting to thank someone, anyone, for this wonderful luck. "I can't wait to tell Robert when he calls that you are staying for the entire two weeks. We are going to have so much fun." Linda followed her through the den and to the stairs. "Follow me upstairs, and I'll show you your room."

Linda followed Josie up the stairs and down a long hallway, until they got to a door at the end on the right.

"This is your room. It's right across from my room, in case you need anything." Josie walked inside and set the suitcase she was carrying down before motioning for Linda to come in.

"This is the room I'll be staying in?" Linda gasped as she set her other suitcase down. She brought both hands to her chest as she took in her living quarters for the next two weeks. "I've never seen such a bed." She walked to the large bed in front of her, topped with a floral bedspread in shades of ivory and rose, and there were four large satin throw pillows resting against two pillows in rose-colored shams. It was too fancy to touch, and Linda couldn't believe she would be sleeping here. She glanced up at the ivory sheer draped over four large posts on each corner of the bed. It peaked in the middle, forming an arch above the bed, like something a princess would sleep in.

Linda moved toward a piece of furniture in the corner. A

hairbrush and hand mirror rested atop the off-white finish, along with a crystal vase filled with bright red roses, the kind Mr. Buckley sold at the flower shop in town, ones that were especially big. Ivory-colored walls were topped with a border consisting of three different shades of roses, and lacy curtains covered two windows. Next to the bed was a small end table with a white lamp. A pink alarm clock and a Bible were on the table next to a telephone.

Josie moved toward a six-drawer dresser along one of the walls, also painted an off-white shade, and pulled open the first drawer. "These are all empty. You can put some of your clothes in here." She pointed to the closet. "The closet is empty as well."

Linda glanced around the room and noticed the television suspended from the wall in the corner of the room. A white rocking chair occupied the other corner of the room. She was afraid to touch anything.

"I hope you like roses." Josie smiled. "I love roses, and I was hoping you did, too, when I started decorating this room for you."

"You decorated this room for *me*?"

Josie nodded, then walked to the closet and swung the door wide. Linda was pretty sure the closet was as big as her entire bedroom at home. "This is probably more room than you need, but every woman should have a big closet."

Linda stared at the couch against the wall across from the dresser. It was an odd-shaped couch, with only half a back that swayed downward, covered in a velvety-looking light pink fabric.

"That's a chaise longue." Josie walked toward the piece of furniture, then sat down. "If you lean back like this, you can see the television really well from here." She twisted her neck back toward the bed. "But you can see it just as well from the bed."

Linda eyed the flat, square television in the corner and wondered if it had a controller to change the channels, like at her *Englisch* friends' houses. Her eyes veered back to the table by the nightstand, and sure enough, there was a television controller beside the alarm clock.

"Do you like the room?" Josie bit her bottom lip.

"Like it? I love it, Josie. I've never seen anything like this." She ran her hand along the delicate bedspread and wondered what it was going to feel like to be wrapped up in the covers with the princess dome overhead. With the television on. She turned around and faced Josie. "*Danki*, Josie, for making this such a beautiful room and for inviting me to come stay with you."

Josie moved toward her and smiled. "You are very welcome." She turned toward the door. "I'll tell you what. Why don't I go finish dinner, and if you'd like, you can take a bath, and then we'll eat, curl up on the couch, and just make it like a slumber party and talk. There's a bathroom down the hall." Josie pointed to her left. "Or, even better, if you'd like to take a bath in our room, there is a big Jacuzzi tub you can soak in."

"*Ya, ya.* I'd like that." Linda didn't even try to contain her excitement. She'd been fantasizing about taking a bath down the hallway, with the big tub, phone, and television set. *But Josie's bathroom is probably even grander.*

"Great. Come on. Follow me. I'll show you where everything is."

Linda crossed the hallway behind Josie, and suddenly her own quarters seemed modest in comparison to Josie's bedroom, if that was possible. Josie's bed angled from a corner of the room and reminded Linda of a sled, the way the base of the bed curved at the bottom. It was much larger than the bed in Linda's room and was covered with a dark blue bedspread and topped with lots of white lacy pillows. Everything in this room was made of dark wood, which made it all seem so formal. There was an entire sitting area off to one side with high-back chairs and a full-sized couch. Why did anyone need all this den furniture in a bedroom?

She wanted to keep looking around Josie's room, study the big framed pictures of landscapes on the wall and the smaller ones of people on her dresser, but she followed Josie into the bathroom.

This is no bathroom. She didn't even see a commode. This room was surely larger than her bedroom at home.

"There are towels in the cabinet." Josie pointed to her left, but Linda could hardly take her eyes from the tub, which she reckoned would hold four people if need be.

"That's some bathtub." Linda eyed the massive, bronzed faucets and water spigots all inside the white enclosure.

Josie walked to the tub, turned the faucet on, then pointed to some buttons on the side of the tub. "You can adjust the jets however you like. Just push these buttons when the tub gets full." She walked to the marble counter and pulled a pretty blue basket full of bottles and tubes toward her. "And there are bubble baths, lotions, and all kinds of goodies in here. Just help yourself to anything."

Linda recalled the baths at her house, lit by lantern if she didn't beat Matt and Luke to bathe in the evenings. Soaps and shampoo that she and *Mamm* made on a regular basis. The small battery-operated fan to keep the sweat from building the minute you stepped from the claw-foot bathtub onto the brown rug. Creaky wooden floor, gas heater in the wintertime, and always, no matter the season, the same towel all week long.

"Here's the remote for the television." Josie handed the

channel changer to Linda. "You should have plenty of time to take a nice soak before I finish dinner." Josie smiled. "Linda, I'm so glad you're here."

Linda glanced around the room, anxious to enjoy a bath in this super fancy tub, but she couldn't shake the feeling that she had forgotten something.

"I'm glad I'm here too."

"Okay. Yell if you need anything."

Linda nodded, then Josie left the bathroom and closed the door behind her. A sweet aroma filled her senses and drew her to the basket of goodies on the counter. She fumbled through the items and chose more than was probably necessary, then set the bubble baths, gels, and shampoo on the platform beside the tub, alongside the channel changer.

She giggled as she pushed the button on the tub. Water started to bubble up like the brook behind her house after a hard rain. She hastily got out of her clothes, tossed them on the tile floor, and removed her *kapp*. Her brown hair fell to her waist, and she dipped her toe into the warm water, then climbed in. As she got comfortable in the tub, she reached for the channel changer and pushed the On button. She wondered what it would be like to take a bath in this tub every day. Hopefully, she'd be doing it for the next two weeks.

She twisted her mouth to one side. Despite the perfect moment, there was something bogging her down, that feeling like you've forgotten something. *What is it? What is it?*

Then she remembered.

12

STEPHEN PASSED THROUGH THE COVERED BRIDGE ON his way to the furniture store on Tuesday evening, anxious to see what Linda's response was to his written proposal. She'd said she would get the note on the way to Josephine's, which would have been way before now since he'd worked late. His stomach swirled and his palms went damp as he pulled the buggy to a stop and reached for the coiled paper. But the swirling turned into a heavy knot in the pit of his belly when he unrolled it.

He sighed, then rolled the note back up and retied the ribbon around it. As he placed it back in between the supports on the bridge, he figured she must have forgotten to pick it up on her way, which irritated him probably more than it should have. She didn't know it was a proposal.

Stephen motioned the horse into action and continued toward the store. He'd check again tomorrow on his way home from work.

He couldn't seem to shake the worry he was feeling about Linda staying with her birth mother for two weeks. It was only natural that she'd want to get to know the woman, but that thought didn't lessen his fear. Stephen saw the way Linda eyed fancy items when they were in town sometimes, and he wasn't sure how strong her attraction to material things was. He shook his head, resolved to trust her. Linda was strong in her beliefs, and he'd keep the faith that she would stay in line with the *Ordnung*.

Still, it irritated him that she didn't swing by the bridge earlier, when she knew there was a note waiting for her.

Linda dried herself off with a towel so plush it felt like silk against her skin. She glanced at the phone in the bathroom and thought about calling Stephen's house and leaving a message on their phone in the barn, but she didn't want someone other than Stephen to get the message, which was most likely what would happen. She'd have to go by the bridge tomorrow to get his note. She was glad she'd remembered what she'd forgotten.

Her suitcases were still across the hall in her room, so she bundled up in the towel, tiptoed out of the bathroom, and walked through Josie's room toward the door. She paused and gazed at the beautiful pictures hanging on the wall, floral landscapes with cottages.

She passed by a large cherry wood dresser with a tall etched mirror. Pictures lined the top of the dresser, and her eyes were drawn to a photo that appeared older than the others and showed a sleeping baby dressed in pink. *Me.* She held the towel in place with one hand and picked up the framed photo with the other and wondered if the picture had always been on Josie's dresser. She set it down and walked to her own room and breathed in the fresh scent from the roses. *This is paradise.*

She pulled a brown dress over her head, brushed out her wet hair, and started to go down the stairs, then she remembered something. Linda went back into Josie's bathroom and reached for the blow-dryer and fumbled to turn it on. She'd never used one before, but she quickly found the On switch and aimed the warm air at her scalp as she raked a hand through her hair. When she was done, her hair was still damp, but it had a smoothness she didn't get from air drying it at home, or when she dried it in front of the battery-operated fan in her room.

She hung the blow-dryer back on the hook beside the sink, then reached for a tube of perfumed lotion she must have missed earlier. She smeared it on her hands until they were soft and felt elegant. If Stephen could see—and smell—her now . . . Linda smiled and then headed down the stairs.

Josie struggled to mash the potatoes. Her entire right hand was numb now and part of her arm. She knew all too well that she was supposed to call the doctor if she began to experience numbness on the right side of her body. *Not tonight.*

She bowed her head as visions of her youth came flooding back, a time when prayer was something she practiced daily. Now, it just felt awkward. But it had worked before, when she had her headache, and she was willing to try anything. *God, please help me to stay well enough to enjoy this time with my daughter. Don't let me get sick—or die—while she's here. Please.*

She raised her head in time to hear Linda coming through the den. Josie took a deep breath, forced a smile, and put the potatoes on the table in the dining room with her left hand.

"Josie, that bathroom is wonderful. That was the best bath I've ever had in my life!" Linda was glowing, and her daughter's youthful zest sucked the fear and worry right out of Josie's mind.

"Good, I'm so glad. I thought you might like taking a bath in my room, in that big tub." Josie felt a bit guilty, knowing that Mary Ellen and Abe couldn't—and wouldn't—offer Linda the kind of luxuries that Josie had enjoyed for most of her life.

"Can I help you do something?" Linda folded her hands in front of her, and Josie didn't think she'd ever seen a more beautiful image. *My daughter. In my home.*

"No." Josie forced herself to look away from Linda. She felt like she could stare at her forever. She'd waited so long for this. "Everything is ready." Josie motioned for Linda to take a seat across from her at the table where she'd arranged two place settings.

Linda hesitated but slowly sat down. She stared at the china, stemware, and serving dishes on the table. Josie had wanted to set the perfect table, but this might be too much for Linda.

"Hey, I said this was going to be like a slumber party, right?" Josie cupped her hips with her hands. "Why don't we take our plates into the den, curl up on the couch, and eat in our laps while we watch TV?"

"Really?" Linda smiled as Josie picked up her own plate with her left hand. "Let's just fill them and take them to the living room."

Josie set her plate on the table beside the meatloaf and then picked up a spatula with her left hand to scoop out a small portion. "Help yourself."

Linda didn't move, though, and her brow creased with worry. "What's wrong with your hand?"

Josie looked down at her arm, swallowed hard, and tried to control the panic she felt when she saw her right arm jerking like it had a mind of its own. "Oh, it's just—oh, it's nothing. It just happens sometimes."

Linda stood up and rounded the table, then stared down at Josie's twitching arm. "It's not nothing. Does it hurt?"

"No. It doesn't hurt at all. I'm just having some motor function issues. It'll go away in a minute." Josie piled some potatoes on her plate, more than she'd ever eat. "Here, sweetie. Fill your plate, and we'll go pick out a movie." She nodded toward the potatoes.

Linda didn't move. "Does the doctor know?"

"Yes, it's really no big deal." Josie shrugged. "I take medicine for it. Sometimes it's worse than others."

"But it doesn't hurt?"

Linda seemed unusually preoccupied with pain, and Josie wasn't sure whether or not to question her about it. "No, it doesn't hurt. I promise."

Hesitantly, Linda went back to the other side of the table, picked up her plate, and began filling it.

"How do you stay so thin, eating like that?" Josie grinned, but she could feel her right hand starting to twitch even more.

Linda was focused on the salad Josie had prepared and helping herself to a nice-size portion. "I reckon it's because we work a lot. There's lots to do on a farm."

"Oh my gosh!" Josie clamped her eyes closed for a moment. When she opened them, Linda had stopped serving herself salad and was staring at Josie. "I almost forgot. The doctor's office left a message and changed an appointment I have from Thursday to tomorrow, so I have a doctor's appointment at ten o'clock in the morning at Lancaster General." She paused and offered Linda what she hoped was a comforting smile. "Just routine." One more doctor confirming what she already knew to be true. *Mrs. Dronberger, the lesion in your brain stem is inoperable, and since all other treatments have failed, we are sorry to tell you* . . . She'd heard it enough to recite it for them.

"Is it for that jerkiness in your hand?" Linda gazed up at her with such concern in her eyes that Josie swallowed a knot in her throat.

"Yes, but it's not a big deal." Josie lifted her plate with her left hand. "Let's go sit on the couch and eat."

"*Mei onkel* is a doctor. Do you want me to have him look at your hand, maybe you won't have to go all the way to Lancaster General? *Mei onkel* has a clinic right here in Paradise."

Josie knew Linda was referring to her husband's friend, Noah Stoltzfus, but she didn't mention it. "Actually, I'm going to see a specialist." Josie nodded for Linda to follow her into the living room. She sat down and tucked her legs beneath her. Robert hated to eat anywhere but the dining room table, so this was a treat for Josie as well, watching television while eating. It angered her that her hand had picked this night to act up, but she'd ask Dr. Phillips about it in the morning.

"Is it serious?" Linda sat down on the opposite end of the couch, keeping her feet together on the floor while balancing her plate in her lap. She stared hard into Josie's eyes.

Josie hated herself for lying, but she was not going to mess up these two weeks. "No, it's not."

"*Gut.*" Linda sighed with relief, then bowed her head.

Josie did the same, but she didn't want to talk to God right now. She opened one eye and watched her right hand twitching. Maybe it wasn't so much that she didn't believe in God; maybe she was just madder than heck at Him. The issue was becoming more and more confusing for her.

Mary Ellen tried to focus on the book she was reading in bed, but she couldn't get her mind off of Linda.

"Mary Ellen, you're tapping your feet together." Abe gently nudged her foot with his. "You always do that when you're upset or worried about something." Her husband pulled off his reading glasses and set the book he was reading aside, the one with a motorcycle on the front. "Linda is fine."

"You don't know that, Abe." Mary Ellen glanced at the book on his nightstand and arched one brow. "There's much temptation in the *Englisch* world."

Abe followed her eyes to the bedside table. "*Ya*, I reckon there is. But Linda will make *gut* choices." He paused, then grinned. "Now quit eyeballing my book like I've turned to the other side." Abe settled back against his pillow and stretched his legs.

"I just don't see why you read such nonsense." She pointed to Abe's reading material. "What could a book like that possibly have to offer you?"

Abe shrugged. "It just interests me, those bikes. How fast they can go, what size motors they have, and how much the *Englisch* will pay for one." He chuckled. "I reckon it's just something to do, Mary Ellen. You worry too much. About everything."

Mary Ellen sat up taller and narrowed her eyes at him. "I do not." She folded her arms across her chest. "I worry about what needs to be worried about."

"Well, my motorcycle book shouldn't be one of those things." He pulled her close. "And I feel like we are past the worst part with Linda. My biggest fear was that she wouldn't forgive us, and she did. Now, let our *maedel* spend some time with Josephine, while she can. And try not to worry."

Mary Ellen sat quietly for a while as shimmering rays of light from the lanterns danced on the clapboard walls. She wondered what Linda and Josephine were doing right now. What did Josephine cook, or had they gone out to eat? Would they stay up late talking or go to bed early? What plans were they making for tomorrow?

She gave her head a quick shake and tried to clear the worry from her heart. Abe was right. She was worrying too much. But one thing scared her more than Linda leaving the community— picking up the pieces of Linda's broken heart if she got too close to Josephine. Did Josephine even think about that before she plowed into their lives?

Linda threw her head back on the couch and couldn't remember the last time she'd laughed so hard or had so much fun.

"That is a funny story. What did your mother do?" Linda tucked her white nightgown underneath her legs on the couch and twisted to face Josie. "I bet you got punished, no?"

"Oh, yeah." Josie smoothed wrinkles from her peach-colored robe with her left hand. Linda could still see Josie's right hand and arm twitching, but she tried not to stare. "I was grounded for a month after that."

"Grounded? Like being punished?"

"Yep. I was punished. I couldn't go anywhere with any of my friends." Josie shook her head, but she was grinning.

"Was it worth it, though? I mean, do you wish you hadn't done it?" Linda tried to picture Josie and her friends filling up a fountain in a nearby town with bubbles, so much so that the bubbles spilled across two blocks into the streets.

"It didn't seem like it at the time because we were in so much trouble." Josie rolled her eyes. "It ended up on television because the bubbles were slowing traffic, then one of the girls bragged to someone, and we all eventually got caught." She giggled, and for a moment, she seemed like she was Linda's age. "But no. No regrets. It's just one of those things we did as kids. No one got hurt, and . . ." She smiled. "And now I can share it with you, something to remember someday when . . ." Josie drew in a long breath, shook her head a bit. "Anyway, it's just a fun story to remember."

Linda had done her share of talking throughout the night too. She'd told Josie all about Stephen, including how she'd forgotten to check for a note by the bridge. "That's so romantic," Josie had said. And she'd shared about her own school years. Josie had already known that Amish children only went to school through the eighth grade, and Linda certainly didn't have any fun stories to share like the ones Josie had. But Josie hung on Linda's every word, in a way that no one had done in a long time. Like she was someone truly special.

"I bet you are not used to staying up this late." Josie glanced at the clock on her mantel. "It's almost midnight."

"It's all right." Linda couldn't take her eyes from the clock. "That's so pretty."

"That clock? Yes, it is. I brought that back from Germany about six years ago when I went with Robert. That mahogany finish is gorgeous."

"I love the way it chimes too. Little chimes every fifteen minutes, longer on the half hour, and then even longer on the hour. I just love that."

They sat quietly for a moment. "You can have it," Josie said sheepishly after a while. "I'd be glad for you to have it."

Linda's eyes widened. "No, I could never." She shook her head, but still couldn't take her eyes off the clock. Sitting about a foot high on the mantel, the timepiece wasn't really fancy, just beautiful. Simple and lovely.

"Linda, I'd really like for you to have it. I don't want to do anything to upset your parents, but I know clocks are allowed. Please take it as a gift from me."

Josie's voice was begging her to reconsider, and Linda could picture how beautiful the clock would look on the mantel at home. *In Mamm's home.* "No, I really can't." She turned to Josie. "But it's nice of you to offer." She tucked her chin.

"You know, Robert says I do that a lot too."

Linda looked up. "What's that?"

"We both lower our heads and look down when we feel uncomfortable and shy about something."

Linda made a conscious effort not to do it again, even though she wanted to do it at this uncomfortable moment.

"When you were born, you had a birthmark above your right knee. Do you still have it?"

Linda untucked her legs from beneath her on the couch and stretched her right leg. She raised her nightgown to reveal the mark. "*Ya*, I still have it all right. It's big too." She shrugged and put her gown down. "But it's all right. It's always covered by my dress."

They were quiet for a few moments again.

"Linda. It's a dream come true for me, you being here. I've dreamed about this since you were born. Thank you for staying with me." Josie's eyes filled with water as she reached over and clasped

Linda's hand, and Linda wished she could feel what Josie was feeling, but it was all just too new. She was still getting used to the idea that Josie was her birth mother, but she didn't remember Josie giving her to her parents, or understand how hard that must have been. She wanted to return the affection Josie had been showing her all evening, but she wasn't sure how. She eased her hand free.

"It is late, no? Maybe we should go to bed." She stood up and cupped a hand over her hair, which she'd pulled into a bun on top of her head.

"Sure. I know it's late." Josie stood up too, but her expression reflected her disappointment. Josie's hand and arm were still shaking.

"Can I come with you to your doctor's appointment in the morning?"

"Oh, I don't know. Don't you want to sleep in, and when I get back we can go do something? You don't want to hang out with me at the hospital. Sometimes, you have to wait, and—"

"I don't mind. I'm sure I'll get up in plenty of time to go."

"Okay." Josie frowned a bit. "If you want to."

"Oh, and Josie?"

"Yes?" Josie blew out a candle on the coffee table.

"Stephen asked me to go swimming at the creek on Thursday. Is that all right with you?"

Josie touched Linda's arm with her left hand. Linda could see her right arm twitching out of the corner of her eye, but she kept her eyes on Josie's.

"I want you to do anything you want to do while you're here. Anything. And by all means, I refuse to interfere with your love life. Definitely go swimming with Stephen."

Linda smiled. "*Danki*, Josie. For everything."

Josie wrapped her arms around Linda and held on for what seemed like forever, and Linda returned the hug. It had been such a wonderful night, hearing about Josie's life, sharing her own life with—with her friend. In Linda's mind, she knew that's all Josie would ever be, and she hoped that Josie would be all right with that too.

Once upstairs, Josie threw herself on the bed. No headache, and she was eternally grateful for that, but the sporadic jerking of her right hand and arm both bothered her and worried her. But tonight, she just wanted to bask in the feel of having Linda under her roof for the first time in twelve years. No, fourteen—fourteen years. No, she's . . .

How old is—is?

Linda. That's her name. Linda. Linda is . . .

Josie grabbed her head with her only good hand. No headache, but something wasn't right. She bolted straight up on the bed, as if sitting up would send a rush of blood to her head and clear the fog that seemed to be wrapping around her brain like a cocoon.

What's happening? Why can't I remember how old she is? I should know this . . .

13

GROGGY FROM SLEEP, JOSIE SAT UP IN BED AND LOOKED down at her hand and arm. She brushed her hand, then her arm, against her leg and smiled at the returned sensation. Closing her eyes, she took a deep breath. "Linda is seventeen years old. Her birthday is the seventeenth of August," she said in a whisper. Everything was back to normal.

She glanced at the clock on her nightstand about the time the phone started ringing, and she answered it on the first ring. A fuzzy voice spoke on the other end of the line.

"Robert, is that you? I can barely hear you."

"Josie, are you okay? Is everything all right?"

"Everything is great. Fabulous. I'm having the best time with Linda." No way she was going to mention the numbness in her hand and arm last night or the slight loss of memory. This trip was important to Robert. "As a matter of fact, I smell bacon. Linda must have gotten up early and made breakfast." *Wow.* She swung her legs over the side of the bed and ran a hand through tousled hair. "How was your trip? Are you at your hotel yet?"

"Josie, can you hear me?"

"Yes, honey. I'm here. Where are you?"

"I'm still on the plane. I've been sitting on the plane for two hours. Something's going on, and they won't let us get off the plane."

Josie's heart thudded hard in her chest. "What do you mean something is going on?"

"I don't know, hon. I can't understand the people speaking in Chinese around me. I'm sure everything is fine, but we aren't being allowed to get off the plane. That's all I know. But . . ."

"Robert, you're breaking up."

"Josie, it looks like they're letting us off. I'll call you tonight, okay? I can barely hear you."

"I love you. Can you hear me?"

"Yes, babe. I love you too. Call you tonight."

Josie sighed a breath of relief as she hung up the phone, though a thread of worry still lingered. She'd feel better when Robert called tonight.

She heard a noise from downstairs and quickly pulled on her robe and headed down the steps.

"Smells like coffee in here." She shuffled across the tile floor in her socks.

"I wasn't sure how to make the cappa cappa—"

"Cappuccino." Josie reached for two cups in the cabinet. "I think regular coffee sounds great this morning. And I smell bacon."

"I already made breakfast, I hope that's okay. It's keeping warm in the oven."

Josie's eyes widened. "Linda, you're my guest. You didn't have to do that."

"*Ach*, I know. But I wanted to. I didn't know if your hand and arm would be . . ."

Josie held up her arm, then wiggled her hand. "Look. Good

as new. And no, I don't mind that you made breakfast. What a treat!"

"I made bacon and eggs with onion, bell pepper, tomatoes, and some bacon bits I found in your refrigerator." She pointed to the other side of the counter. "And some toast." Linda smiled as she stared at the toaster. "Much better than broiling it in the oven."

"Thank you. You must have gotten up early. I'm sorry I didn't get up in time to help you."

"No. I like to cook. *Mamm* says it's important to be able to cook *gut* for a husband."

"She's right. Although . . . I'm afraid that if I had counted on that for Robert to marry me, I'd still be waiting." She tipped her head to one side and twisted her mouth. "I'm not a great cook. If the truth be told, I was worried about the meatloaf."

"No, it was *gut*."

"Are you s-u-r-e?"

Linda giggled. "*Ya*, I reckon I'm sure." She pulled a skillet of eggs from the oven and placed it on the kitchen counter. Then retrieved a plate of bacon.

"Do you want to eat on the patio?" Josie pointed to the large window in the kitchen. "It's lovely out there this time of day. The birds are just starting to wake up, and it's not too hot."

"Sure."

"We probably need to leave for Lancaster about nine fifteen." She paused. "Are you sure you want to go?"

"*Ya*. I'll just wait for you. It's no problem."

Josie wanted Linda by her side constantly; she just didn't want to take a chance that Linda would find out about her illness. Not yet. "Okay. We'll do something fun afterward."

They filled their plates and moved to the patio. The glass table was surrounded by flowering potted plants, and it offered a nice view of Robert's garden.

"What do you have planted?" Linda pointed to the garden as she took a seat in one of the chairs.

"Oh, that's Robert's garden. I think he has tomatoes, cucumbers, and some peppers. I'm not sure exactly."

"We musn't forget to water it while he's gone." Linda smiled, then bowed her head.

Josie lowered her chin. *I'm dying. If you're there, stop me from dying.* Her silent plea was laced with bitterness, and an instant pang of guilt stabbed at her heart, which caused uncertainty. *If I don't believe, why do I feel guilty?* She didn't need this type of confusion this morning. She raised her head and waited for Linda to do the same, then they both began to eat.

Josie and her daughter. On her patio. She was determined to live in each special moment without dreading the future.

———

Josie sat in an oak chair with a worn leather seat, facing a desk covered with papers and file folders, and she wondered how Dr. Phillips kept anything straight in this mess.

"Mrs. Dronberger." Dr. Phillips walked in and extended his hand. "It's nice to meet you."

"Nice to meet you too." Josie stood up to shake his hand, then sat back down when Dr. Phillips took a seat behind the desk.

"I've reviewed all your files and test results. Has anything changed since Dr. Stoltzfus had your records forwarded to me? Any new symptoms or problems?"

Josie knew if she told Dr. Phillips about the numbness in her hand and arm, he most likely would subject her to further testing, or worse—admit her to the hospital. She'd waited too long to spend time with Linda. "No. Still just a lot of headaches."

"Well, I'm going to recommend that you stay on your current meds for now, and I really don't see the need for another MRI just yet, since you just had one a couple of weeks ago. But I would like to schedule you for one thirty days from now, so we can see what that tumor is doing." He pulled off a pair of dark-rimmed reading glasses and placed them on the desk. Dr. Phillips was a well-built man of around fifty, Josie assumed, with a full head of gray hair and eyes that seemed careful not to reveal too much information. Josie assumed they trained for that in medical school.

Josie nodded and waited for the doctor to go on. He rubbed his eyes, then replaced his glasses with a sigh. Josie knew what was coming.

Dr. Phillips opened a file and read for a moment. "I see where you had radiation therapy two years ago." He glanced up at Josie.

"Yes. I did. And I was hopeful for a while. The tumor regressed, and my symptoms subsided. For a while." She paused, crossed her legs. "But then I had a seizure."

He read some more, then removed his glasses again. "Mrs. Dronberger, I see where you've also had chemo, and that failed as well. The only option left would be for me to try to remove that tumor, and . . ." He shook his head. "I don't think I could give you more than a five percent chance of surviving the surgery." He paused, as if waiting for a reaction that wasn't coming. "Is this even an option for you?"

"No. I want to live out however long I have, not die on an

operating table." She folded her hands in her lap. "This is what I've been told repeatedly. Five percent."

"That lesion is located in an . . ." He stopped and pulled a large envelope from underneath the file. "Here, let me show you." Dr. Phillips pulled her MRI out and faced it toward her. "Do you see this?" He pointed to the lesion that Josie had seen a hundred times before.

She smiled politely. "Yes."

"Where it's located in the brain stem makes it almost impossible to get to. I imagine most doctors wouldn't even consider it. And I'll be honest with you, I've never successfully taken out a lesion of this size in this location, but there is a small window of hope should you ever feel that you want me to try."

"Five percent isn't much of a window, Dr. Phillips." She folded her arms across her chest. She knew this would be a waste of time, but she'd endure for Robert, who couldn't pass up any opportunity to get another opinion, even though they were all the same.

"No. It's not." He gazed at her, in the familiar, sympathetic way she'd gotten used to. "But, Mrs. Dron—"

"Just Josie."

"All right. Josie, if your quality of life should come to a point where you are willing to take the risk, you should have that documented." He paused. "For example. If you should lose the ability to remember, to think clearly, and it's evident to your husband that your quality of life is suffering greatly, you might want to make sure that he has power of attorney to make decisions for you. It might be that at that point, the surgery would be an option. Do you understand?"

"Yes, I understand. My husband already has my power of

attorney for such things." She glanced out the window and wished she'd never come here, never allowed herself to have the tiniest glimmer of hope. She just wanted to pretend for two weeks that everything was normal.

They sat quietly for a few moments.

"Josie, have you had any type of counseling? Perhaps a support group of others who are going through what you are?"

"I've been in counseling, Dr. Phillips. I understand what's happening."

"Understanding it and dealing with it are two separate things."

Josie stared out the window of the eight-story building. "I'm dealing with it the best anyone can, I suppose."

They were quiet again.

"Do you have any questions?"

"Nope." She turned toward Dr. Phillips. "I appreciate you seeing me on such short notice, but honestly, Dr. Phillips, you aren't telling me anything that I haven't already heard."

"Then you do realize how your body will begin to shut down? Numbness, particularly on the right side. Motor functions will be affected, and even memory disturbances." He wiped his forehead with his hand, then continued. "There will be increased brain pressure as the lesion expands, Josie. The headaches will become debilitating and could even cause some changes to your personality. I'm assuming all of this has been covered by your doctors before me?"

"Yes. It has." She forced a smile. "I understand."

Dr. Phillips tilted his brow and looked at her uncertainly, waiting for more. Finally, he said, "Well, all right. Then I suppose we'll have another look in a month."

Josie nodded, stood up, and extended her hand. "Again, thank you for seeing me on such short notice."

What Dr. Phillips didn't understand was her ability to program herself for the situation. She'd learned that a long time ago. When she didn't want Robert to worry, there was a program for that. When she didn't want a doctor to see her cry, there was a program for that. When she needed to pretend that this was all a false reality, a program for that. She'd been doing it for so long, sometimes she actually believed she'd never have to face the grim reality before her.

She rubbed her hands together as she walked down the hallway. *Good.* Complete feeling. It had been like that all morning. She was glad she didn't mention anything about the numbness to Dr. Phillips.

After she made her appointment for an MRI in a month, she walked into the waiting room to find Linda surrounded by four women. They all had their heads bowed and were holding hands. Linda looked up when she entered the room.

"I'm sorry. I have to go." Linda stood up. "I will pray for each of your loved ones."

One woman hugged her. "Thank you."

Josie waited until Linda walked to where she was standing a few feet away.

"Normally, it's not our place to minister to others, but all these women are sad about a very sick loved one, so we all prayed together. I told them of the Lord's peace and how he never abandons us in our time of need." She smiled, then her expression grew serious. "What did the doctor say about your hand and arm?"

"Oh, it's fine. Just a neurological problem from the headache.

No biggie." *If there is a hell, I'm going there for lying.* "Let's forget all this and go do something fun."

Linda didn't move. "Are you sure that's all he said?"

Josie nodded. "I told you, no biggie. How about a trip to the mall? Does that sound good? And maybe get some lunch after that? By then, we'll be hungry after that fabulous breakfast you made." She headed toward the exit. Linda followed, waving at her new friends on the way out.

"Sure. That all sounds fine."

Linda had been to the mall plenty of times with her *Englisch* friends since she'd begun her *rumschpringe* almost two years ago, but her friends clearly didn't have the wealth that Josie had.

Linda thumbed through the blue jeans on the rack while Josie was in the dressing room.

"No one has to know if you want to try them on."

Linda turned to see Josie standing beside her with several pairs of pants and a couple of shirts draped over her arms.

"*Ach,* I couldn't." Linda wondered if she would look like the women in the fashion magazines, or even like Josie. She smiled. "Or could I?"

"It's only clothes. And you're just giving them a try. It's your running-around period, right?"

Linda thought for a moment, tried to visualize herself wearing the stylish blue jeans. "Okay." She picked out a size she thought might fit and also grabbed a pink, lacy blouse, then walked to the dressing room.

After she slipped out of her dress, she pulled the tight blue jeans on, then slipped the blouse over her head. She had a slender figure like Josie's, but enough curves to fill out the *Englisch* clothes. Vanity and pride were forbidden, and guilt rose to the surface as Linda studied herself in the mirror, but she pushed it aside, and just for this moment, she pretended she was one of the fashion models in the magazines. She put her hand on her hip and turned slightly to one side, the way the girls in the magazines did. She pushed her chest out a bit, puckered her lips, and wished she could pull her hair from the prayer covering to make the look complete.

"Can I come in?"

Linda's heart jumped in her chest when she heard Josie's voice, and she could feel the red taking over her cheeks. "Uh, wait. Um. Just a minute." She gathered herself, then opened the curtain.

"You look adorable." Josie smiled. "Do you want me to get them for you?"

"*Ach*, no. I'm not allowed."

"Okay. I understand. Like I've told you, I don't want to do anything to upset your parents. I just wasn't sure if you were allowed since it's your *rumschpringe*."

Linda recalled the time Marian Kauffman wore blue jeans into town while she was in her running-around period. Her parents had found out, and even though they weren't happy, they didn't do anything because certain behavior is allowed during that time. Josie closed the curtain.

"Wait." Linda pulled it open again. "I reckon, maybe it might be all right." She lowered her head, but quickly raised it, now that she was aware she tended to do that.

"Great. I'll meet you at the register."

Linda stood looking at herself in the *Englisch* clothes, and suddenly she thought of her mother. Her *real* mother.

"Where are the clothes?" Josie asked when Linda met her by the register.

"I changed my mind."

Josie's brow crinkled as she spoke. "Are you sure?"

"*Ya*, I'm sure."

"Okay." Josie looked at her own pile on the counter, then glanced at Linda. "You know, I think I have plenty of clothes." She turned to the clerk. "I've changed my mind too."

As they exited the mall, the sun felt good against Linda's cheeks, a welcome contrast to the cold in the mall. Josie draped an arm around Linda's shoulder, and for whatever reason, Linda thought of *Mamm* again.

Late that afternoon, Linda helped Josie fold clothes she'd pulled from the electric tumble dryer. How much easier wash day would be with such modern conveniences, but she noticed right away that Josie's dried clothes didn't smell the same as her clothes at home, a certain freshness that could only come from line drying.

She handed Josie a folded pair of blue jeans.

"Those used to be my favorite jeans, but I've lost about ten pounds, and they don't fit very well any more."

"I like the beads along the waist." Linda studied the sleek design, then glanced around the room, making double sure they were alone. "Can I try them on?"

Josie handed her the jeans. "Of course you can. You can have them, if they fit, but only if you're comfortable with that."

"No. I just want to try them on."

"Here try on this blouse with them. That's one of my favorites." She handed Linda a bright red blouse with lace on the collar. "It'll be our secret."

Linda darted up the stairs with the clothes and returned feeling as pretty as Josie. She'd left her hair in a bun atop her head but shed her *kapp*. "What do you think?"

"I think you look beautiful! But Linda . . ." Josie's expression softened into a nurturing look she'd seen on her mother's face. "I think you look beautiful in your Plain dresses too. Simply gorgeous."

Linda knew that looks were of no concern. They shouldn't be anyway. It's how she'd been raised and what she truly believed. But it felt good to bend the rules just a bit. She'd never been in any real trouble, and if this was the worse thing she ever did during her *rumschpringe*, her conscience could handle it.

Josie had turned on some music. Another thing they didn't have at home. Songs of worship during church service were only sung in High German. There was some harmonizing at Sunday singings, but nothing like this. Instruments were forbidden in their community, said to invoke too much unnecessary emotion. But when Josie's hips started swaying to the music, Linda found her hips moving to the tune as well.

"Oops. I forgot to turn on the dryer after I pulled this load out. Be right back." Josie headed past the kitchen to the large laundry room. Linda kept swaying her hips to the music until she heard a knock at the door.

"Can you get that?" Josie yelled from the back part of the house.

Linda walked to the front door, pulled on the knob, and swung the door wide.

Without even thinking about how she was dressed.

14

"STEPHEN!" LINDA STOOD FROZEN IN THE DOORWAY. "What are you doing here?"

Stephen eyed Linda up and down in the blue jeans and bright red shirt. He was speechless, but he could feel his mouth curving upward into a smile. This is exactly what he'd feared, his Linda succumbing to temptation. But seeing her in the tight jeans and lacy red shirt showed off curves he didn't know she had, a figure she'd kept hidden beneath her Plain dresses. It wasn't anger bubbling to the surface, something entirely different. Stephen swallowed hard.

"I just wanted to make sure you were all right. You told me Monday that you'd go by the bridge, and my note was still there tonight on my way home from work." He frowned. "I reckon you weren't that interested in what I had to say."

She stepped onto the front porch and closed the door behind her. "Of course I'm interested in what you have to say. You know how much I love your poems."

"You don't even have your *kapp* on." He looped his thumbs beneath his suspenders and scowled.

She mumbled something under her breath, shook her head, then folded her arms across her chest. "I know what you must be thinkin', but I'm not straying from our ways. I was just trying some of Josie's clothes on. For fun." Her expression challenged him to quiz her further, so he just shrugged.

"If you say so." He tipped his straw hat in her direction. "I'll let you get back to what you were doin'."

She grabbed his arm. "No, wait." Then she threw him a smile, the kind that always made him melt. "Where's my note? Is it still there?"

Stephen recalled the proposal he'd written. "No. I threw it away."

"Why?" Her lip folded into a pout.

"Because it just didn't seem important anymore." Stephen wondered how much of the *Englisch* life Linda was going to get involved in. Maybe he should just walk away from her for good. What if his grandfather saw the way she was dressed? Another part of him wanted to drop to his knee right then, to assure that she would marry him and remain a part of the community. But he shifted his weight and stared back at her with the same challenging look.

Her expression softened. "Anything you write to me is important. I'm sorry that you're mad."

"I'm not mad, Linda. I just figured you would have been by our spot under the bridge before now, and . . ." He paused with a sigh. "I'm just surprised to see you in Josie's *Englisch* clothes. You sure you ain't gonna jump to the other side?"

She stepped forward, her arms still crossed. "Stephen, I cannot believe you would even ask me that."

He shrugged again. "Well, it just wonders me to see ya dressed like this."

"It ain't . . ."

Linda stopped when the front door swung open. "Hello."

If Stephen wanted to know what Linda would look like when she got older, now he knew. Linda looked exactly like her birth mother, but with darker hair instead of blonde, and minus the lines around the older woman's eyes.

"You must be Stephen," the woman said with a smile. "I recognize you from Linda's description. I'm Josie." She shook Stephen's hand, then turned to Linda. "You're right. He is very handsome."

Linda's cheeks reddened, but it warmed Stephen's heart to know Linda had said that, even though vanity was to be avoided. He forced a half-smile.

"Come in." Josie stepped backward and pushed the door wide.

Stephen raised one brow at Linda, who nodded.

Once inside, Linda excused herself. "I'm going to go change clothes." She scurried up the stairs, and Josie motioned for him to sit down on the couch. Josie sat down in a chair on the other side of the coffee table. He glanced around the fancy home, not comfortable in it and not comfortable being alone with Josie. He resented the time Linda was spending with her, and he was afraid it would show. Too much temptation for Linda. Then he recalled his reaction to Linda in the *Englisch* clothes and decided maybe he'd best just work on his own temptations.

"It's so nice to meet you . . . um . . . oh gosh. Um . . ." Josie rubbed her temples with both hands. "I'm sorry. It's nice to meet you . . ."

"Stephen."

Josie closed her eyes, slowly reopened them, and dropped her hands in her lap. "I'm sorry. I knew that." She attempted a smile.

"So, I understand that tomorrow you and Linda are going swimming at the creek?"

"*Ya.*"

"That should be fun. I know Linda is looking forward to it." She appeared as if she was trying to smile again, but instead cringed so badly that Stephen felt himself cringing just watching her.

"You all right?"

"Actually, I have a really bad headache." She stood up. "I need to go take something for this. I apologize for leaving you downstairs by yourself."

Before Stephen could answer, she was hurrying up the stairs with one hand holding her head. It was only a moment later when Linda came down the stairs.

"Josie said to apologize again for leaving you." Linda sat down beside Stephen on the couch. "She gets really bad headaches sometimes."

Stephen was glad to see Linda back in a dark blue dress and black apron. "You look beautiful." He reached for her hand and squeezed. "You don't need all that fancy stuff."

"I know that. I was just, you know . . . playing dress up." She smiled.

Stephen decided to take advantage of them being alone, in the nice air-conditioned house. He leaned over and kissed Linda softly on the lips, then said, "I just don't want you to get too used to all this."

"I'm not. I'm just trying to get to know Josie, and all this comes along with Josie. That's all."

"You plannin' to see your folks during the two weeks?"

"*Ya.* I thought I'd go spend the day Sunday with them. There's no worship service, but I'd like to just be there." She scowled, then leaned closer and whispered. "We don't have any kind of devotions here, and I miss that. I really do."

Stephen was glad to hear that she missed it. "Maybe you should bring it up, see if she'll share devotion time with you."

Linda tipped her head to one side. "I think I will. I'd enjoy that."

Josie popped two Vicodin in her mouth and downed the pills with some water she had on her bedside table. This was a bad one, and when the phone started to ring beside her, she thought her head might explode. She grabbed it on the first ring.

"Josie?"

"Robert? I can barely hear you." It hurt to talk, and as much as she wanted to talk to Robert, she was hoping he'd keep it short.

"Honey, listen. Something's happened. Have you been watching TV?"

Josie took a deep, cleansing breath and tried to fight the pain enough to understand what Robert was saying. "No. What do you mean something's happened? Are you all right?"

"Yes. I'm okay. But they are having their own version of 9-11 over here, and over eleven hundred people are dead from an explosion at last count. Turn on CNN."

"What? Oh, my gosh! But you're okay? Robert, you're in a safe place, right? Should you come home?" Josie stood up, kept one hand to her head, and wandered restlessly around the room.

"Josie, listen to me. I am in a very safe place, far from where the explosion occurred, so don't worry. Things will settle down again soon, but I just didn't want you to see all that on television and worry. I am perfectly safe where I'm at."

"Thank God," she whispered.

"What?"

"Thank goodness." She spoke loud and clear. "Thank goodness you're safe."

"I love you, babe. I'll try to call you later, but if not, we'll talk tomorrow."

"I love you too, Robert. Be safe."

Josie hung up the phone and decided to head downstairs to check on Linda and Stephen and to turn on the television. Her head was still killing her, but she knew the meds would take effect soon, and she wanted to see what was going on in China.

"Where's Stephen?" Josie glanced around the living room.

"He went on home. Said to tell you it was nice to meet you."

"I feel badly that I had to leave him like that, but I had a really bad headache come on." She reached for her temple and could feel the sharp pulse against her fingertip.

"Is it better?"

"No. But it will be. I just took some pills." She reached for the remote. "Robert just called, and there's been a big explosion in China. He's far away from the action, but he said it's just like 9-11 was here." Josie pushed the On button.

"Oh, no. Really?"

"Well, I don't think planes crashed into buildings, but there was an explosion, and Robert compared it to 9-11."

Josie began flipping channels until she reached CNN. She focused on the television, thankful that the Vicodin was kicking in. "That's horrible."

Live coverage from Beijing showed bodies covered with dark sheets among the wreckage of the explosion. It had occurred at a twenty-six-story high-rise not far from Peking University. The newscaster said that a well-known terrorist group had already taken credit for the despicable act.

Josie watched the details unfolding. "I'm glad Robert called to tell me he was okay. I'd have been worried to death if I'd turned on the TV and saw this." She shook her head. "So many dead. So tragic." Josie continued to view the devastation. Her heart hurt for all of them. "As bad as this is, at least it wasn't a direct hit on the university where all those young people go to school."

Josie heard a sniffle and turned to Linda. Tears were streaming down her daughter's cheeks, then she began to sob loudly. Josie ran to her side and threw her arms around her.

"Linda?" Josie held her tightly; she was trembling. "Sweetheart, are you all right?"

"Those people, they are dead, no?" Linda pulled away from her, swiped at her eyes, and pointed to the television. "The ones covered up."

Josie gazed into Linda's eyes as her daughter stared in horror at the disturbing images on the television, right about the time the newscaster said, "The death toll has now reached twelve hundred and twenty-two."

"Yes. I believe those people are dead."

Linda shook her head and covered her face with her hands. "I can't watch any more. I'm sorry, Josie."

"No, it's all right. We don't have to watch it." Josie clicked the remote and the screen went black. "I'm sorry. I didn't realize you would get so upset or I would have never turned it on, Linda. I'm sorry."

"We read about 9-11 in the newspaper when it happened here, but it's so much worse to see it on television. We need to pray." Linda reached for Josie's hand. "We need to pray for all those people in that place and for all those families who lost loved ones." Linda sniffled and bowed her head.

As Josie lowered her head, she squeezed Linda's hand tightly. Maybe some of Linda's faith would rub off on her.

Stephen scrubbed his courting buggy with soap and water so it would be nice and clean tomorrow when he picked up Linda to go swimming at the creek. Every time he envisioned the two of them in their swim clothes, and him without his elevated shoe, his stomach twisted with anxiety. But if he was going to marry Linda, this was something he knew he was going to have to get past.

He glanced over his shoulder when he heard a buggy pulling onto the driveway, then dried his hands and waited until his grandfather came to a stop.

"*Gut-n-owed.*" The elderly bishop stepped with care from the buggy, his gray beard spanning the length of his chest.

"Good evening to you, *Daadi.*"

"Where is the rest of the family?" His grandfather tipped his straw hat back as he approached Stephen, his back curved forward as he walked.

"Hannah and Annie are helping *Mamm* make supper," Stephen responded about his only two siblings, "and I reckon *Daed* is bathing already."

"*Gut.* We can talk before your supper."

Stephen removed his hat, wiped sweat from his brow, then placed it back on his head. "Is something wrong?" Stephen recognized the expression on his grandfather's face. Usually, it was directed at a member of the district who had displeased him. Stephen couldn't think of anything he'd done to warrant it.

"No, nothing is wrong, but I have concerns, Stephen."

Stephen's brows shot upward. "About me?"

His grandfather stroked his beard. "I understand Linda is staying in the *Englisch* woman's house for two weeks, no?"

"*Ya,* she is." Stephen was wondering who told him but surmised it could have been anyone. Nothing stayed a secret around here for long.

"Does this concern you? Her being there?"

"No. Not at all." Stephen's stomach flipped a bit when he realized he'd just lied to his grandfather. "I mean, maybe a little. But Linda's faith is strong, and she'll only be there for two weeks."

"Don't underestimate the bonds of blood. That woman is Linda's kin." Bishop Ebersol stood taller as he spoke and lifted his chin. "Linda is at a time in her life when she can choose the life she wants to live." His eyes narrowed in speculation. "Do you think she is continuing to practice the ways of the *Ordnung?*"

"*Ya, Daadi.* I reckon Linda just wants to get to know her mother. That's all. Then she'll come home."

"Very *gut* then. I was just on my way home from the Miller farm."

"How is Jonas?" Stephen knew that when Jonas passed, lots of people would be devastated. He was such a fixture in the community, such a wise soul, and everyone loved him. Linda would be very upset.

"Jonas is doing poorly. The doctor told the family that he is rapidly declining." His grandfather shook his head. "He will be greatly missed."

Stephen hung his head, not wanting to think about Jonas passing.

"I know it is almost suppertime. Tell the rest of the family I will be by with your *mammi* on Sunday for a visit." He turned to leave, but turned briefly around. "Keep Linda on course, Stephen. This is a delicate situation, her being with the *Englisch* woman."

"I will, *Daadi*."

Stephen recalled seeing Linda in Josie's *Englisch* clothes. He sure hoped he could keep Linda on track.

Linda couldn't sleep that night. All tucked in under the covers of the princess bed, her mind raced with thoughts of what she'd seen on television. There was much in the *Englisch* world she didn't understand. She'd enjoyed her bath for the second night in Josie's big bathroom, but if all this sadness came with Josie's world, Linda was sure she didn't want any part of it for long.

She was disappointed that she'd been so caught up in her new surroundings that she'd forgotten to check the bridge for Stephen's note. But at least they would have tomorrow, an afternoon swimming in the creek. Linda didn't really care what they did, as long as they were together. Tomorrow, she'd reassure Stephen that the only things she wanted were to be in his arms and to be a member of the community. Maybe soon, he would think about asking her to marry him.

Linda closed her eyes and tried to sleep, but her mind was as restless as her body. She missed *Mamm* and *Daed*, even Luke and Matthew. She'd only been there since Tuesday, but it seemed longer.

Josie looked at the clock on her nightstand. Eleven thirty, and each minute seemed to be ticking by a hundred times faster than the last one. She'd never been more frantic to get her affairs in order than she was right now. She scanned the pile of personal mementos and keepsakes in front of her on the floor as her right hand began to shake again, something it had done several times during the course of the evening.

Linda had gone to bed early, and Josie sensed something was wrong. She wasn't sure how much of it had to do with the tragedy on television or if it was something else. Either way, Josie wanted Linda to know everything about her, and her entire life was poured out on the floor of her bedroom. With her left hand, she picked up a picture of her and her mother at the beach. Josie remembered her father taking the picture when she was about ten. She and her mom had made a sand castle together and were proudly displaying it for the camera.

Josie tossed the picture into the pile she didn't plan to leave for Linda, but then picked it up again and wondered if her mother would speak to Linda at Josie's funeral. Would they establish any kind of relationship after Josie was gone? Mom was not the kind of influence Josie wanted for Linda. All Mom cared about was status and what people thought, nothing like sweet Linda. Josie supposed she'd die without seeing her mother again, and sadly, that was all right with her.

Robert didn't call again tonight, but he'd said it might be tomorrow, so she tried not to worry. She had the television volume in her bedroom on low, and at last count, fatalities were at fifteen hundred. She recalled Linda's reaction to the news again and wondered if bringing her here was a mistake. Such innocence. And Josie was exposing her to life in a world she'd been sheltered from.

She slammed her right hand down hard on the carpeted floor, hoping the blow would jar some feeling into the numb limb. Nothing. She picked up a picture of her and Robert on vacation in Italy. It was one of her favorite pictures of Robert, handsomely dressed in cargo shorts and a white T-shirt, and she was wearing a yellow sundress and looked so happy. Robert was going to be a lost soul when she was gone. She recalled the first time she met Robert, through mutual friends, and the only blind date she'd ever been on. He'd stolen her heart on that first encounter at the Italian restaurant on Mason Boulevard.

Josie lay down in the middle of the floor, surrounded by tokens of her life lived thus far, a life soon to end, and she allowed herself to feel the pain in her heart, the fear of the unknown, and the absolute sense of loss she felt about not growing old with Robert and not being able to spend more time with her daughter. It was her most pitiful moment, she was sure, as she pulled her knees to her chest and sobbed.

"I don't want to die." She tucked her blue satin pajamas tight around her knees and hugged her legs. "Please, God. I don't want to die. I don't want to die. I'm afraid. I'm so scared." She sobbed hard, stifling her cries so as not to wake Linda.

And then she felt it.

His presence.

And then she heard it.

His voice.

I am here My child. The fool hath said in his heart, There is no God.

15

JOSIE AND LINDA SPENT THE MORNING WATCHING television, mostly sweet loves stories. Josie didn't turn on the news, and while she tried to focus on the movies she and Linda had picked out, her mind wandered. Linda had asked her if she was worried about Robert, and she said a little bit, which was true.

Josie could tell that Linda was anxious to see Stephen, mentioning their planned swimming trip several times. Linda seemed nervous as well and explained that girls in her district wore either shorts and a shirt to swim in or a one-piece bathing suit. She also said some of the girls wore a two-piece swimsuit, but she didn't own that kind and didn't think she'd wear it if she did.

Linda had left to try on her suit for Josie, and when she entered the room wearing her swimsuit, Josie rose from the couch. "That looks really good on you." Linda had chosen a dark blue, one-piece bathing suit.

"*Danki. Mamm* approved of this one when we went shopping in the city."

"Are you going to Pequea Creek?"

"*Ya.*" Linda tugged on her swimsuit in an effort to cover more of herself. Josie remembered her own breasts being larger than most girls' too.

"Sweetie, you're all in there. I promise." Josie smiled warmly. "Stephen will think you look great."

Linda blushed slightly. "It feels strange not to have my *kapp* on." She reached up and touched the clip that held her hair in a tight bun on top of her head. "What are you gonna do this afternoon, Josie?"

"Well, I thought I might take a little nap and then make us some dinner for later. Do you like lasagna?"

"*Ya!* I have that when we go to Paradiso. *Mamm* and *Daed* take us there about once a month. Do you know how to make lasagna?"

Josie smiled. "Actually, I make pretty good lasagna. So, I'll make that, a salad, and some garlic bread for us to eat when you get home from your swim with Stephen. How's that?"

"Sounds *gut.*"

Josie heard the clippety-clop of horse hooves.

"There's Stephen." Linda headed toward the door. "I'll see you later."

"Have fun."

———※———

Josie watched out the window as Stephen pulled away with Linda beside him in the buggy. It was a bright, sunny afternoon, and the cool water in the creek would be a welcome relief from the heat. Josie remembered those days from her own youth. But twenty years ago, Amish girls wouldn't have been caught dead in a swimsuit like Linda was wearing, no matter how conservative. Times were changing. Even for the Amish.

Though she didn't have a headache this afternoon, Josie lay down on the couch anyway. She hadn't slept much last night. She couldn't shake that voice she'd heard. Her religious background had certainly taught her everything she needed to know about God, about Jesus. She'd studied the Bible. She'd gone to Bible study. And for a time, it seemed to make sense, even though she never felt any real connection to God, even back then.

Robert had so many valid arguments against the concept of God. "Josie, some humans need something to believe in, or there would be even more chaos than there already is," he'd said. "I'm not one of those people. My mind just can't grasp the concept of this higher power." He'd talk about evolution, how an all-powerful God wouldn't let people suffer this way, and on more than one occasion, he'd mentioned the possibility of otherworldly entities being in control. "There are too many pieces of the puzzle missing, parts of the Bible missing, cover-ups by religious rulers. It's just not an idea I can buy into."

But what if Robert was wrong? He was the most giving, loving, generous, and sincere person she'd ever known. Robert wasn't capable of telling a lie, and he lived each day to serve others. If what she'd been taught in Sunday school was correct, Robert was going straight to hell for not believing in God and His son, Jesus. And if there is a God, how could such an entity send such a good man to the depths of hell for all eternity?

What about me? What do I really believe? Am I changing my tune at the eleventh hour on the off chance that there might be a God, so that I'm not damned to hell? Is it too late for me? Again, she recalled the feeling she'd had the night before, the voice she thought she'd heard, and the calm that had spread over her. She'd felt like a child, wrapped in the comforting arms of a parent, unconditional love that could be felt to the core of her being.

She closed her eyes and tried to reconcile her thoughts, her feelings. But nothing made sense anymore.

Linda dipped her toe into the cool water at Pequea Creek and wondered when Stephen was going to shed his trousers, shirt, and shoes. She knew this was uncomfortable for him, but if they were going to be married someday, he was going to need to get past this. *If I can wear this bathing suit . . .*

Reflections of everything around them bounced off the clear blue water as sunshine streamed down through the trees, leaving patches of glassy stillness on the creek's surface. Linda poked the water with her foot until it made ripples across the reflection of her face.

"It's chilly." She turned to Stephen. "You coming in?" Linda eased down the creek bed until she was knee-deep in water.

"*Ya.*" Stephen sat down on the ground and fumbled with his shoes. Linda made it a point not to watch. She heard him toss his boots to the side and then the sound of him pulling off his trousers. She was sure Stephen had a bathing suit on underneath his brown pants, but the sound of him pulling them off, then tossing them on the ground, sent a ripple of anticipation through her. She turned around in time to see him toss his blue shirt and suspenders onto the pile and shivered at the sight of his beautifully proportioned body in nothing but a pair of gray and white swim trunks. He held his head high above a confident set of shoulders and broad chest, even though his square jaw tensed visibly. A gentle breeze blew his tawny-gold, bobbed hair as he stepped toward the water's edge with precise footing—as if he'd practiced it a thousand times.

Linda eased backward in the water until she was chest deep,

and it only took Stephen a few moments before he was facing her. Their eyes met in a new and unexplored way, and Linda wondered what was going through Stephen's mind. He leaned forward and kissed her tenderly on the lips, and the feel of his naked chest against her invoked both excitement and fear. She backed away, bit her bottom lip, and eased herself into deeper water.

Then without warning, she cupped her hands in the water and splashed Stephen in the face. Things were getting too intense, too serious.

"Hey!" He splashed her back, and in no time, they were carrying on like playful kids, instead of the young adults they were. And this felt better. There'd been enough serious moments in her life lately, and today she just wanted to play and have fun, put her worries aside.

And that's exactly what they did for the next two hours.

Abe wished he could do something to ease the worry in Mary Ellen's heart. His wife wasn't sleeping well, tossing and turning all night long, and during the day, she worked so hard he thought she might keel over.

"Mary Ellen, if everything isn't perfect while Linda is away, the boys and I will survive. You don't need to work so hard." He watched her scrubbing the floor after they'd finished supper Thursday evening.

"I reckon I can't have the *haus* a mess, Abe." She scrubbed the wood floor even harder with the sponge in her hand, although Abe hadn't a clue what she was scrubbing. It looked clean to him.

He squatted down beside her and eyed the floor. "What ya scrubbing, Mary Ellen? It ain't dirty."

She stopped abruptly and fired him a look. "Luke spilled orange juice here earlier, if you must know." Mary Ellen resumed the scrubbing as if she was mad at that floor.

He grabbed both her shoulders and pulled her to her feet even as she resisted. "Abe, what are you doing?"

Then he wrapped his arms around her. "I'm giving you a hug and hoping to pull some of the worry from your heart." He eased away and cupped her cheek. "I know you are working so hard to keep your mind off of Linda, but I worry *mei fraa* is going to just fall over with exhaustion." He kissed her on the cheek. "*Mei lieb*, everything is going to be all right."

Mary Ellen shrugged. "I know that, Abe. There's just lots to be done, that's all. I am still expected to have a clean home, and that is just what I plan to do." She dropped to her knees and began to scrub again.

Abe blew out a breath of exasperation. "All right, Mary Ellen. I'm going to go secure things outside. Paper says we're in for a nasty storm later. Luke and Matt are already out there tending to the animals."

"Fine."

Abe shook his head as he headed out the kitchen door. Poor woman was going to be exhausted if she kept on like this. But, truth be told, he was missing his Linda more than he cared to let on, and it had only been two days.

Mary Ellen rubbed the sponge across the floor with a vengeance God wouldn't approve of, anger and bitterness with every swipe. Sending Linda for two weeks was her idea, and Mary Ellen didn't think she'd regretted anything more in her life. She'd never been away from her daughter, for starters, but every time she envisioned Linda with Josie and all her fancy things, she went into some sort of jealous tailspin that was not in her normal character. Jealousy is a sin, and she'd prayed that God take away these feelings ever since she'd dropped Linda off on Tuesday.

The woman is dying. How can I be harboring such nasty thoughts toward her? She'd been praying constantly to rid herself of such notions. Mary Ellen knew she'd been selfish and mean-spirited, but Josephine Dronberger hadn't thought things through either. Linda would be devastated when Josephine passed. Didn't Josephine ever stop to think that maybe it would have been best for Linda if she'd never shown up here?

Linda was terrified of pain and saw pain as the gateway to death. Mary Ellen reckoned all that started when Linda was a young girl and witnessed their cow having a troubled birth, which killed both the momma and the calf. Mary Ellen had reprimanded Abe repeatedly for allowing Linda to see that. Mary Ellen had been at market when it happened, and six-year-old Linda cried for days afterward. Once Luke sliced his finger on a saw blade in the barn, not even enough for a stitch, and Linda passed smooth out and busted her chin. Linda couldn't stand to see someone in pain.

Mary Ellen stopped scouring the spot, took a deep breath, and bowed her head.

Dear Lord, release me of the bitterness I feel for Josephine, this woman who so graciously gave us Linda to raise. Now, in her time of need, please guide me to do right by her, to shed all jealousy where she is concerned, and to help her any way I can as her time to join You draws near. In Jesus' name I pray, God. Give me strength.

Mary Ellen stood up, dropped the sponge in the sink, and headed out to see if she could help Abe and the boys get things ready for the storm.

<hr />

Stephen hobbled out of the water, anxious to get his shoes back on. He towel dried as best he could before pulling on his pants and shirt over his swim shorts, then quickly pulled his work boots back on. He'd felt confident in the water where Linda couldn't see his awkwardness, but back on land, he needed his shoes on to feel normal.

"You worry too much about that." Linda waded her way out of the water, thrust her hands on her hips and stared at him. "About your foot."

Aw, don't bring it up. "I ain't worrying." He pulled his suspenders up over his blue short-sleeved shirt.

"I reckon you seem like you're worried about it." She pointed to her leg. "What about my birthmark? Should I be trying to cover that up around you?"

"It ain't the same, Linda." That birthmark was the last thing he'd been looking at.

She reached for a towel she'd left on the bank and wrapped it around herself. "I just want you to know that I love you just the way you are."

He turned quickly toward her. She was white as snow, her eyes wide, and biting her lip. "What did you say?"

"I, uh . . . you know what I mean. I just like you for being you." She turned away from him, and Stephen walked to her, wrapped his arms around her waist.

"No, that's not what you said." He kissed the back of her neck. "You said—"

"No I didn't!" She spun around. "Because I would never say something like that first, Stephen. It just—it just slipped out, and—"

"Linda." He cupped her beautiful, soft, pale cheeks in his hands. "I love you."

She didn't smile. "Are you just saying that because I did? On accident?" She twisted her mouth sideways, lifted her chin.

"Don't you even read my poems? I've done everything but scream it to you. I love you, Linda. With all my heart. I've loved you for a long time."

She giggled. "Since when?"

Stephen smiled. "I reckon since you stubbed your toe on the playground in first grade. You cried so hard, I wanted to hug you, even back then. And don't you remember, I gave you the pie in my lunch that day?" Stephen chuckled. "I loved you then, 'cause I reckon rhubarb pie is my favorite, and I gave it to you."

"I do remember that." She lowered her head for a moment. When she looked up, her eyes were teary, but in a good way. "I love you, Stephen Ebersol."

Now is the time to ask her. Stephen opened his mouth to ask her to be his wife, the way he'd so romantically—or cowardly—done in the letter, but the words just weren't coming. "Linda . . ."

She waited.

"Linda . . ."

Just then, thunder boomed overhead amidst clouds that had darkened within the last few minutes.

"I love you, Linda." He kissed her gently. "But we better get home."

"*Ya*, look at the clouds coming from the west." She pointed to a large mass of blackness moving in their direction.

They hurried to Stephen's topless courting buggy. "It's gonna make wet before I get you back to Josie's, I reckon."

Linda shrugged. "We're already wet anyway." There was a loud clap of thunder. "But thunder and lightning scare me." She squeezed her shoulders together and closed her eyes.

Stephen flicked the horse into action. "Don't worry. I'll get you home safely."

They'd barely pulled out onto the road when the sky opened up.

When they got to Josie's, Linda gave Stephen a quick kiss in the driveway. "Don't come in. Get home before the storm gets worse. And be careful." She turned to leave, but spun back around, as if waiting for something.

"I love you, Linda."

Her face brightened beneath the droplets of rain. "I love you too, Stephen!"

He watched her run up the walkway, turn the doorknob, and get safely inside before he turned to leave. Blackness engulfed the skies above him, and the thunder was so loud he jolted every time it echoed overhead. He considered asking Linda if he could stay for a while, but his house was less than fifteen minutes by buggy. Surely, it'd be all right. Stephen backed the buggy out of the driveway.

Mary Ellen closed the window above the kitchen sink when rain began to spray through the screen.

"Luke and Matt, go close the windows upstairs. I know it

might be hot for a spell with all the windows shut, but otherwise we're going to be sleeping on wet linens later."

Both boys headed toward the stairs as Abe came in from outside. He pushed the wooden door closed behind him.

"What a storm. We sure need the rain but maybe not so much of it at once." Abe pulled off his soaked straw hat and hung it on the rack by the door, then raked a hand through his hair. "Everything is secure outside."

A loud clap of thunder rocked the house and rattled the china in her cabinet. "That was close." Mary Ellen walked to the window and peered outside. "And it's raining so hard, can't see a thing." She paused, turned to Abe. "You think Linda is all right? She gets scared during storms like this, even at her age."

"She's fine, I'm sure, Mary Ellen." Abe headed toward the back of the house, presumably to check the other windows.

"I hope Josephine doesn't leave her alone during the storm for anything. Linda would be terrified." She shook her head. "She might pretend otherwise, but I know my daughter, and every time it storms, I coddle her like a baby. She puts her hands over her ears, Abe, and she gets very scared."

"Mary Ellen, Linda is fine."

"I know she thinks she's grown up, but in so many ways she is still so young."

"She's a big baby. She always gets scared when there's a storm." Matt rolled his eyes as he walked into the kitchen. He opened the refrigerator and pulled out a pitcher of tea, then pulled a glass from the cabinet.

Luke followed his older brother. "She ain't no baby. She just don't like thunder."

Mary Ellen narrowed her eyes in Matt's direction. Then she turned to Luke. "That's right, Luke. She just doesn't like thunder."

"Hope she's havin' fun on her little vacation." Matt walked to the window by the kitchen door and looked outside. "Sure ain't fun around here, having to help with girl chores." He sat down on a bench at the table and drank his meadow tea.

"*Ach*, Matt. I've asked you to do very little since your sister has been gone. Now stop your complaining."

Her oldest son rolled his eyes again.

"You will find your *daed* taking you out to the woodshed if he catches you rollin' your eyes at me like that." Mary Ellen knew Matt was much too old for that type of discipline, but as of late, he'd developed a disrespectful attitude.

Luke pulled the wooden door in the kitchen open and watched the lightning flash for a moment before holding his hand up in everyone's direction. "Listen. Do you hear that? I think it's the phone ringing in the barn."

Linda. "I'll go." Mary Ellen closed the door, reached for the umbrella behind it, then swung it wide again.

"You will do no such thing, Mary Ellen." Abe latched onto her arm. "Do you hear how close that lightning is? You'll get soaked, and by the time you get there, that phone will have stopped ringing."

Mary Ellen jerked from his grasp and stepped into Abe's galoshes that were by the door. "I told you. Linda gets scared when there is a storm, and the sound of my voice will comfort her. I'll just call her right back and talk to her for a minute."

Abe was shaking his head as she brushed past him. She stood on the porch staring at the torrential rain and cringed as another burst of lightning lit up the sky, followed by a deafening eruption of thunder. Her heart thudded hard as she made her way across the yard to the barn. Like her daughter, she was not a fan of raucous storms.

As Abe predicted, the phone had stopped ringing by the time she got to the barn. The answering machine light flashed one. Mary Ellen set the umbrella down and pushed the button.

"*Mamm*, I'm so scared. *Mamm*, I'm really scared!"

I knew it. Mary Ellen reached for the phone to call and comfort her daughter, but she stopped when she heard Linda go on.

"*Mamm*, call me back. It's about Josie. I'm scared. She's not breathing."

16

LINDA WATCHED TWO MEN IN WHITE UNIFORMS HUDDLE over Josie, and lights from the ambulance flashed through the window of the house. The rain continued to pound outside, and one of the men had placed a plastic mask over Josie's face and said it would help her to breathe.

"*Onkel* Noah, is she going to be all right?" Linda had known to dial 9-1-1 when she walked into the house and found Josie lying on the kitchen floor in the middle of red sauce and a broken casserole dish. Lasagna noodles and meat were strewn across the tile floor. After she called the emergency number for help, she'd called her uncle, and then her mother.

"Josie had a seizure." Noah put his hand on her shoulder. "But she is going to be all right."

Linda didn't have any idea what that was, but she knew she'd never been so scared in her entire life. "What is that? What caused it? Did her bad headaches cause her to have a seizure? What now? Is she going to the hospital?"

"I'm not going to the hospital. I'm fine."

Linda turned to see that Josie had pulled the mask from her face. Linda pushed her uncle out of the way and squatted down beside Josie on the floor. "Josie, oh Josie. Are you okay?" She latched onto her hand. "Are you hurting? Are you in pain?"

"No, sweetheart. I'm not in any pain. This has happened before, but it hasn't happened in a long time. I'm sorry you had to see this."

"Mrs. Dronberger, we're going to have to take you to the hospital for evaluation."

"No. I'm not going."

Her uncle moved toward them and knelt down. "Linda, Josie was breathing, but she was unconscious when you found her." Her uncle leaned down closer to Josie. "How long has it been since you've had a seizure, Josie?"

Josie reached up with her left hand and rubbed her eyes. Linda noticed Josie's right hand was jerking like before. "I don't know, Noah. I guess maybe about a year. They were pretty regular back when—" Josie stopped and looked at Linda for a moment, then back at her uncle. She didn't go on.

"When is Robert due back in town?"

"Not for another week and a half." Josie sighed. "He was far enough away from the attacks in China, and he was going to try to finish his business since he made the long trip."

Linda glanced back and forth between her uncle and Josie. *Do they know each other?*

Linda had called her uncle because he was a doctor, but he and Josie sure seemed familiar with each other.

"I think we need him to come home sooner, Josie. You shouldn't be alone." Her uncle's forehead wrinkled with worry.

"She's not alone. She has me. I'm staying here for the whole two weeks, while Robert is in China."

"Honey, I think Josie is going to need more care than you can probably give her." Uncle Noah was talking to her like she was a child.

"I can take care of you, Josie." Linda folded her hands in her lap as she began to wonder what was wrong with Josie. She turned toward her uncle. "Did this happen 'cause of her headaches?"

Linda watched Uncle Noah and Josie lock eyes briefly.

"Yes, it happened because of my headaches." Josie smiled at Linda. "You know how bad they get sometimes."

The men in the uniforms were packed up and looked like they were ready to leave. The taller man handed Uncle Noah a piece of paper. "Dr. Stoltzfus, she really should go to the hospital, but we'll leave her in your care if she'll sign this release form saying she refused to go."

"Josie . . ." Uncle Noah sighed. "How about it?"

"I'm not going, Noah. And you know why. This is going to happen again, and . . ." Josie looked at Linda again, then back at Uncle Noah. "And there's nothing that can be done."

"I can take care of you Josie," Linda repeated, although the thought terrified her. "Just tell me what to do."

"Linda!"

Linda turned and saw her mother's comforting face. She jumped up and ran into her mother's arms as Mary Ellen walked into Josie's kitchen. "Are you all right?" *Mamm* held her tight.

"I was so scared," Linda whispered in her mother's ear. "I didn't know what to do. I called 9-1-1 like you always told us."

"You did the right thing." *Mamm* eased out of the hug and made her way toward Josie and Noah.

"Is she all right?" *Mamm* directed the question to Noah.

"I'm fine." Josie sat up, then looked at the mess in her kitchen and at her clothes. "I sure made a mess, though."

"We're going." The two uniformed men waved and headed

out the front door. "Take care, Mrs. Dronberger," the taller man said before he closed the door behind them.

"Josie, you can't stay here by yourself. What about your mother? Do you want me to call your mother?" Noah stood up.

Linda watched Josie's face turn a bright shade of red. "No. Do not call my mother. I don't want her around me."

Noah let out another sigh. "Then let's get Robert on the phone and have him come home early."

"I don't want to do that." Josie's eyes filled with tears. "This case is so important to him." She paused and looked at Linda. "But I know it's not fair for Linda to stay."

"I have told everyone that I can take care of Josie." Linda glared at Noah, then looked at her mother with pleading eyes. "Besides, maybe it won't happen again. Josie's had some headaches but nothing like this."

"It will happen again." Josie turned her head away from everyone, and Linda was sure they were not telling her something.

"Does Robert have his cell phone over there? I'll go give him a call." Uncle Noah stood up and pulled his cell phone from the pocket of his white doctor's coat.

"Yes, he does."

"He wasn't near any of the trouble, was he?" Noah took a few steps toward the other side of the room.

Josie was still facing away from everyone, and Linda saw her wipe away a tear. "No. He wasn't near there."

Linda wasn't sure what to do. *What is happening?* Her uncle walked into the next room. Linda could hear him talking but couldn't understand what he was saying.

"Here, let's get you cleaned up." *Mamm* squatted down beside

Josie on the floor. Josie wiped her hands, covered with sauce, on her blue jeans, then covered her face with both hands. "I'm sorry, Mary Ellen. I'm sorry for everything. I should have never . . ."

Normally, if someone was crying, *Mamm* was the first one to offer comfort, but *Mamm* just sat there and seemed unsure of what to do. Linda knelt down beside her mother.

"Josie, it's all right." Linda grabbed her hand and squeezed at about the same time her mother wrapped an arm around Josie. Together, *Mamm* and Linda pulled Josie to her feet.

"Linda, why don't you clean up this mess, and I'll help Josie upstairs to get some fresh clothes on." *Mamm* said it in a tone that meant there'd be no argument. Linda nodded.

Mary Ellen kept an arm around Josephine's waist as they headed up the stairs. Josephine grasped the handrail with one hand and draped her other arm across Mary Ellen's shoulder. Mary Ellen could feel her struggling to pull herself up the steps with each heavy step they took. Josephine kept mumbling how sorry she was. For everything.

"Are you sure you didn't get cut by all that glass in the kitchen?" Mary Ellen paused on the step when she felt Josephine leaning on her even more. Josephine took a few moments to catch her breath, then shook her head.

"No. I didn't get cut." She sighed. "I'm just really tired."

"Can you keep going?"

Josephine nodded. "I think so."

Mary Ellen tightened her hold around her and edged them upward.

When they walked into Josephine's room, Mary Ellen couldn't believe her eyes. She hadn't really noticed the downstairs too much with all the ruckus going on, but now that things had settled down a bit, she took in her surroundings. She'd been in plenty of *Englisch* homes over the years, but nothing like this. Why in the world would anyone need all this?

Mary Ellen cringed when Josephine sat down on the bed and smeared what appeared to be spaghetti sauce all over her blue bedspread, even getting a little on one of the white throw pillows. But she didn't seem to care. Josephine wasn't crying anymore. Her expression was blank as she stared into the far corner of the room.

"I never should have come here." She turned to Mary Ellen. "This is all going to be too hard on Linda, and it was selfish of me to want to get to know her. Selfish of me to put her through all this."

Mary Ellen didn't say anything.

"But now I don't know how to undo it." She shrugged. "I guess Robert and I could just leave, and—"

"And leave Linda hanging, thinking her mother abandoned her?" Mary Ellen stared hard into Josie's eyes. "I don't think that's an option at this point."

"Then what should I do, Mary Ellen?" Josephine threw her hands in the air, then slammed them down beside her. "I've already said how sorry I am about everything." Then Josephine started to cry again. Mary Ellen sat down on the bed beside her. Her own dress was covered in sauce anyway.

"I just want to protect my daughter. That's all I've ever wanted to do." Mary Ellen felt her own eyes watering, but she was not about to let herself cry. "We are going to have to tell Linda about your—your condition at some point. But today is not that day. She has been through enough for one day."

Josephine sniffled. "I agree." She stood up. "I'm going to go get cleaned up. You can go downstairs if you want. I'll be down in a minute."

"I'll wait for you." Mary Ellen met Josephine's eyes. "In case— in case you need help or feel ill."

"Thank you."

Mary Ellen glanced around the room after Josephine went to the bathroom to change. So many things. So many things she has exposed young Linda to. Mary Ellen shook her head. Then she just waited. Wondering. Worrying.

"Okay." Josephine came out of the bathroom wearing a fresh pair of blue jeans and a pink pullover shirt. She stopped in the middle of the room. "I guess I better go see when my husband will be home." But she didn't move and instead started to tear up again. "I hate this. I just hate it. I hate all of it. If there is a God, He wouldn't let all this happen!" Then she dropped to her knees right there in her bedroom, as if she could no longer carry the weight of her situation. Mary Ellen put her hands on her chest and wondered if she'd heard correctly.

She walked to Josephine, who was sitting on her heels, covering her face with her hands. "I have no hope, Mary Ellen. Do you know what it's like to face death with no hope?"

Mary Ellen dropped down beside her. "Josephine, what are you saying?"

Josephine uncovered her face and brushed away tears with only her left hand. Mary Ellen could see her right hand twitching in her lap. "You heard me, Mary Ellen. You can add that to your list of reasons to hate me."

"That's not fair, Josephine. I never said I hated you." Mary Ellen took a deep breath. "These are hard times for all of us, but I never said—"

"It doesn't matter." She lifted her head, then stood up, sniffling, struggling to gain control of her emotions. "I miss my husband very much. Let's go downstairs. I want to know when he'll be home."

Mary Ellen followed Josephine downstairs. How could anyone face death and make such comments? It was the saddest thing she'd ever heard.

When they got downstairs, Linda was scooping up the last of the broken glass and Mary Ellen heard Noah telling Linda how he knew Josie, that he was friends with Josie's husband.

Noah walked toward Josephine. "Josie, there're more problems in China. Robert is fine, though."

"What? Did something else happen? More attacks? Robert said he was far away from everything."

Mary Ellen was thinking that this woman really couldn't take any more today.

"No, nothing else happened, but the airports are closed indefinitely for those who aren't citizens, those traveling with a passport."

"What?" Josephine looked like she might collapse again. Mary Ellen stepped toward her but stopped when Linda rushed to Josephine's side.

She watched her daughter—*their* daughter—put her arm around Josephine. "It's all right. We'll figure something out. I'll stay here with you."

Mary Ellen's eyes welled with emotion at the nurturing kindness in Linda's voice. And she knew right away what she needed to do.

She raised her chin, folded her hands in front of her, and spoke directly to Noah. "Josephine will come and stay with us. In our home." She swallowed hard, then glanced at Linda. A smile spread across her daughter's face. Josephine, however, was staring at Mary Ellen as if she'd lost her mind.

"Mary Ellen, I don't know if . . ." Noah's brows furrowed as he spoke. "Are you sure that's a good idea?"

"Absolutely not," Josephine interjected.

"Why?" Linda was quick to ask. Mary Ellen watched her daughter gaze at Josephine with eyes that begged her to reconsider. "You can stay in my room. I have two beds. It would still be like a sleepover, but at my house."

"She's right." Mary Ellen moved toward them. "It makes the most sense. Until Josephine's husband gets home, she should stay with us. She can still . . ." Mary Ellen looked down for a brief moment, then faced Josephine. "You can still get to know Linda, and there will be several of us around so that you are not alone, just in case this should happen again."

"Mary Ellen, can I talk to you outside?" Noah's voice was firm, but Mary Ellen didn't care. She knew that this was the right thing to do for all concerned.

"Of course. We can talk outside while Linda helps Josephine pack a few things."

Josephine moved away from Linda, walked toward Mary Ellen, and faced her. Mary Ellen couldn't tell if she was angry, relieved, or a combination of some other emotions that Mary Ellen wasn't familiar with.

"Mary Ellen, I appreciate the offer, but I—"

"Do you have a better one? Offer, that is," Mary Ellen asked in a challenging tone.

Josephine just stared at her. Speechless.

"Scoot. Both of you. Go pack while I go talk to Noah." She turned around. "Noah, let's talk." She marched out of the kitchen and into the living room. Or den. Or family room. Or whatever this oversized room filled with unnecessary items was.

"What is it, Noah?" Mary Ellen folded her hands across her chest.

"You have no idea what you are getting into." Noah shook his head. "It's noble what you're trying to do, Mary Ellen, but if Josie is starting to have seizures, she is going to start going down quickly. Are you really prepared to take care of her? What if it's weeks before her husband can get back?" Noah leaned closer and whispered. "Not to mention, that no one in this charade has told Linda that Josie is going to die."

"The Lord will guide us, Noah. And I believe this to be His will."

Noah put his hand on his hip, then ran a hand through his wavy dark hair.

"You need a haircut." Mary Ellen smiled at her brother.

"Seriously, Mary Ellen. This could be a huge undertaking if her husband doesn't come back soon. I will give you some literature that explains all about seizures and what to do if she has another one, but the best thing to do would be to call 9-1-1 if Josie begins to exhibit any symptoms that another seizure is forthcoming." Noah shook his head and sighed. "This is too much for you, Mary Ellen. Maybe after a day or two with you, you can convince her to call her mother. I understand from her husband that they don't have a relationship. He told me once that her parents forced her to give up Linda for adoption, and she never forgave them. But who knows . . . there might be more to it than that. At this time in her life, I would think that she needs her family."

"Linda is her family, and in that respect, I reckon I will have to be her stand-in family."

Noah leaned over and hugged her. "You're a *gut* woman, Mary Ellen."

"*Ach*, I see you still speaka the *Deitsch* sometimes," she teased.

"*Ya*. I do."

She stayed in Noah's arms, his words lingering in her head . . . *You're a gut woman.* She hadn't felt like a very good woman lately. And maybe inviting Josephine to stay at their home was a mistake. But one thing bothered Mary Ellen far more than her own troubles.

If there is a God, He wouldn't let all this happen. I have no hope, Mary Ellen. Do you know what it's like to face death with no hope?

Josie loaded clothes into a red suitcase while Linda sat on the bed and waited.

"What do you think your father will say about me coming to stay?"

Linda stretched her arms behind her and leaned back. "I reckon it'll be just fine with him." She nodded her head with confidence and smiled.

Josie smiled back at her, even though she wasn't convinced. "I'm surprised that your mother asked me to come stay. But it's very kind of her."

"*Mamm* is wonderful. You'll love her cooking too."

Josie looked down at her suitcase. "I think that's probably all I'll need." She zipped it closed, then sat down on the bed beside Linda, away from the splattered sauce. She put her hand on Linda's knee. "I'm sorry about today. We didn't get to eat lasagna, and I didn't get to hear about your day with Stephen at the creek."

Linda smiled again. "We'll have lots of time to talk since you'll be staying in my room."

"Sure that's okay with you?"

"I'm sure. It'll be fun." She giggled. "You don't snore or anything, do you?"

Josie chuckled lightly. "Robert says I do sometimes." Then she thought about Robert being so far away, near all the chaos. "I hope he's all right."

"We will say special prayers for him. I'm sure he'll be fine." Linda paused. "Josie, there's something I want to ask you."

Josie pulled her hand from Linda's knee, smoothed wrinkles from her pink shirt, and twisted to face her. "What's that?"

Linda locked eyes with Josie. "Tell me what's really wrong with you. I want to know the truth."

17

JOSIE PULLED HERSELF TO A STANDING POSITION BUT kept her back to Linda. She squeezed her eyes closed for a moment and pondered how to avoid a lie and still stay true to Mary Ellen's wishes.

"I have really bad headaches that cause me to lose control of my motor functions, and sometimes I have seizures." Josie turned to face Linda and shrugged. "And that's the truth. Sometimes I feel really bad. Other days are good."

Linda's accusing gaze burned through Josie, and she wondered just how mad Linda was going to be when she became privy to the entire truth, not just bits and pieces of the truth. She didn't want Linda to look at her the way Robert did sometimes, with pity in his eyes.

"What causes these headaches?" Linda stood up and folded her arms across her chest. Then she slammed them to her side and stomped one foot. "Please, Josie. I know you're all not telling me something, and I'm not a child!"

Josie jumped, caught off guard by Linda's display. "I know you're not a child. I never said—"

"Then tell me!" Linda took a step toward her. "Just tell me what's wrong with you."

Josie turned her head toward the bedroom door as it swung open.

"What's all this yelling in here?" Mary Ellen's lips thinned with irritation as she shifted her gaze back and forth between Josie and Linda, finally centering on Linda. "What are you yelling about?"

Linda lowered her head, then looked back up at Mary Ellen. "I know there is something else wrong with Josie. Something she's not telling me. Do you know too, *Mamm*? Is there something you're all not telling me?"

Mary Ellen's face clouded with unease. She glanced at Josie, then back at Linda. "Why do you ask such a thing, Linda?"

"I can just tell, *Mamm*. By the way you are all behaving. Even *Onkel* Noah. And I am old enough to know what's going on."

Mary Ellen moved across the room until she was right in front of Linda. "Everything will be fine." She reached out to touch Linda's arm, but Linda backed away as she gritted her teeth and released a heavy breath through her nose.

"Linda." Mary Ellen's voice was disciplinary. Josie got the impression that this was not Linda's normal behavior. "Why are you acting in such a manner?"

"Because you are not telling me the truth!"

"Hey, hey." Noah walked into the room. "What's going on?"

Linda ran to her uncle and threw her arms around him. "*Onkel* Noah, please tell me the truth. Everyone is treating me like a child. There's something wrong with Josie, and you all aren't telling me."

Noah eased her away, cupped her cheek in his hand, and stared lovingly into her eyes. Then his eyes locked with Josie's. "Tell her."

Mary Ellen took a step toward him. "But Noah, I don't think this is—"

Noah silenced her with narrowed eyes. "There is never going to be a good time, Mary Ellen."

"Tell me what?" Linda ripped out the words as she faced her mother, then shifted her angry gaze to Josie. "Tell me what, Josie?"

Josie was frozen in limbo, in a place where no good would come from whatever response she offered. A war of emotions raged within her, but she knew the time of reckoning was upon them, so she tried to mask her inner turmoil with a deceptive calmness. "Linda, what we've told you is true. We just didn't tell you everything, because I wanted time for you to get to know me. Time for me to get to know you." She searched Mary Ellen's eyes for guidance, but Mary Ellen was biting her lip, holding her breath. "Linda, I have a brain tumor. A tumor that they can't operate on or take out, and . . ." She searched for the words as her bottom lip began to tremble. "I'm sorry."

"What do you mean, *sorry*?" Linda choked out the words in a small voice.

Josie knew that a good mother would keep her raw emotions in check, keep in tempo with what needed to be said, but the words caught in her throat. "I'm—I'm dying, Linda."

A black silence surrounded them as they waited for Linda to react, and then Josie saw Linda's mouth begin to move, but she couldn't grasp what she was saying. Josie could feel the color draining from her face as tiny bolts of light shimmied in front her, purple rods of warning, a sign that another seizure was forthcoming. *I've never had two in one day.*

She could see Linda moving toward her through eyes she was

struggling to keep open, and the tip of her tongue edged toward the roof of her mouth as if magnetized by something out of her control.

"She's having another seizure," Noah said.

It was the last thing Josie heard.

When Josie opened her eyes, it took her a few minutes to figure out where she was, then she hazily remembered Noah carrying her to his car. She blinked her eyes into focus to find a room full of people hovering around her, and she scanned the rustic room until she saw Linda. Josie could tell Linda had been crying, and she longed to ease her suffering.

"How are you feeling?" Mary Ellen was standing at the foot of the bed. To her left were Noah and Linda. A man she didn't know and two teenage boys were standing to her right.

"Tired." She reached up and touched the side of her head, then pulled back when pain speared through her temple.

"You fell before we could get to you." Noah sighed. "You've got a pretty good knot on your head, but luckily the floor was carpeted."

"Josephine, I'd like you to meet my family." Mary Ellen walked to the older man's side. "This is my husband, Abe. And these are our two boys, Matthew and Luke."

They each moved forward and shook her hand, then she studied them for a moment. The taller boy, Matthew, was wearing a dark brown shirt, and his brother was wearing a dark blue shirt like their father. They all had on black pants and suspenders and made for a handsome trio.

"Your family is lovely." Josie forced a smile for each of them, even though her head was splitting. Then she homed in on Linda, and tried to fight the tears building in her eyes as she whispered, "I'm sorry."

Linda shuffled closer to the bed and reached for Josie's hand. "*Danki* for telling me." She smiled. "We are all going to be praying for you constantly."

"Prayers are being offered across a broad network of prayer groups as we speak." Noah smiled. "I've already called Carley, and she's put the wheels in motion. Before we even hit the driveway, thousands of people had started praying for you, Josie."

Josie glanced at Mary Ellen, and for a moment, the women just stared at each other. No words were necessary. Mary Ellen knew her secret. Thankfully, it didn't appear that Mary Ellen had shared Josie's lack of faith with the other members of her family. Josie wasn't sure how Mary Ellen's husband would feel about having a nonbeliever under their roof. Josie knew how devout the Amish were. If Mary Ellen didn't want her here, she certainly could have used that as an excuse.

Josie finally pulled her gaze from Mary Ellen's when the oldest boy turned to his father and spoke. "*Daed*, I'm gonna go get the horses put up."

"You boys go ahead." Abe nodded at the boys, who seemed anxious to be on their way.

"Josie, I'm going to go," Noah said. "If you have any problems at all, call me on my cell phone." Then he eased closer, touched her arm. "These seizures are going to come with more frequency, but I'm going to talk to a neurologist I know and see if we can get you something stronger to help with that. And I'm going to give

Mary Ellen some information about what she needs to do if it looks like you might have another one. It's important that you get lots of rest too." He paused, his brows wrinkling. "I'm sure plenty of doctors have told you what to expect?"

She nodded and wondered if she should be in the hospital, although she knew that realistically this could drag on for months. This was such an imposition on Linda's family until Robert returned. She tugged at her pink blouse with her left hand and pulled it away from her body, shaking it. *So hot.* A tiny fan on the nightstand blew full force in her direction, but it did little to help with the still heat inside the room. Green shades were drawn high above two open windows on the wall to Josie's right, but no breeze blew through the screens. *How can they sleep in this heat?*

Josie scanned her surroundings. As Linda had told her, there were two beds in the room. In between the beds was a wooden nightstand with one drawer—a simple but lovely piece of furniture, with a pitcher of water, two glasses, a Bible, and a box of tissue on top. And a lantern. Josie eyed the relic and wondered if she was making a mistake. No electricity. The heat. No television. Sometimes, television was the only thing that kept her mind on something other than her own fate.

An oak dresser was against the wall opposite the beds, another well-crafted piece of furniture. One rocking chair was in the corner, and there were no wall hangings except for a calendar and a small mirror.

Then she glanced up at Linda and realized that none of that mattered if she could spend time with her daughter.

After Noah left, Mary Ellen asked Linda to go start supper

while she spoke with Josie. Linda pouted a bit, but left, promising to return shortly.

"How is she?" Josie propped herself up higher in the bed. "I don't really remember anything."

Mary Ellen walked to the window and lowered the blind a few inches to block out the sun as it began to set. Then she turned to Josie. "You were in such bad shape at the time, she said very little. I will try to talk with her more later." She paused. "Or . . . she'll be in here with you. Perhaps you would like to talk with her about it."

Josie nodded. "Thank you for having me in your home, Mary Ellen. I know this must seem awkward—"

"The bathroom is down the hall to your left. You'll find everything you need in there if you'd like to bathe later."

"Okay." Besides the obvious, Josie could feel the other elephant in the room. "Thank you for not saying anything about my—my lack of faith."

Mary Ellen stared blankly at her for a few moments. "Is it something you're ashamed of?"

"No." Josie didn't mean to sound so defensive, but Mary Ellen didn't seem affected by her tone.

"Do you not know of the Lord? Were you not educated as a child?"

"Oh, I was educated. I just don't think I ever really *got* it." Josie pushed back the light sheet that was covering her legs. "And then I married Robert, and he doesn't believe in God. At all. And his arguments against a higher power seemed valid." She leaned her head backward against the wall. "I guess it's been so long now since I've thought about God, I just—I just figure it's too late for me. Although, the other day . . ."

Mary Ellen sat down on the edge of the bed, waited for Josie to go on.

"I felt something." Josie recalled the voice in her head. *I am here My child. The fool hath said in his heart, There is no God.* "I was praying, and I heard something, and it seemed so real."

"I thought you didn't believe." Mary Ellen arched her brows.

"I don't, but . . ."

"Then why would you pray?"

She shrugged. "I'm dying, Mary Ellen. I guess I was willing to try anything."

They sat quietly for a moment.

"My husband is a good man." Josie reached for the cup on the nightstand, poured herself some water, and took a big gulp. "He really is. He does for everyone but himself. He is the most kind-hearted, loving, generous person I've ever known. Robert is full of goodness."

Mary Ellen's expression was somber. "Why do you feel the need to defend him?"

"I know how strong your faith is, Mary Ellen. All the Amish. I just don't want you to think he's a bad man. Or . . . that I'm a bad person for not believing."

"It's not my place to judge. Only God can do that."

It grew quiet again, and Mary Ellen stood up. "I'll let you rest." She turned to leave.

"Mary Ellen?"

She turned to face her. "*Ya?*"

"What if I'm wrong? About God?" She pulled her knees to her chest.

Mary Ellen locked eyes with her, a kindness in her expression that Josie hadn't seen from her before. Softly, she said, "Exactly. What if you are wrong?"

Then she turned and left.

———※———

Mary Ellen met Linda coming up the stairs.

"I put the chicken in the oven and peeled the potatoes. Can I go visit with Josie for a little while?"

"*Ya*. But first . . ." Mary Ellen pushed back a loose strand of hair that had fallen from beneath her daughter's *kapp*. "Are you all right?"

"*Ya*." She sighed. "I reckon it just doesn't make any sense. For me to get to know her, only to have the Lord call her home. And she's so young."

"You know we don't question His will."

"I know, *Mamm*. I just wish things could be different, and I'm going to pray that God will heal Josie."

Mary Ellen kissed her on the cheek. "You're *mei gut maedel*." Then she brushed past her down the stairs and crossed the den to the kitchen. Abe was sitting at the kitchen table.

Mary Ellen picked up a fork and poked the potatoes that were simmering in a pot on the stove. "It won't be ready for at least thirty minutes."

Abe picked up the *Die Botschaft* and began to flip through the pages. "Sure smells *gut*."

After only a few moments, he closed the newspaper. "Mary Ellen, I reckon I gotta tell ya . . ." He peered into the den to see if anyone was there, then lowered his voice. "I'm surprised 'bout you asking her to stay here."

Mary Ellen set the fork on the counter and took a seat across from her husband. Keeping her voice low, she said, "She doesn't have anyone to tend to her until her husband can get home from China. Might only be for a day or two."

Abe looped his thumbs under his suspenders. "It's a *gut* thing you are doing, especially for Linda." He paused and rubbed his tired eyes. "I suspect Linda knows by now what's happening with Josephine?"

"*Ya.* She does. And Abe . . . she seems to be handling the news better than I would have expected." She reached over and put her hand on his. "And, of course, she is praying for the Lord not to call Josephine home just yet."

"We should all pray that the Lord's will be done, whatever that might be. But it's only human to pray for extra time for those we care about."

"Like Jonas. You know I've been praying extra hard for that old man since he was first diagnosed with the cancer years ago. I reckon all the prayers from everyone in the community have kept him alive, do you think?"

"We must be careful what we pray for. Jonas is hurting these days, and to pray for him to stay on this earth doesn't seem right."

"That's true."

They sat quietly, and Mary Ellen considered telling her husband about Josephine's lack of faith but decided against it. It wasn't their way to minister to others, to teach them about God.

But Josephine had said she didn't have any hope. Everyone should have hope.

<hr />

Linda walked into her bedroom, and Josie was standing by the window looking out. She turned around when Linda entered.

"It's beautiful here."

"What are you doing out of bed?" Linda lifted the pitcher to see if Josie still had water, then joined her by the window. "*Onkel* Noah said you need to rest."

"My headache is better, and I can't just stay in bed."

Linda's stomach twisted with anxiety. First Jonas. Now her own—mother. So much loss. She worried how much her heart could take. Why would God introduce her to this woman, only to take her away?

"Josie, how long—how long do you—how much time . . ."

"A few months. Maybe six."

Linda sat down on Josie's bed; her knees felt like they might give beneath her. Josie sat next to her.

"But I plan to sing loudly at your birthday and watch you blow out your candles this year."

Linda covered her face with her hands and started to cry. "This seems so unfair."

Josie put her arm around Linda's shoulder and squeezed as her own eyes welled with tears. "You know what they say, life isn't fair."

Linda wiped her eyes and turned to face Josie. "Are you scared?"

"Yes."

They sat quietly for a few moments. Linda could see Josie's right hand twitching. *Please God, don't let her have another seizure. Please keep the pain away and help her not to be scared.*

"Maybe you will get better, no?"

Josie shook her head, then cupped Linda's cheek and gazed into

her beautiful sapphire eyes. "No, Linda. I'm not going to get better. I have an inoperable brain tumor in my brain stem. Eventually,
it's going to disrupt my motor skills much more"—she glanced
down at her trembling hand—"much more than just my hand and
arm. I'll forget things, won't be able to keep my mind clear, and the
seizures will come more often. I'll most likely slip into a coma at
some point." She paused when a tear rolled down Linda's cheek.
"The highlight of my life is this time I have with you."

"Oh, Josie." Linda threw her arms around her neck.

"My sweet baby girl."

Then Josie cried in a way Linda had never heard a grown-
up cry. Deep sobs that caused her whole body to shake. Linda
fought her own emotions and held Josie as tight as she'd ever held
anyone.

"Don't be scared," Linda whispered. But Josie just cried harder.

Linda thought about what might make things easier for Josie.
Then she had a thought.

Josie joined the family for breakfast the next morning, even though
Mary Ellen offered to bring her breakfast in bed. Josie remembered
eating the morning meal with her Amish friends on occasion when
she was younger. There was always a bountiful layout of food, just
like Mary Ellen's table now. Eggs, bacon, homemade biscuits, lots
of jams and jellies, and a traditional dish called scrapple, a mushy
cornmeal mix made with leftover parts of a pig, something Josie
didn't like as a child and didn't plan to eat this morning. She didn't
have much appetite, but would try to eat some eggs and maybe a
biscuit just to keep her strength up.

After Mary Ellen filled the last glass with orange juice, she sat down at the head of the table across from her husband. Josie was sitting beside Linda on one of the wooden benches across from Matthew and Luke. They bowed their heads in silent prayer. Josie clamped her eyes closed.

I don't want to die. I'm scared. Please, help me. It was wrong to ask for help from an entity she wasn't sure was even real. But the "what if" of the situation was gnawing at her, and again, she recalled the voice she'd thought she heard. She drew in a deep breath. *Thank you for this time with my daughter.*

She opened her eyes when she heard the clanking of silverware across the table. Both boys were diving into the scrapple as if afraid they wouldn't get enough, then scooped generous amounts of scrambled eggs onto their plates. Josie helped herself to a small spoonful of eggs and reached for a biscuit after the boys were done.

"That's rhubarb jam." Mary Ellen pointed to a small jar in the middle of the table.

Josie smiled, then reached for the jar and spread some of the bright red mixture onto her biscuit.

Matthew grabbed two biscuits and began loading them up with jam. "We got a rooster that's *ab im kopp, Daed.*" He reached across his brother and pulled back a handful of bacon. "He's crazy as I've ever seen."

"I noticed that bird didn't seem to be acting right the other day," Abe said as he eyed his son's helping of bacon. "I'm sure everyone would like some bacon, Matt." Abe arched his brows and a slight grin formed.

"Oh." Matt put two pieces back.

"*Ya*, that rooster done slammed into the barn the other day," Luke added with a chuckle. "I know it ain't funny, but after it did that, it got up and ran all around the yard, chasing them hens."

"Like a drunkard," Matt said.

Linda giggled, which was music to Josie's ears. "You've never even seen a drunkard, Matt."

"Have so. At the Mud Sale in Gordonville last year. He was wobbling and ran into a wall. Just like that rooster."

Everyone laughed in between bites, and Josie recalled family breakfasts at her house when she was growing up. They'd certainly lacked the warmth of this family's. Her family's meals had been about appearance and formality, and even though Josie and Robert were fortunate to have nice things, Josie had always tried to make their home seem warm and inviting. She looked around at everyone at the table—this perfect family—and smiled. *Linda's had a good life.*

Josie did the best she could, picking at her food enough to not hurt Mary Ellen's feelings, although she avoided the scrapple.

"I can't eat another bite." Josie waved her hand in front of her when Mary Ellen placed some apple turnovers on the table next to Josie. "It was all wonderful, Mary Ellen."

Mary Ellen smiled, then pushed the plate toward her boys. "These are Matt's favorite."

Josie watched Mary Ellen serving her family, and she didn't think she'd ever seen anyone more cut out for mothering than Mary Ellen. Josie looked down at all the food left on her plate, then folded her arm across her stomach which was upset to the point that she fought the urge to leave the table.

When Abe and the boys finished their apple turnovers, they

excused themselves, and Josie picked up a few dishes to help Mary Ellen and Linda clear the table.

"You don't have to do that," Mary Ellen said to Josie. "You're our guest. And you should rest."

"Please don't treat me like a guest. I want to help. It's the least I can do, Mary Ellen. Really."

"How are you feeling?" Linda narrowed her brows at Josie, like a little mother hen.

"Pretty good." Except for her stomach, that was the truth. Josie's head wasn't hurting, and she could certainly handle a tummy ache in comparison to the headaches.

Linda turned to her mother and whispered something Josie couldn't hear. Mary Ellen nodded, turned to Josie, then back to Linda. "I think that's a *gut* idea," Mary Ellen said.

"Josie, there's someone I'd like for you to meet." Linda stashed a jar of jam in the refrigerator. "Do you feel up to a ride in the buggy to go visit a friend of mine?"

"Sure." Josie wasn't sure about any sort of travel, but Linda looked so anxious and excited for them to go that Josie would just hope her stomach didn't get any worse.

"I'm gonna go ask the boys to get the buggy ready." Linda scurried across the kitchen and bolted out the door.

Josie picked up a kitchen towel and started drying the plates that Mary Ellen was putting in the rack to drain. "Who does she want me to meet?"

Mary Ellen handed Josie a clean plate and smiled. "A very special man. His name is Jonas."

18

JONAS SHIFTED HIS BODY IN THE BED AND RECONCILED that there was no comfortable position anymore. Not a part of his body that wasn't hurting these days. He had one thing left to do, and then he hoped that the Lord would call him home. Clenching as another wave of pain overtook him, Jonas tried to focus on the life he'd led. He wondered if there was a man alive who'd been as blessed as he had. He'd shared the majority of his life with a wonderful woman, his beloved Irma Rose. And when God saw fit to call her home, he'd been blessed with his Lizzie.

So many people he'd loved, and he'd been loved by so many. His daughter, Sarah Jane; his granddaughter, Lillian, and her family; and a community full of family and friends whom he'd watched grow up, marry, and have families of their own. Yes, he'd been a blessed man. *But I'm ready, Lord.* Just this one last thing to do.

"They're here." Lizzie pushed the bedroom door open.

Jonas could see his friends standing behind Lizzie, and he forced a smile, determined to hide the constant ache in his bones while he visited with Sadie and Kade.

"Come in, you two." He wearily motioned with his hand for them to come closer. "*Danki* for coming."

Lizzie smiled at her husband, then eased out of the room.

Kade moved ahead of his wife and latched onto Jonas's hand. As Kade stood before him in traditional Amish clothing, Jonas recalled the first time he met Kade. He was a fancy, rich, *Englisch* man without a clue about real life. More money than any man could spend in a lifetime but as miserable as any a person could be. Jonas recalled mentoring Kade, teaching him about the *Ordnung*, and helping him to grow his faith. An Amish man teaching an *Englischer* about the *Ordnung* was out of the ordinary, but Jonas had seen something in Kade worth the effort. And he was right. Kade donated his wealth wisely within the district and to those outside the community in need. He'd set up a fine school for children with special needs, like his own son, Tyler, who was autistic. And he'd married the lovely Sadie, a woman most deserving of a good man. Like Jonas, Sadie had been widowed. Her first love passed on at a young age, so Jonas was glad that she was able to start anew with Kade, and Jonas had recently heard that Sadie was pregnant again.

"I brought the letters." Kade handed a large envelope to Jonas, and Sadie joined her husband at Jonas's bedside. Sadie leaned down and kissed Jonas on the forehead.

"Hello, Jonas."

"Dear Sadie. You look lovely."

She rubbed her slightly expanded belly. "*Danki*, Jonas."

Jonas reached into the envelope and pulled out the letter addressed to Linda. "Kade, reach into that drawer." He pointed to the bedside table. "Pull out that letter addressed to Linda. I'd like to replace Linda's letter with a new one."

Kade pulled out the letter Jonas had written to Linda when he heard her birth mother was in town.

"Jonas, these letters are a beautiful idea," Sadie said as her eyes filled with tears.

"No tears, my sweet Sadie. This old man has lived a blessed, full life. I'm ready." Jonas paused and looked back and forth between his friends, knowing this could be the last time he saw them. He could feel his body shutting down. And he'd seen Irma Rose twice this week just sitting across the room smiling.

Jonas had written the letters four years ago, figuring he'd be gone way before now. The letters told each person what they'd meant in his life. He'd never been good at expressing his feelings, and he wanted all of them to know that his life was blessed and he was a better man for knowing them all. He'd updated the letters over the years—most recently Linda's. The arrival of Linda's birth mother was surely an upset to his young friend, and he wasn't going to be around to see her through this.

There was a letter for Lizzie and one for his daughter, Sarah Jane. There were letters for Kade and Sadie, Carley and Noah, his beloved granddaughter, Lillian, and her husband, Samuel. Plus there were letters for all the children, young and old, whom he'd loved and watched grow, many of whom he'd never see marry and have children of their own. He was going to particularly miss seeing his great-grandson, David, marry and have *kinner*. The boy had survived a kidney transplant and was now a grown man of nineteen. But this is how it was supposed to be. A man can't live forever.

"I hear we have another young one on the way," Jonas said when he saw Kade's eyes filling with water. His good friend tried hard to blink back the tear, but it spilled onto his cheek anyway. Jonas reached for Kade's hand and held it tightly.

"*Ya*, we do." Sadie swiped at her eyes. "Jonas . . ." Her voiced cracked a bit, but then she smiled. "If it's a boy, we would like to name him Jonas."

Jonas wasn't sure he could keep his own emotions in check. He took a deep, labored breath. "Nothing would please me more."

They all shifted their eyes to the bedroom door when it creaked open.

"Jonas, you have two more visitors." Lizzie smiled. "I just wanted to let you know. Linda is here. And she's brought—she's brought a friend. But you take your time, Sadie and Kade. Sarah Jane and I will visit with them downstairs." Lizzie closed the door.

Kade said he would like for them all to pray, and Jonas was pleased that it was Kade who made the suggestion.

Jonas realized this was going to be harder than he'd suspected, saying good-bye to his loved ones.

Josie wasn't sure about Linda's reasoning for bringing her to a dying man's house. Nor could she understand Mary Ellen's way of thinking, agreeing that it was a good idea. Didn't Linda or Mary Ellen consider that Josie wouldn't want to see this in particular? Sadness filled the air around them and threatened to suffocate Josie. She'd have enough of this when her own time came.

"More coffee, dear?" Jonas's wife, Lizzie, offered to refill Josie's cup, but Josie shook her head.

"No, I'm fine."

For nearly fifteen minutes, Josie and Linda made small talk with Lizzie and Jonas's daughter, Sarah Jane. Josie's stomach was better, but she really just wanted to go home. She was starting to get tired already, and she missed Robert.

A few minutes later, a couple descended the stairs. Sarah Jane made introductions, and while Josie suspected Sadie and Kade knew she was Linda's birth mother, no mention was made. Sarah Jane had simply introduced Josie as a friend of Linda's, and once Kade and Sadie were gone, Lizzie escorted them up the stairs.

"I know this man is a friend of yours, Linda," Josie whispered to Linda, "but maybe I should just stay downstairs."

"Everyone should meet Jonas." Linda smiled. "Jonas has something for everyone, whether it's words of wisdom, or just a simple prayer to offer on their behalf. He's a special person."

"But he's so sick and I don't want to intrude." *Mostly, I don't want to stare death in the face.* If it had been anyone else dragging her up the stairs, Josie would have refused to go, but it seemed important to Linda that Josie meet this man.

Lizzie turned her head around. "You're not intruding, dear." Then she chuckled. "My Huggy Bear can be a bit gruff sometimes, so if he acts like that, you just ignore him."

Josie nodded. *Great. An old, dying man, who is also gruff.* She was getting more and more upset that Linda brought her here. But when they reached the top of the stairs, Linda grabbed Josie's hand and smiled, and any anxiety Josie felt melted away.

"You are a popular old man this morning," Lizzie said when she pushed the door open. "Linda and a friend of hers, Josie, have come for a visit." She turned to Linda and grinned. "You make him behave, Linda."

"I will, Lizzie."

The older woman left the room—a room that smelled of disinfectant and sickness. Josie hoped they wouldn't stay long, and she lagged behind near the door as Linda walked to the bedside and kissed the old man on the cheek. Josie suspected he must have been a handsome man at one time with his square jaw and big blue eyes, but now shades of gray beneath his lower lids were accentuated by his pale color, and his features were sunken in beneath a tangled mass of gray beard.

"Sweet Linda," he whispered. He attempted a smile, but Josie saw him cringing with pain.

"Jonas, are you in pain?" Linda clasped his hand within hers. "I thought Noah was changing your medications and that you would feel better."

The old man sighed. "He lied." Then he grunted but with the corner of his mouth tipped up on one side. "They did change my medicines, but turns out this old body just has too much going on inside to hold up much longer."

"We will pray right now, Jonas." Linda's voice was desperate as she bowed her head.

Jonas gently lifted her chin and gazed into her eyes. "Don't pray for me to stay on this earth, dear Linda. I'm ready to go home." He tenderly brushed a tear from her cheek with his thumb. "You are a special one." Jonas glanced at Josie, then back at Linda. "Introduce me to your birth mother."

Josie straightened, shocked that he would verbalize her true relationship to Linda.

"Jonas, this is Josie." Linda waved Josie to move closer, and she inched forward. She extended her hand to Jonas.

"Nice to meet you, Jonas."

His touch was frail, but he locked onto her hand and stared into her eyes. "Nice to meet you too."

"Oh, no!" Linda slapped her hands to her sides. "I forgot

something in the buggy. Stay here, Josie. I'll be right back." Linda
scurried across the floor, opened the door, slammed it closed, and
left Josie with her mouth hanging open, prepared to oppose being
left alone with Jonas.

She pulled her gaze from the closed door and slowly turned
to face Jonas. She smiled and glanced at the water pitcher on his
nightstand, just like the one in Linda's room. "Can I get you a cup
of water?" She moved toward the nightstand.

Jonas shook his head and scowled. "Now, why do you reckon
that girl left you here with me? You do realize we've been set
up?"

Josie couldn't help but smile at his honesty. "Yes, it appears
that way."

Jonas arched one brow high. "Why is that?"

Josie shrugged. "I—I don't know." But she had a pretty good
idea. "Probably because I have cancer too."

He cringed, but raised his chin as he spoke. "Ah, yes."

"You say that like you already know."

"*Ya*, I do. Noah was worried about Linda, and he told me you
were ill."

"Did Noah tell you that I am staying with Linda and her family until my husband returns from overseas?"

His eyes widened. "No. I didn't know that."

Josie looked toward the floor. "I had a seizure while Linda
was staying with me. I guess everyone got worried, because I don't
really have any family here, and I passed out and spilled spaghetti
sauce everywhere, and—and I'm sorry. I know I'm rambling." She
looked up and locked eyes with this man, and the strangest feeling
came over her. "Why am I here?"

"I don't know."

Josie shook her head and sat down in a chair by Jonas's bed. "I'm sorry I asked that. What a strange thing for me to say."

"Why do you think you're here?" His face twisted in pain.

"Oh, no. What can I do?" Josie leaned forward, but he waved his hand and seemed to let the pain take its course, then took a deep breath and refocused on Josie.

"So? Why do you think you're here?"

Josie leaned back against the chair and sighed. "I think Linda is hoping that by talking to you, that I won't be afraid of dying." She locked eyes with his. "Are you afraid?"

"No."

"Just like that? Just no? You don't have the least bit of apprehension about dying? Because, I have to tell you . . . it terrifies me."

Jonas smiled. "Now we know why you are here and why we've been set up to have this little chat."

"Why?"

He grimaced. "Because you are afraid of dying, and I'm not."

"Sir, with all due respect . . ." Josie paused and thought about whether or not she should speak her mind. "You are much older than me. I'm only thirty-four-years-old, and I've recently met my biological daughter. I'll never see her marry, have children, or any of that. I feel cheated."

"By who?"

"By God!" It just slipped out, and Josie regretted immediately that she'd said it. "I'm sorry, I just . . ." She fought the knot building in her throat. "If there is a God, I don't understand why He'd cut my life short after I get the only thing I've ever wanted, a relationship with my daughter. I have six months, at the most!

That's not long enough. I want more time. I'm afraid." Josie didn't understand what was happening to her, why she'd opened up to this complete stranger who had enough problems of his own. She cupped her face in her hands, embarrassed at her display, but too upset to have any dignity.

Jonas twisted his mouth to one side and stared at the woman before him, a woman with no hope. *I guess there are two things I have left to do, instead of just one.*

Jonas reached his hand straight out. "Take my hand." She was hesitant, pulling her hands away from her tear-streaked face, but she eventually latched onto his hand. "You are afraid because you don't believe, is that it?"

"What if there is nothing after this?"

"What if there is?" Jonas tilted his head slightly.

"But there's no way to know, one way or the other."

"Of course there is." *Oh, Lord, I need more time with this one.*

You don't have much time, My son.

Jonas sighed. "Does Linda know this? Is that why she brought you here?"

"No. Linda just knows that I'm afraid. Mary Ellen knows, though."

Jonas lay quietly for a moment. "Listen to me, Josie. Listen very carefully. I don't have much time. Mary Ellen is a *gut* woman. Listen to her. Trust her. She will show you the way. Oh, dear child. Learn of our Lord and His son, Jesus. While you can."

"I want to believe. I need to believe. I need hope, Jonas. I need something . . . I need . . . I don't know . . . I just need . . ."

"God." He squeezed her hand as best he could. "Open your heart, not your mind. Forge out falsities, and make way for His words to reach you. Once that happens, you will be filled with hope, and your fears will be no more."

She shook her head. "You seem like a very kind man, and I very much regret that I won't get to know you better. But I don't know how to do that."

"Then I will show you."

Lord, give me the strength, the knowledge, and the words to perform this last task for You, to help this soul find her way to You through Jesus.

"Close your eyes and picture the most perfect place imaginable, and then add the happiest moment in your life to that picture."

Josie closed her eyes and whispered, "When Linda was born."

"How do you feel?"

Her eyes were still closed, and Jonas gave her a reassuring squeeze with his hand, glad she couldn't see the look of agony on his face as another shot of pain seared down his spine.

Josie smiled. "I feel like I want to love unconditionally, this beautiful child, for the rest of my life."

"That is how God thinks of you. He loves you now, the same way He loved you when you felt His love through the gift of a child."

Her eyes opened, and her face filled with anger. "But He took that child away from me."

"Did He?"

"Yes, God took my baby away from me to be raised by someone I didn't even know. My own flesh and blood. And now I am dying, and I won't even get to see her grow into a mature woman."

"This angers you that God would do this?"

"Yes!" She stared at him with tears pouring down his face. "I am angry with God!"

Jonas breathed a sigh of relief. "Then tell Him that."

"What?" Her face twisted into confusion.

"Tell God that you're mad at Him. If you don't believe in Him, what harm can it do?"

"I don't know. It doesn't seem right to blame . . ." She let go of Jonas's hand and brought both hands to her head. He could see her right hand trembling, and Jonas worried he might be pushing her too hard.

"And yet, you do. Blame Him."

"I'm confused. I'm scared. I need something, and I don't know what it is. I feel lost."

"We all feel lost before we are found, dear Josie." Jonas sighed. "Look at me."

She sniffled, then pulled her hands away from her face.

"I'm leaving soon. I can feel it. And I regret that you and I won't have more time together. So, I'm going to offer you these parting words." He took a deep breath, hoping, praying that Josie would understand what he was saying. "*The fool hath said in his heart, There is no God.*"

Josie felt like she might faint when she heard Jonas speak the words she'd heard before—words not harsh, threatening, or fearful, but a declaration that brought on emotions Josie couldn't quite identify.

She stared at Jonas, wishing she would have more time with this man. Linda and Mary Ellen were right. There was something special about him.

"Jonas, is it too late for me? Too late for me to reconcile with God?"

His eyes were barely open, and his lips moved slowly. "It's never too late."

"But won't God think I'm just trying to get in His good graces because I am—I am not going to be here long?"

Jonas fought to keep his eyes open. "Josie, you don't sound like a woman who doesn't believe, but a woman who has lost her faith somewhere along the line. God doesn't care what brings you to Him, just that you go to Him. Pray, Josie. And talk to Mary Ellen. She is a wise woman."

Josie couldn't picture chatting with Mary Ellen about God. Then Robert flashed into her mind. *I miss you so much, Robert.* What would Robert think about her attempt to have a relationship with God? Would he think she was silly? She stood up from the chair and walked back and forth across the room, eventually zoning in on a calendar on the far wall with bright yellow flowers for the month of June. She stared at the colorful blooms as her mind raced.

"How will I know I've connected with God?"

"You will know."

Her back was still to Jonas as she folded her arms across her chest. She noticed her right hand trembling. "I don't think I could ever believe in miracles, but I want to go with an inner peace in my heart, hope for something after this life. My husband doesn't believe, but I should make my own choice. I haven't really allowed myself to explore the possibilities." She sighed. "I'm confused, I admit, but Jonas, I feel something I haven't felt throughout all of this." She relaxed her arms and reached up and touched the yellow flowers on the calendar. "I feel a glimmer of hope. Thank you for talking with me." She turned and faced him.

"Jonas?"

He smiled as he stared off in space at the rocker in the corner of the room. "Irma Rose is here. God's peace to you, Josie."

And he closed his eyes.

19

JOSIE'S VISIT WITH JONAS WORE HER OUT MORE THAN she'd expected it would, and she'd spent the remainder of the day napping on and off. It was eleven that night when Josie's cell phone buzzed on the nightstand between her and Linda, and she quickly reached for it.

"Robert, I miss you. Hold on." She jumped from the bed, tiptoed across the wooden floor, and stumbled down the stairs in the dark. "I'm going outside so I don't wake Linda up," she whispered. "Are you all right?" She groped her way through the den and onto the front porch.

"I'm fine, sweetie, but I am so frustrated. Still trying to get out of here. Are you all right? How are you feeling? Any more seizures?"

"I'm okay. I had another seizure after Noah called you, but I haven't had one since then. No headache either. I miss you so much, Robert. But don't worry about coming home. I'm with Linda, sleeping in the same room with her. If anything happens, she's right there, plus I'll really get to know her this way. So you should plan to finish your business there. Really. Even if the airports open in the next few days."

"No, Josie. I should have never come. I should have never, ever left you. I just want to come home and be with you. Maybe Linda could stay with us some of the time, but I don't want to be away from you. This whole trip was a bad idea. I love you so much, baby. I'm going to hope the airports reopen soon, and I'll be on the first flight."

"I love you too, Robert." She paused. "You're never going to believe what happened this morning."

"What's that?"

"Linda took me to meet a friend of the family. Well, actually, I think he's a relative by marriage, but anyway . . . he was a wonderful old man, and Robert—he died right in front of me in his bed at home."

"What? Oh my gosh! Are you all right? That must have been horrible."

Josie thought for a moment. "You know, I'd just met the man, but I cried when he passed. Strange, huh?"

"Why would Linda take you there, to a dying man's home?"

She sighed as she recalled Jonas taking his last breath, unsure how much to share with Robert. "She said he was special and that she wanted me to meet him."

"Hmm . . . Seems odd."

"I wish I would have had more time to spend with him." She paused with a smile. "His name is Jonas. This entire community seems rocked by the loss. Poor Linda cried really hard earlier tonight. And, Robert, she climbed in the bed with me, and I just held her. It was the first time I felt like—like a mother."

"Oh, baby. I'm so glad you're getting to spend time with her. I know how much you wanted that."

"And you made it possible. You are the best husband in the entire world, and I don't deserve you."

"I'll do anything for you, Josie. You know that. You're my wife, and I love you."

Josie had thought a lot about her life all day, on and off between naps, about the possibilities of something to look forward to. She'd prayed tonight, really prayed. Prayed for strength and courage, for Linda, for Jonas's family, and for the knowledge to understand what having a relationship with God really means. Maybe she'd imagined it, or was just relieved not to have a headache, but a calm had settled over her.

"Jonas talked with me about God, Robert."

"He's Amish. They have a very strong faith. I'm not surprised."

Silence dredged a gap between them, and Josie felt oddly detached from Robert for a moment. "Linda and I prayed together tonight too. For quite a while." More silence. "Maybe we're wrong, Robert. About God. I mean, who's to say that just because we don't have something tangible, that a higher being doesn't exist?"

"Sweetheart, I have told you from the day we met that it's important for you to form your own opinion about this. I don't think I ever forced my beliefs on you, did I?"

Josie knew he hadn't. She'd just listened to his arguments against God and decided for herself that no God of hers would strip her of her child and deny her the ability to have another one. She recalled when Jonas said she was angry with God. Josie wondered if she'd always been angry, which made it easier to pull away from Him. Maybe she'd always believed.

"No, you didn't force anything on me," she finally said. "But I think I want to investigate the possibility of something after this, Robert."

Another silence, then Robert said, "Then you should." He paused. "But Josie, I won't change what I believe."

"I know."

She'd been married to Robert for twelve years, and at this moment, his last comment bothered her more than any harsh words they'd ever exchanged. How would this affect their relationship?

"I'm hoping the airports will reopen in a day or so, and I'll keep you posted. Josie, I am keeping my phone with me at all times. Please, baby, call me if you need to anytime, and make sure Linda and her family have my phone number to call if anything—happens. I mean, if you have a seizure or something."

"I will." She took a deep breath. *Please God, keep Robert safe.* Josie realized that prayer came easier with each passing moment, and she wondered why.

"Well, I guess I better go, but I'll call you tomorrow. I love you."

"I love you too, Robert."

The next day, the community celebrated the life of a man they'd all loved. There was much admonition for the living as well as respect offered for Jonas. A hymn was spoken, not sung, and following the service, Jonas was laid to rest in a hand-dug grave next to his beloved Irma Rose, his wooden coffin plain and simple with no ornate carvings. As customary, friends and family gathered for a meal at Jonas's home following the service.

Linda didn't think she'd ever stop crying, plus the thought of going through this again with Josie was overwhelming.

She glanced around the kitchen as the womenfolk worked to set out the meal and fill tea glasses. Jonas's wife, poor Lizzie, had only shared a few years of marriage with Jonas, but Linda didn't doubt for a minute that her love for Jonas was immeasurable. Linda watched the frail, gray-haired woman pouring tea with shaky hands and swollen eyes. Linda scanned the room to see where she might be needed, but everything to do with the meal was being handled. She slowly walked from the kitchen to the den and scanned those mourning.

Her *Onkel* Noah and *Aenti* Carley were sitting on the couch, entertaining their daughter, Jenna. Kade, Sadie, and their two children sat on the far side of the den, with Kade's arm wrapped around Sadie who was crying softly. Jonas's daughter, Sarah Jane, brushed past Linda and offered tea to several of the men. Linda heard her sniffling as she passed back by her. Uncle Samuel was sitting in a rocking chair with his two young girls in his lap, and her cousin, David, stood nearby. Linda had already seen Lillian in the kitchen, not much good to anyone. Her poor aunt could barely function.

Jonas was going to be missed, and Linda's heart hurt for all the friends and family who'd gathered at his home today. She passed back through the den and into the kitchen. Josie was helping her mother line up loaves of homemade bread on the counter, assisted by two other *Englisch* women, Barbie Beiler and Lucy Turner. Linda didn't think Josie and her mother were exactly friends, but they were respectful of one another, and Linda was just glad that Josie felt well enough to come today. Yesterday had been a bad day, and Josie hardly got out of bed after they'd visited Jonas. Another headache.

Linda wasn't sure how Josie would feel about coming to a funeral, but she'd insisted that she wanted to pay her respects to this very special man.

"Linda, can you open that door?" Her *Aenti* Rebecca nodded toward the door in the kitchen as she carried a tray with full glasses of tea. "I want to get these to those outside in this heat."

"*Ya.*" Linda pushed the screen door open and let it slam behind her. She walked down the porch steps and into the yard. When she stepped around to the side of the house to have a moment to herself, she heard voices coming from the back.

"I don't care, Ivan."

Linda recognized the voice to be her *Aenti* Katie Ann.

"Please, Katie Ann . . ." her *Onkel* Ivan said. "I've said I'm sorry a hundred times."

"And it wonders me if you mean it one bit. The fact that Lucy Turner is even here turns my stomach."

"It's a funeral, Katie Ann. I reckon it's not like I invited her or nothin'."

"She's not even friends with Jonas. Barbie Beiler has been a wonderful friend to Jonas, and of course, she should be here. But that Lucy woman is only here for one reason, and you know what it is!"

Her aunt rounded the corner, and her eyes widened when she saw Linda. "Linda!"

"Uh, sorry. I was just trying to get away from the crowd for a few minutes." Linda could feel the heat building in her cheeks, unsure if it was from being caught listening or from the conversation she'd just overheard.

Katie Ann folded her arms across her chest and marched past Linda mumbling something under her breath. Linda quickly followed before Ivan came around the corner.

Stephen drank a glass of tea out in the front yard following the meal. He watched Linda and Josephine walk to her car and get inside. It appeared they were enjoying some air-conditioning for a few minutes. Stephen sighed as he recalled seeing Linda in the fancy blue jeans and red blouse at Josie's house.

Two more times, his grandfather had spoken with him about Linda and shared his concerns about her relationship with her birth mother and about stretching privileges during *rumschpringe*. Plenty of times, Stephen had watched his grandfather warn parents when their children were stepping outside the boundaries set forth by the *Ordnung*, but lately Stephen found himself worrying about Linda and her role within the community. Stephen had never felt the need to explore the *Englisch* world. His place was here. With Linda. Or so he'd thought.

He took another sip of tea. "Avoid getting too close to those who are unequally yoked," his grandfather had told him.

His thoughts were interrupted when he saw Kade Saunders gathering the immediate family on the front porch. Most everyone else had gone home, but a few people were still cleaning up for Lizzie and Sarah Jane, including Stephen's mother and sisters.

Stephen sipped his tea and held his position, not wanting to intrude. But he could hear from where he was standing. He could also see Linda included in the group.

"Jonas left some special instructions for me to share with those he was particularly close to." Kade reached into a large envelope and began distributing smaller envelopes. When he was done, he addressed the entire group. "Before you open your letter, I have this note to read to you from Jonas."

My dear friends and family,

I am a blessed man to have shared in all of your lives. I've watched many of you grow up and have families of your own. We've celebrated the gut times and struggled through the bad times together through prayer and fellowship. I reckon each letter is my way of letting you know what you mean to me.

Take care of each other through love and prayer.

In His Name,
Jonas

Stephen regretted the fact that he wasn't getting a letter and that he hadn't been closer to Jonas, since Jonas was often called upon like he were the bishop himself. Everyone spoke of Jonas's wisdom and fun-loving personality. Perhaps, that was why his grandfather had never encouraged his family to be close to Jonas. *Jealousy?* But that's a sin. Surely *Daadi* wouldn't think like that. Stephen watched each person walk away with their letter to a quiet spot. Linda went to the far side of the yard and sat down in the grass underneath a shade tree.

Linda peeled open her envelope and eased out the letter, knowing she would treasure Jonas's final words for the rest of her life. She took a deep breath and read.

My Sweet Linda,

If you're reading this, I'm dead and buried, six feet under. Everyone is probably moping around, crying and the like. Now, no need for all that, mei maedel. *I'm with our Lord, and I reckon by the time you get this, me and Irma Rose will be sipping cider on the front porch of our heavenly home, looking down on our loved ones, and hoping you folks can behave yourselves.*

Although, it ain't likely that you'll disappoint me. What a fine young woman you are. Always polite and eager to help others, much like your mother. You will be a fine fraa and mamm some day, and I regret that I won't be around to see you in this role, but I will be smiling from above. I'm not sure if there is a greater love than that of a mother, and as of recently, I reckon you have two. How blessed you are, even though I know it is a confusing time. Somehow in all of this, I see you as the strong one, the binding glue so to speak, in this threesome.

And be not conformed to this world: but be ye transformed by the renewing of your mind, that ye may prove what is that good, and acceptable, and perfect will of God.

May the will of God be done, and may you grow and prosper in His name.

Now, I have some final thoughts for you. I reckon you'll end up marrying Stephen Ebersol. Don't let that scary grandfather of his get you worked up. You young folks don't see Bishop Ebersol as the man he truly is, with three times the wisdom as your old friend Jonas here. Bishop Ebersol just ain't all warm and fuzzy like I am.

Linda grinned. She could picture Jonas roaring with laughter as he wrote the comment about his warm and fuzzy self.

Go to him, Linda, if you need to. For anything. He is a wise man who has much to offer.

I have always thought of you as one of my grandchildren, Sweet Linda. You've always been precious to me.

> *Loving thoughts from above,*
> *Jonas*

Linda pulled her knees to her chest, then buried her head and wept.

She jumped and lifted her head when she felt a hand on her shoulder. Stephen brushed away a tear on her cheek.

"I wish I had received a letter from Jonas. I know he was a *gut* man."

Linda swallowed back tears. "*Ya*, he was. The best."

"Let's go to the creek when we leave here and get away from all this sadness and just be together for a while."

"*Ach*, I don't know. Josie is staying with us. I don't know." Although there was nothing she wanted more. She could tell Stephen wanted to kiss her, but there were too many people around, and public affection of that type was frowned upon.

"I understand. How's it going with Josie at your house?"

"So far, so *gut*." Linda felt tears building again. "I just can't believe that we'll be having a funeral for Josie. I don't know how I'm going to get through that."

He reached for her hand and squeezed. "I will be by your side, you won't be alone. Let's pray for Josie." Stephen bowed his head and closed his eyes. Linda did the same.

Dear Lord, please don't let Josie be in pain, and please let her stay with me for as long as it is Your will. If You could see fit to let her stay with me for a long time, that would be so gut. *Say hi to Jonas for me. Aamen.*

They both lifted their heads when they heard footsteps.

"Hello you two." Carley squatted down beside them. "Jonas will certainly be missed."

"*Ya*, he will," Linda said as Stephen nodded.

"Linda, I've already spoken with Josie, and there is something I want you to know. There are so many people praying for Josie.

I know you don't have a computer, but prayers for her are flying across the Internet and people of every denomination are praying for her. She is on our prayer list at church. Barbie Beiler has also added her to their church list, and tons of people you've never even met are praying for Josie. I just wanted you to know that."

Linda let a tear spill over, then hugged her aunt. "*Danki,* Carley."

"You're welcome."

Josie sat down at the bench in the kitchen when the strobes of light began to flash. *Please, not now.* A few women were finishing the cleanup, including Mary Ellen. Josie thought about what Noah's wife, Carley, had said. About all the people praying for her. What a sweet gesture from so many people whom she'd never meet.

It had been a long day, and Josie could feel the weight of her emotions turning into a bad headache. But she had no regrets at coming. She didn't know Jonas, but something about their one encounter propelled her to be present at his funeral.

"Josie, look at me." Josie tried to blink her eyes into focus. Mary Ellen had a hand on her shoulder. "Are you all right?"

"I—I think so. It's just my head. I'm sorry. I don't want to cut your time short. I'll be fine."

"Nonsense. We're done. I'll find Abe and gather Linda and the boys."

Josie watched Mary Ellen quickly walk away, and she pondered the oddity of this situation—Mary Ellen taking care of her. And, to her surprise, Josie welcomed Mary Ellen's nurturing ways, something she'd never had from her own mother. Even though Mary Ellen was only a few years older than Josie, she felt safe in her presence. *This must be how Linda has always felt. I wonder if I could have been as motherly and nurturing as Mary Ellen.*

"Hi, Josie. *Danki* for coming. I'm Lillian." The woman Josie already knew to be Jonas's granddaughter sat down beside her.

"I hope I'm not intruding, but I met Jonas one time, and I just felt something . . . and I—I don't know. I just wanted to be here. And also for Linda."

Lillian's eyes were swollen from crying. "Grandpa had that effect on people." She smiled. "He would be glad to know you're here."

They sat quietly for a moment.

"Linda thinks the world of you," Josie finally said.

"Linda is very special. When I first came to the community, after being in the *Englisch* world for most of my life, Linda was so welcoming. I liked her right away."

Josie fought the pressure in her head. The strobe lights had stopped, but the pain in her temples was making her stomach churn. "Was it hard for you to leave, I mean, leave the *Englisch* world and become Amish?"

"Hmm. I wouldn't say it was hard." Lillian twisted her mouth to one side. "Challenging, perhaps. But once I realized that the only way to true inner peace was through a relationship with God, then it was easy."

"So, you didn't always believe?" This piqued Josie's interest.

"No, I didn't. I didn't understand." Lillian paused and twisted on the bench to face Josie. "My grandparents taught me about the *Ordnung*, about trusting in God's will, and ultimately I became a Daughter of the Promise."

"What is that?"

"It's when a woman takes a spiritual journey to find the meanings of faith, hope, and love."

Hope. I need that more than anything. "It sounds wonderful."

"It is an amazing journey, especially when you are first establishing a true relationship with God and you see the immense changes in your life." Lillian stared off in space for a moment. "My grandpa was a huge part of that process for me, and of course my grandma, Irma Rose, who died several years ago. Without them, I'm not sure where I'd be." Then she smiled. "And, my husband, Samuel, was right by my side while I learned about the Lord."

"I understand from Linda that you and your husband went through a lot with his—I mean *your* son, David. Linda thinks the world of David too."

"It was tough times four years ago. David needed a kidney, and Noah was the only one who was a match in our family. Noah had been shunned, and it was a rather big mess for a while. But David is healthy now, and over time the community has welcomed Noah into their hearts and homes."

"I can't help but notice how everyone in this community joins together, in good times and in bad. I remember that from when I was growing up here. I had a few Amish friends."

"How is it going, staying with Linda and her family in their home? Miss that air-conditioning?" Lillian smiled. "It was the hardest thing for me to give up."

Josie liked Lillian. Even during this difficult time, she was making an effort to get to know Josie, and Josie was touched. "It was a little warm last night. Although I suspect my husband will be home from overseas soon, and I'll be returning home."

"I'd like to pray with you, if that's all right," Lillian said.

"I'd like that."

"Normally, we pray silently, but I'd like to offer a prayer aloud for you."

Josie nodded, welcoming this thoughtful gesture.

"Please Heavenly Father, be with my new friend, Josie, and stay close to her during difficult times, both now and in the future. Bless her with Your healing touch, and wrap Your loving arms around her. In Your name we pray."

Josie tried to stifle her sobs, which would only make her head hurt worse. "Thank you. I don't know why that's making me cry." She faced Lillian. "I just appreciate it so much. And it's such a sweet thing to do."

Lillian gazed long and hard into Josie's eyes, and Josie had the strangest feeling that Lillian knew her secret, although she was sure Mary Ellen would never share something so private. "When I first came to know the Lord, I cried a lot. It's a spiritual cleansing of sorts. Maybe that's the case with you." Lillian smiled.

Josie didn't respond. She swiped her eyes and wondered what was taking Mary Ellen so long, even though she was enjoying this time with Lillian.

"Lillian, I've been looking for you. I thought you were out-side." Sarah Jane hurried into the kitchen. "Hello, Josie. I'm sorry to interrupt."

Josie remembered Jonas's daughter from her visit to see Jonas. "No, that's fine," Josie said as she stood up.

"*Mamm*, what is it? You look frantic." Lillian rose from the bench also.

"This!" Sarah Jane held up an envelope, much like the ones several family members and friends had received earlier.

"Your letter? What about it? I got one too."

"Not like this, you didn't." Sarah Jane's eyes widened as she grinned. "I already opened my personal letter from Pop. But this is a second letter addressed to you, me, and Lizzie. You're never going to believe this." She pushed the letter toward Lillian. "Read it. See for yourself!"

20

LILLIAN OPENED THE ENVELOPE HER MOTHER HANDED to her just as Lizzie walked into the kitchen and after Josie excused herself to go look for Mary Ellen.

"My Huggy Bear is just full of surprises." Lizzie sat down in a chair at the far end of the table. "I couldn't believe my eyes when Sarah Jane showed me the letter."

"Leave it to Pop to do something like this without telling us." Sarah Jane sat down on the wooden bench, propped her elbows on the table, and rested her chin on her hands. "What was he thinking?"

Lillian unfolded the white piece of paper and read.

Lizzie, Sarah Jane, and Lillian,

You three girls have probably given me more grief over the past few years than all the folks I've ever known—always hovering over me, trying to take care of me, and bossing me around.

Lillian covered her growing smile with her hand. She couldn't help but laugh at her grandfather's ways, even at the end.

But I love you girls with all my heart, and I hate that I won't be around to take care of you all—especially you, Lizzie. Lillian, you have Samuel; and

Sarah Jane, I reckon you do all right on your own, but you two take care of my Lizzie.

Now, for the matter at hand. Lancaster County is growing more and more populated, with less farmland for future generations, which makes the land prices mighty high. I reckon by the time Lillian's young girls are grown and married, their husbands will be forced to work only in the Englisch *world, unable to tend to the land we love and make a* gut *living at it. We are getting further and further away from our Amish roots with each passing year, and it wonders me if generations to come will hold steadfast to our deep satisfaction to work the land in hopes of a plentiful harvest.*

In the valley beneath Colorado's Sangre de Cristo mountains, small Amish communities are gathering. I've purchased one thousand acres there, in a place called Canaan, Colorado. There are two farmhouses on the property, over two hundred years old and in need of much repair. I believe that more and more of our people will move west due to overcrowding and high land prices here. So, my girls . . . this is my way of safeguarding future generations.

Beautiful country there, and it's available to you if you should want or need it. Kade Saunders has all the details.

Calm down, Sarah Jane. I can see your face as you read, wondering how I did this. There's this thing called the Internet down at the local library. Puts you in touch with anyone, anywhere. I had to bend a rule on my way out.

> *In His Name, and loving you all,*
> *Pop—Grandpa—Huggy Bear*

"Close your mouth, Lillian," her mother teased in reference to Lillian's jaw, which hung to the floor. "I had the same reaction."

"*Ya*, I was shocked as well." Lizzie shook her head.

"Why would Grandpa think that any of us would split the

family up and leave? We all love it here." Lillian cringed. "Does this mean Grandpa hasn't even seen the property he bought?"

"Hello, ladies." Kade walked into the room. He chuckled. "Leave it to Jonas to do something like this. I didn't know about this until an attorney knocked on my door yesterday with this letter and deed to the property, with instructions from Jonas for me to deliver it all to you. And to answer your question— apparently Jonas has not seen his purchase. Amazing that he would buy property over the Internet, sight unseen, and not tell anyone."

"Well, we'll just sell it," Lillian said. "We don't need a thousand acres in Colorado. That's the craziest thing I've ever heard of."

"I agree." Lizzie shook her head again. "Silly old Huggy Bear knows I could never make a trip like that."

"Kade, would you be able to handle the details of selling the property for us?" Sarah Jane folded her hands in front of her. "We'd pay you, of course."

"I would be glad to." Kade rubbed his chin. "Although . . . I did some research last night and never underestimate Jonas. He got a great deal on this property, in a beautiful location. Land in Lancaster County is almost six times as much as in Colorado. It's not as crowded there, and the acreage Jonas purchased is in a very rural area. I know exactly where Canaan is, I've been there. It's near Monte Vista. You might not want to make this decision so hastily."

"What decision?" Samuel walked into the kitchen carting Elizabeth in his arms and with Anna by his side.

Lillian covered her face with her hands for a moment, then blew out a breath of frustration. "Can you believe that Grandpa bought a thousand acres in Colorado without telling anyone? Property with two farmhouses in a rural area. He left a letter for *Mamm*, Lizzie, and me. We just were just telling Kade to make the arrangements to sell the property."

Samuel stroked his beard and didn't say anything, and Lillian watched his brows narrow speculatively.

"Samuel? Doesn't it shock you that Grandpa would do something like this?"

"*Ya.*" Samuel glanced back and forth between Lillian and her mother. "But I think we should go. Move to Colorado."

Lillian thought she might fall off the bench. "What?" She sat up taller. "We're not going anywhere."

"Samuel, why would you say that?" Sarah Jane edged closer to him and extended her arms to take Elizabeth. "Come here, sweetie. Come see your *mammi*." Then she narrowed her eyes at Samuel. "I love you, Samuel, but the thought of you taking my grandbabies makes me want to smack you."

"I reckon we can talk about it later." Samuel looped his thumbs under his suspenders. "Are you ready to go, Lillian?"

Lillian stood from the table. "I guess so, but I'll tell you right now, Samuel Stoltzfus, we aren't going anywhere, so there is nothing to talk about later." Lillian eased Elizabeth out of her mother's arms, kissed her *mamm* on the cheek, and said, "Let me know if you or Lizzie need anything."

She said her good-byes to the others, then she and Samuel loaded the girls into the buggy. David would be leaving in his own courting buggy. She waited until they were heading home on Black Horse Road before she broached the subject of Colorado.

"Samuel, why would you say that about moving to Colorado?"

She curled her mouth into a frown. "Our families are here. We could never do that."

Her husband was quiet for a moment. "I guess you're right."

Lillian could see their farm up ahead, and she thought about all the work Samuel had done to the property and everything she'd done to make it a home for all of them. "There must have been some reason you said that, Samuel." She cut her eyes in his direction.

Samuel shrugged. "*Ach*, I don't know. It was just a thought."

Lillian sat taller as they pulled onto the driveway. "I could never leave here."

Samuel didn't say anything.

<hr />

Josie felt drained by the time they returned from the funeral, and after helping Mary Ellen carry in casserole dishes she'd taken to the funeral, Josie sat down in one of the rockers in the den and pushed herself into motion.

Mary Ellen walked into the den and put her hands on her hips. "You look terrible."

Josie lifted her brows. "Thanks."

"You've done too much today. Why don't you go lie down before supper?"

"No. I'm fine. A little tired, but I'm just thankful that my headache went away." She pointed to her hand. "And look. No bothersome jerking either."

Mary Ellen pushed back a strand of hair that had fallen from beneath her prayer covering, then she wiped her hands on her apron. "I'm making a very simple supper, so I don't need any help, if you'd like to rest. Besides, Linda should be home from her walk with Stephen soon."

Josie kept rocking. "Your bishop didn't have much to say to me today. I tried to talk to him."

"Bishop Ebersol? *Ya*, that's Stephen's grandfather. He's been the strictest bishop we've ever had." Mary Ellen shook her head. "Too strict, if ya ask me."

Josie thought for a moment. "He probably wouldn't like me staying here, would he?"

"I doubt it. But it isn't for long."

Ouch. Mary Ellen had made the statement as if she were relieved of that fact. "Where are Abe and the boys?"

"In the far pasture. One of the cows is due any day, and they went to check on her."

Josie nodded, then Mary Ellen turned to go into the kitchen. Josie followed her.

"Mary Ellen, why did you ask me to stay here when I get the distinct impression you'd rather me not be here?" Josie folded her arms across her chest and waited for Mary Ellen to answer. She appeared in no hurry as she opened the refrigerator door and pulled out a stick of butter. Josie continued to wait.

Finally, Mary Ellen turned to face her. "I've asked myself that a hundred times." Josie's heart sank, but then Mary Ellen smiled before she walked to the stove. "I have a sense that you are meant to be here, Josie. Not just because you are Linda's birth mother either."

Josie sat down on the bench while Mary Ellen pulled two pots down from a rack near the stove. "What kind of sense?"

"The kind that comes from God." She turned her head around,

and her eyes flashed a gentle warning. "But I do not want Linda to be tempted by your ways." Then she turned back around and placed the pots atop the stove.

"That doesn't make sense, Mary Ellen." Josie scowled. "If you're so worried about that, then why did you invite me here?"

"Honestly?"

"Yes, honestly. I'd like to know." Josie paused. "You offered for Linda's sake, I suppose. Or just out of pity."

Mary Ellen turned around and twirled the wooden spoon in her hand as she spoke. "Because you are—ill. And because you don't know Jesus and His Father. I think that's tragic, and I thought perhaps you might learn from us. It's normally not our way to minister to others about the Lord, but I have a strong feeling that you are the exception."

"But how much could you teach me in only a day or two? Robert thinks he can catch a flight home from China any day now." Josie raised her shoulders and let out an exasperated breath. "I wish . . ."

Mary Ellen stood waiting.

Josie tapped her finger to her chin. "I wish I knew what was going on with me. I've felt different lately. Especially today, at the funeral. All those people together at one time, praying." She pulled her eyes from Mary Ellen's and focused on the brown mat in front of the sink. "I've even been praying." Then she shook her head. "I'm conflicted, I guess."

"There is much power in prayer, Josephine." Then Mary Ellen smiled. "A lot can be covered in a day or two."

Josie returned the smile. "I'm all ears."

If Mary Ellen could help her attain the hopefulness that she'd felt on brief occasions lately, Josie was willing to open her heart and her mind to the possibilities.

The days stretched into more than a week, but Robert was due home midmorning the next day. She missed Robert terribly, but until the end she'd treasure her time in this house, with this family. She spent lots of time during the day with Linda, by her side doing laundry, mending, or housecleaning. She'd only had two really bad headaches, and neither had lasted very long. The new medication Dr. Phillips prescribed for the seizures seemed to be working since she hadn't had one. Getting to know her daughter was all she wished for.

Late in the afternoons, Josie helped Mary Ellen with supper. Linda was glad that it gave her an opportunity to spend some extra time with Stephen. Each day she walked about a half mile to meet Stephen when he drove over the bridge in Ronks, and they would talk for about an hour before Stephen would bring her home.

In an ironic twist, Josie had never felt as alive as she had the past week, and something had changed between her and Mary Ellen as well. During the couple of hours that it took to prepare supper, Mary Ellen talked with Josie about the Bible and about the *Ordnung*, an unwritten code of conduct that most Amish know by heart. And they'd prayed. A lot. And with each prayer, Josie felt more hopeful about her circumstances. She'd begun to have dreams about heaven, and in her dreams it was the most beautiful place she could imagine.

As she felt possibilities springing forth around her, she fought a building resentment at Robert. Josie knew she was a grown woman perfectly capable of forming her own opinions, but she couldn't help but wonder how differently her life might have been if she'd married a man who had a strong faith like Mary Ellen did. But each time the thought presented itself, she worked to push it aside. Robert was the best man she'd ever known.

Josie was chopping tomatoes while she sat at the kitchen table that evening, sweat dripping down her face, and thinking how good it felt to not wear any makeup. It had seemed pointless after about the second day, as she only sweated it off, and no one else around here wore any.

Since Abe and the boys had gone into town and Linda was with Stephen, Josie wanted to share with Mary Ellen something that had been on her mind before she left in the morning.

"I want to thank you, Mary Ellen. For everything." Josie sliced the end off a tomato and began to chop it into tiny squares for the stew that night. "I know that my being here has been difficult for you from day one. But I just—just wanted to know her. That's all."

Mary Ellen stirred meat in a pot on top of the stove. She didn't turn around. "You're welcome."

"I guess I really didn't need to be here. I mean, I've had a couple of headaches, but no seizures, and overall I've felt pretty good."

Mary Ellen turned around. "*Ach*, I feel quite sure you needed to be here. For several reasons, no?" She smiled, then turned to stirring again.

"I guess you're right."

Josie continued chopping the tomatoes, but her mind was a whirlwind of activity. What if she hadn't stayed here, learned from Mary Ellen, opened herself up to a relationship with God? She'd even been fortunate enough to attend worship service with them all at Mary Ellen's sister's house. Rebecca and her husband, Aaron, hosted the Sunday service at their home. It was a long three hours, sitting on the wooden benches, but Josie felt honored to have been invited. Even though she didn't understand most of the service spoken in High German, there was a sense of amazing fellowship. She still couldn't say that she wasn't afraid to die, but alongside her fears there was now hope, hope at an everlasting life.

"Do you mind if I keep seeing Linda in the next few months?" She piled the tomatoes on a plate to her left.

"Of course not." Mary Ellen was adding potatoes that Josie had peeled earlier to the stew, but she didn't turn around.

Josie stood up, picked up the plate, and took them to Mary Ellen. "Time for the tomatoes?" She held the plate over the pot.

Mary Ellen nodded but turned her face away from Josie. But not enough that Josie couldn't see the tears in her eyes.

"Mary Ellen? What is it?" Josie set the plate on the counter, latched onto Mary Ellen's shoulders, and gently turned her until Josie could see her face. Mary Ellen swiped at her eyes and shook her head.

"I'm fine."

"You're not fine. You're crying. What is it? What's wrong?"

Mary Ellen covered her face with her hands and sobbed. Then she looked up at Josie with tear-filled eyes. "Josephine . . ." She hung her head for a moment before she lifted her chin and locked eyes with Josie. "I've committed a sin against you, against God. I reckon I never wanted you here. I never wanted you to search for Linda, I never wanted her to know you, and I didn't want you to disrupt our lives."

None of this surprised Josie, but she wondered why Mary Ellen was telling her this now, when they seemed to have come so far. She waited for her to go on, hoping there would be a *but* coming.

"But I've grown to care deeply for you, and I would have never wished this on—on you, never, Josephine. Do you hear me? I never wanted something like this to happen, and . . ." Mary Ellen slumped over, crying hard.

"Mary Ellen." Josie spoke firmly, squeezed her arms gently, and nudged her to look up. "I know that. Do you hear me? I understand everything you are saying. I don't think you've experienced an emotion yet that wouldn't be human in this situation. You didn't make me sick, Mary Ellen. And I *did* disrupt your life. And I never expected to care for you like . . ." A lump in Josie's throat prevented her from going on. Instead, the women embraced, and Josie held on to Mary Ellen while her own tears spilled.

Mary Ellen eased away from Josie and gathered herself. "I know that God's will is to be done, but I will miss you, and it saddens me to think—to think . . ."

"I will miss you too." She dabbed at her eyes and smiled. "But if everything you are telling me is true, which I believe to be so, I'm going to a wonderful place, and we'll see each other again in heaven."

"*Ya, ya.*" Mary Ellen nodded as she sniffled.

A loud crash startled them both. They spun around to see a rooster slam through the screen in the door, ripping it in every direction as the winged animal hurtled toward them. Josie screamed.

Mary Ellen grabbed Josie's hand and pulled her to the other side of the kitchen just as the rooster rounded the corner and headed into the den.

"What do we do?" Josie yelled over the shrill squawking that echoed through the house.

Mary Ellen grabbed a broom in the corner. "Not sure! Something is wrong with that bird!" She ran into the den, and Josie followed behind. Then Mary Ellen screamed, and turned around, bumping right into Josie. "It's coming back!"

They ran back through the den, and Josie threw her hands over her head as the rooster began to flap his wings and lift off the ground, spewing horrible sounds. Josie didn't know much about roosters, but this didn't sound good at all. The bird skimmed the coffee table; books, Abe's glasses, and a lantern went crashing to the floor. Josie kept running until she got to the kitchen, but Mary Ellen stayed behind. Then it got very quiet.

"Mary Ellen, are you okay?" Josie peeked around the corner, and Mary Ellen had her shoulders scrunched up to her ears as she pointed to the couch.

Josie jerked her head to the left. That bird had perched itself on the back of the couch. Still and quiet. Josie didn't move. She looked back at Mary Ellen. "What do we do?"

That's all it took. The bird was in flight, and both women started screaming and trying to stay out of its path as it flew around the den, then into the kitchen, then back to the den. Josie even jumped over the coffee table to get out of the bird's way, toppling the wooden table over when her foot didn't quite clear it. Mary Ellen was trying to use the rocking chair to block the bird as it dove toward her, eventually toppling the chair over as well.

Mary Ellen began screaming something in Pennsylvania *Deitsch* when the bird slammed into the china cabinet up against the wall in between the kitchen and den. Then she yelled, "That's my wedding china!"

Josie was hovering on the couch with her hands over her head, but when she looked up and saw Mary Ellen holding the broom like a weapon and protecting her china, Josie burst into laughter, the type of laughter that causes you to snort and make all kinds of sounds you wouldn't necessarily want anyone to hear.

"You think this is funny?" Mary Ellen still had her hands gripped firmly around the broom, but her eyes were looking to the left, then to the right. "Where is that bird?"

Josie rolled onto her side on the couch, struggling to catch her breath because she was laughing so hard.

They both turned toward the kitchen when they heard the screen door slam. Linda's mouth dropped open. She looked back and forth between Josie and Mary Ellen. Then her hands moved over her mouth as she surveyed the area, which, Josie knew, looked like a war zone. When Linda looked at Josie lying on the couch, with tears streaming down her face, she turned to her mother.

Placing her hands on her hips, she said, "*Mamm*, put that broom down right now! What could you two possibly be fighting about? Look at this mess." She walked toward Josie, mumbling to herself in Pennsylvania *Deitsch*, before she addressed Josie directly. "Are you all right?"

Josie burst into laughter at Linda's assumption and, through watery eyes, noticed that Mary Ellen was bent over at the waist, laughing as hard as she was.

"Linda!" Mary Ellen yelled between gasps for air and laughter. "Do you really think I would hit Josie with a broom?"

Mary Ellen went to the couch and sat down beside Josie, who sat up next to her. Both women continued to laugh, but Linda didn't seem to see the humor.

"It smells like something is burning in the oven, and look at this mess!"

"Oops. Forgot to take the bread out." Mary Ellen started laughing again.

Linda walked toward them, laughing like school girls on the couch. She folded her hands across her chest. "Well, I reckon the two of you better get this mess cleaned up before *Daed* gets here and sees you carrying on this way. He'll think you've been hitting the wine, I reckon."

Josie heard the flapping of wings, and evidently Mary Ellen did too. "Cover your head," Mary Ellen yelled to her daughter as she scooted closer to Josie and held her hands above her head.

"What is that—" Linda looked toward the mudroom just in time to see that crazy bird come flying through. She screamed, then joined them both on the couch. All three were still huddled together when Abe walked through the door. He grabbed the rooster by the neck, then eyed the women on the couch, who were trying not to laugh but were unsuccessful.

He shook his head and walked out the door mumbling.

It took a few moments for Josie to gather herself. She took several deep breaths, then she looked to her left at—at—

Her head started to hurt in a way that it had never hurt before, and she slammed her hands to her temples. She could vaguely hear the women asking her if she was all right.

She panicked as her heart began to race, and her head was surely going to explode. *Please, dear God, help me. Oh, please help.*

I am here, My child.

Then everything went black.

21

JOSIE BLINKED HER EYES INTO FOCUS AND SQUINTED from the bright lights in the drafty room. She recognized the smell of the hospital right away.

"Hello, sleepyhead." Robert ran his hand through Josie's hair, then leaned down and kissed her on the lips. "How are you feeling?"

"I don't remember getting here. There was this bird, and . . ."

"You had a seizure last night, and Mary Ellen called an ambulance from their phone in the barn." Robert pulled a chair closer to the bed and sat down. "Mary Ellen stayed with you all night, until I got here this morning."

"She did?" Josie lifted her arm and eyed the IV. "I don't remember much." She reached for Robert's hand. "I'm so glad you're home. So very glad."

He leaned down and kissed her again. "Me too. And I'm not leaving you again. I don't care what kind of business presents itself." Robert hung his head. "I'm so sorry, babe."

Josie reached up and cupped his cheek with her hand. "It's all right, honey. I had an amazing time getting to know Linda. And Mary Ellen . . . well, who would have ever thought that we might become friends? She's a wonderful woman. And Robert, she taught me so much while I was there."

Robert smiled. "I imagine she did. I bet it was interesting to find out about their ways, live the life for a while."

"We prayed, she explained some of the *Ordnung*, their way of conduct, and we read the Bible. It was wonderful."

Robert stopped smiling, and his expression filled with concern. Then he seemed to be forcing a smile. "I'm glad you had a good time."

"I did." She paused, seeing the hurt in his eyes. "But I missed you terribly."

"The doctor said you can go home. They're sending home yet another new medication that hopefully will help with the seizures."

"Robert, I want you to get to know Linda."

"I'd like that."

"Maybe she can come stay with us some over the next few— few months."

"Josie, we can do anything you want to do. Anything." He ran a hand through her tangled hair again. "My precious Josie."

"She'll be eighteen in August. And I'll be praying that I make it to her birthday party."

Robert tried to hide the shadow that crossed his face, but Josie knew him too well for that.

"That bothers you, doesn't it?"

"What's that?"

"That I would mention praying."

Robert shrugged. "No."

She intertwined her fingers within his and stared into his eyes. "Do you know that people all over the country are praying for me? I know you don't believe, Robert, but I think that is just amazing."

Robert lifted her hand and kissed her fingers tenderly. "Josie, if you think it's amazing, then I think it's amazing."

"Get me out of here." She grinned. "Take me home and hold me all night long."

"Deal. We're just waiting for the nurse to come take out your IV. Then we can go."

Josie gazed into Robert's eyes, the love of her life. *Please help him to believe, God. Even if just a little.*

The door swung open, and the nurse walked in. "I understand someone is ready to go home?"

"Yes! Release me, please." Josie playfully lifted her hand with the IV up and down.

"You got it."

With Josie's IV out, Robert helped her dress and took her home.

Linda pushed herself along on the foot scooter, pumping her leg faster the closer she got to the bridge in Ronks. Stephen had told her he'd left a poem for her there, and sure enough, she saw a pink ribbon as soon as she entered the shade from the covered bridge. She fought to catch her breath and pulled the note from between the slats.

> *My heart belongs to the recipient of this letter; the one who makes my heart feel better.*
> *My emotions for you I cannot hide; as you are the warmth I feel inside.*
> *Please believe me as this is true; my entire world revolves around you.*
>
> *I love you, Stephen*

She smiled at Stephen's gentle words. "I love you too," she whispered, and she wrote those same words on the note before stuffing it back in place. As much as she loved these exchanges on the bridge, her heart ached for Stephen to propose. She worried that Bishop Ebersol didn't think she was a suitable choice for a *fraa*, and perhaps Stephen would never get around to asking her to marry him. They'd been dating for over a year and were in love.

It was bothering her more and more, and even though she was only approaching her eighteenth birthday, she was sure she wanted to spend the rest of her life with Stephen. She sighed, then kicked the scooter forward, wishing she'd taken the time to hook the horse to the buggy. This July heat was almost unbearable. Lines of sweat rolled down her cheeks as she continued to Josie's house. She hadn't seen Josie in three days, and she knew that tomorrow Josie would get the results from the special test she'd had last week, the test to check the tumor inside her head.

"Hey, there," Robert said when Linda rolled onto the driveway. "Josie will be so glad to see you. She's had a great couple of days."

"*Ach, gut!*" Linda dragged her foot a bit, pulling the scooter to a stop. "What ya doing?"

Robert's hands were on his hips and he was staring at a leafy green plant in a big red container. "Wondering why this thing looks so sickly. I water it every day since it's so hot."

"Maybe it doesn't need water every day." Linda propped the scooter up on the stand, then leaned forward. "I reckon I've never seen a plant like that."

Robert chuckled. "Me either. It was actually here when we bought the place." He lifted his head and pointed toward the front door. "Go on in. Josie's making a shoofly pie."

"She learned that from me," Linda said.

"I'm quite sure I don't need to eat all the molasses in those things, but I sure enjoy her making them. You're probably just in time to have a warm slice." Linda turned to head toward the front door. "Save me a piece," Robert said.

"I will."

Over the past few weeks, she'd had time to get to know Robert. He was so good to Josie. He waited on her constantly, went out of his way to make her happy, and just the way he looked at her caused Linda's heart to fill with anticipation. *I want to live my life with Stephen like that.*

She entered the house, walked through the living room, and made her way to the kitchen. Josie was just pulling the pie out of the oven.

Linda walked to Josie's side as Josie placed the pie on a cooling rack. "Smells *gut.*"

"Linda!" She threw her arms around her. "I'm so glad you stopped by. You're just in time for pie."

"Robert said you've had a *gut* couple of days. I'm glad."

Josie eased out of the hug, then studied her pie. "A very special young lady showed me how to make the perfect shoofly pie, so let's have a piece." She paused. "And yes . . . it's been a great couple of days."

Linda nodded and went to the cabinet where she knew the plates were stored, and she pulled out two small ones. Josie sliced the pie, and they took a seat at the kitchen table. They both bowed their heads in silent prayer, and Linda added an extra special one for Josie. *Please God, leave her with me for a long time.*

"This air-conditioning feels so *gut.*" Linda took a bite of her pie, then grinned.

Josie chuckled. "I have to admit, I never appreciated air-conditioning so much until recently. Stay as long as you like."

"Tomorrow you find out about your test, no?" Linda tried to sound upbeat as she made the statement, but Josie's expression soured just the same.

"Yes. The results from my MRI. They'll be able to tell how fast the tumor is growing." Josie shrugged. "Whatever. I feel good today, so I'm going to enjoy it."

Linda watched Josie shoveling the rest of the pie into her mouth. "I guess you do feel better." She brought her hand up to stifle a giggle.

Josie chuckled. "Think I've put on a few pounds too."

Linda didn't want to focus on anything negative. For now, she was going to pretend that Josie would be around forever. "Guess what?"

"What?" Josie put her plate in the sink, then returned to the table.

"My birthday party is in two and half weeks. *Mamm* wanted me to tell you to come over at four o'clock that day, Saturday. She's going to make meatloaf. All my aunts and uncles and cousins will be there too. *Ach*, she's also making yellow cake with chocolate icing. My favorite."

Josie's face shriveled up until she looked like she might cry.

"What's wrong?" Linda reached across the table and touched her hand.

Josie sniffed. "I'm just incredibly grateful to be included. This year, I'll get to see you blow out your candles." Then she gasped. "You do blow out candles, right?"

Linda giggled. *Englisch folks, they can never keep things straight.* "*Ya.* We have birthday parties just like everyone else. Cake, candles, and homemade ice cream. We're making vanilla ice cream. Luke and Matt will take turns churning the ice cream during the afternoon, like I do when it's one of their birthdays."

"And singing?"

"*Ya*, singing too."

Josie smiled. "It will be a wonderful day."

Linda gazed into Josie's eyes, eyes still filled with happy tears. *Please God, don't let anything happen to her before my birthday.*

Stephen pulled the buggy to a stop in front of his house and wished he could see Linda's face one of the times she read his notes from the bridge. As he stepped down from the buggy, he heard wagon wheels churning the gravel on the driveway, and he turned to see his grandfather pulling up to the house.

Daadi pulled beside Stephen, but didn't get out of the buggy, so Stephen walked closer.

"Hello, *Daadi*. Are you here for supper?"

"No, I was just on my way home from Bird-In-Hand, and I saw you pulling in." He stroked his long gray beard. "How are things at the Huyard home? I understand the *Englisch* woman is back at her home, no?"

"*Ya*, she is."

"This pleases me, as I don't think it was appropriate for her to be their guest. Too complicated." He shook his head.

Stephen took a deep breath and smiled, too tired to argue with his grandfather.

"Does Linda plan to continue a relationship with this woman?"

"That *woman* is her birth mother. I reckon so." Stephen's heart started pounding in his chest the moment he made the wise comment, and he could tell by the look on *Daadi's* face that his statement was not well received.

His grandfather narrowed his eyes in Stephen's direction. "I was against Mary Ellen and Abe adopting Linda for reasons such as this. Linda is a fine *maedel*, but I worried something like this would happen, the girl's *mamm* showing up to claim her."

"She's not claiming her, just being friends with her."

Daadi's forehead wrinkled with concern. "We all have *Englisch* friends, Stephen, but this is not the same. Are you sure that Linda still plans to be baptized into the faith?"

"*Ya.* For sure she is."

Stephen knew his parents didn't have any concerns about Linda, but he worried his grandfather might persuade them.

"Even before this woman entered Linda's life, I heard many stories of Linda stretching her *rumschpringe* to the limit. Much time at the movies and malls with *Englisch* girlfriends. It wonders me if she will be able to stay on course with her studies of the *Ordnung*."

Stephen fought the anger building, but also realized he'd been guilty of having these same thoughts where Linda was concerned. But that was in the past.

"*Daadi*, Linda will not stray from her faith, even if she is friends with Josie. I'm sure of it." Stephen recalled briefly the scene with Linda wearing Josie's blue jeans, but quickly wiped it from his mind.

His grandfather tipped back the rim of his straw hat with his thumb. "I hope you're right."

I know I'm right.

If that was the case, why couldn't he bring himself to propose to Linda? He'd gotten up his nerve once, only to have her disappoint him.

"Besides, *Daadi* . . ." Stephen looked down and kicked the gravel with one foot. "Josie is sick."

"*Ya*, I know. God's peace be with her."

Stephen knew how much Josie's passing was going to affect Linda, and he was planning to be by her side.

"*Ya*, God's peace be with her," Stephen echoed.

The next morning in Dr. Phillips's office, Josie took a deep breath and crossed her legs while she and Robert waited for the doctor to bring in her MRI results. She'd thrown up earlier that morning but she attributed it to nerves. *I just want to make it to Linda's birthday in a couple of weeks. Please God.* And she felt hopeful, since she'd had a good few days. Surely she couldn't go down that fast, although she was well aware that the pressure on her brain stem could cause her to slip into a coma with little warning.

"What's taking so long?" Robert stood up and began to pace. "He's kept us waiting in here for thirty minutes."

Fear twisted around Josie's heart. Maybe things had worsened. She gazed at Robert, whose expression was filled with concern. "I'm sure he'll be here soon."

He walked up behind her and rubbed her shoulders. "Sorry, babe. I know this waiting is hard on you too." Robert leaned down from behind her and kissed her on the cheek.

"I guess I'm used to it."

Robert walked around Dr. Phillips's desk and eyed all the plaques on the wall. "He is one of the best in his field." He turned to face Josie. "And who knows, Josie. Who knows. Maybe it's taking so long because they are trying to decide whether or not surgery will be possible."

"Or maybe it's taking so long because they are deciding how to tell me that my time is shorter than they think." She knew she shouldn't have voiced her thoughts, and as Robert turned around, his eyes glazed with despair, she said, "Sorry."

Robert walked back to his chair and sat down. He stared straight ahead and didn't say anything, resting his head in his hand which he'd propped on the arm of the chair.

Please, God, be with Robert when I'm gone. He is going to be so lost. Please help him find his way to You.

They waited another ten minutes before Dr. Phillips entered the office, accompanied by two other doctors.

This must be bad.

Robert, always the optimist, didn't even wait for introductions. "Can you operate?"

"Hello, Josie . . . Robert." Dr. Phillips didn't answer Robert's question, but instead extended his hand to Robert, then Josie. "This is Dr. Bissmeyer and Dr. Simpson. I've invited them to join us."

Dr. Phillips eased back behind his desk and sat down. The two other doctors stayed standing by the door. After Dr. Phillips slid on his pair of dark-rimmed reading glasses, he pulled Josie's MRI films from a large envelope, then hung them over a lighted panel to his left for Josie and Robert to see.

As Dr. Phillips scratched his forehead, the other two doctors moved closer so they could also see the large X-rays.

"Sorry to keep you both waiting." Dr. Phillips leaned across his desk. "I wanted to confer with Dr. Bissmeyer and Dr. Simpson to make sure I wasn't missing something, but we're all in agreement about these results. You may want to do another test, but we're confident that these are accurate."

"Just tell us, Dr. Phillips," Robert said as he shook his head. "Has the situation changed? Is there any chance you can operate?"

Josie's heart was beating out of her chest, and her stomach churned with anxiety as she watched Dr. Phillips point to the middle of the film.

"See this?"

Josie and Robert leaned forward as the two doctors hovered above them. She focused on the spot above Dr. Phillips's fingertip.

"There won't be an operation, Josie." Dr. Phillips took a deep breath.

22

LINDA OPENED THE SCREEN DOOR AND GREETED HER Uncle Samuel and Aunt Lillian, then David and the girls when they arrived for her birthday party. After giving each of them a hug on the front porch, she could see her Uncle Noah and his family pulling up the driveway in their car, followed by another buggy that looked like it was carrying Sarah Jane and Lizzie.

"I can't believe you're eighteen today," Lillian said. "All grown up."

Linda smiled. "*Ya*, eighteen today." She loved when the entire family was together. Aunt Rebecca and her family showed up next, followed by Uncle Ivan and Aunt Katie Ann.

"Snacks are in the kitchen, and there's also some chips on the coffee table." Linda's mother had been busy that morning, readying everything for the party, and as she scurried around the kitchen making sure everything was perfect, Linda wondered when Josie would get here. She'd only seen Josie twice in the past two weeks, and Josie had been unusually quiet. However, during their last visit, Josie had assured Linda she would be here. *Please God, I hope Josie is having a good day.*

"Matt, go help your brother with the ice cream," her father instructed as he walked into the kitchen. Then Abe gave Linda a big hug. "I reckon you'll always be *mei boppli*," he whispered in her ear.

"I know, *Daed*."

Only one thing kept the day from being perfect. Stephen had to work, but he'd promised to leave her something special at the bridge later.

Linda eyed the large cake in the center of the kitchen table—yellow cake with chocolate icing and eighteen candles ready for her to blow out. This would be a big day for her and Josie. *Where is she?*

Robert was coming with Josie, and it would be the family's first time to meet him. No doubt, everyone would like him. Linda had been fond of him from the very beginning, particularly the way he treated Josie. That made her thoughts roll back to the conversation she'd overheard between Aunt Katie Ann and Uncle Ivan, and she wondered if everything was all right.

She walked onto the porch and saw her brother working up a sweat. "You have to keep turning the handle, Matt." She thought about how good the homemade vanilla ice cream would taste with the cake later.

"*Ya*, I know." Matt pushed back his straw hat and wiped beads of sweat from his brow. "Maybe you could bring me a glass of tea, no?"

"Sure." Linda walked back into the house, and by the time she got back with Matt's tea, she saw Josie's SUV pulling into the driveway. She headed down the porch steps and waited for her to get out of the car.

"Sorry I'm late." Josie was holding the clock from the mantel. "I thought you might like to have this as a birthday present. Sorry I didn't get it wrapped. I couldn't find a box it would fit in."

Linda accepted the clock, cradled it on her hip, and then gave Josie a hug. "*Danki*, Josie." She stepped back after a moment and held the clock at arm's length to see it better. "I love this." Then she looked back at Josie. "Where's Robert?"

Josie sighed, wove her hands together in front of her, and looked down. "He couldn't come." When she raised her head, Linda could see the disappointment in her eyes. "But he said to wish you a very happy birthday." Josie smiled. "I'm here, though, and I've waited for this day for a very long time." She threw an arm around Linda's shoulder. "And I bet your mother has made all sorts of good food."

"*Ach, ya*, she has." They walked toward the house together, and Linda silently asked God to bless this day for Josie above all else.

Josie wound her way through Linda's family, who in many ways felt like the only family she had. Some of them she knew better than others, but Linda's home was a place where she felt comfortable. When the entire family got together, their fellowship seemed to spill over in abundance and touch anyone who was blessed enough to be present. More than anything, she wished Robert could be here to feel this. Maybe then he wouldn't be so confused and sad, when in reality, there was so much to be thankful for.

She recalled Dr. Phillips's conversation with her and Robert—and Robert's reaction. He'd broken into tears right there in the office.

Josie stood tall as everyone gathered in the kitchen to watch Linda blow out her candles. She refused to let his absence sadden this day that she'd waited so long for—for eighteen years—and today there would be no shadows across her heart. *This is a perfect day.*

Linda blew out her candles, and as celebrated in other homes outside of this peaceful community, everyone sang "Happy Birthday." Josie's words choked in her throat as her eyes filled with tears of joy. She felt a hand grab tightly to hers, and she looked to her left to see Mary Ellen singing at the top of her lungs. Mary Ellen squeezed her hand, then turned to her and smiled. Josie let the tears flow.

After the cake and ice cream, Josie watched Linda open her gifts. Her cousin David had made her a small wooden box to keep special trinkets in, and he'd etched her name on the front. Mary Ellen gave Linda a lovely black sweater that she'd knitted herself, and all her aunts had made her a special quilt for her bed. Then everyone gasped when Abe and the boys walked in with a cedar chest.

"We normally don't do this much for birthdays," Mary Ellen whispered to Josie as the boys placed the cedar chest in front of Linda, "but it's her eighteenth."

Linda cupped her mouth with her hands. "*Ach, Daed!* It's beautiful."

"We helped too," Luke said, breathing hard.

"*Danki,* Luke and Matthew, and *Mamm* too!" She gave each of them a hug. "*Danki,* all of you, for everything. What a wonderful birthday."

Josie knew she was about to steal the show, but she'd waited over two weeks to share her news with those she loved, and it had taken everything she had to hold back until now.

"I—I have some news," she said, barely in a whisper. She looked directly at Linda.

Linda's glowing expression left her beautiful face instantly. "Oh, no."

Josie walked closer to Linda, pushed back a strand of hair that had fallen across her cheek, and gazed into her daughter's eyes. Then she looked at Mary Ellen, and glanced around at all the others, before she turned back to Linda.

A tear rolled down her cheek and she clenched her jaw to stunt the sob in her throat.

She opened her mouth to try to speak, but everyone turned their attention toward the porch when they heard footsteps. Mary Ellen walked to the door in the kitchen and opened it. When Josie saw her husband walk into the den, she ran into his arms.

"Thank you for coming. Oh, Robert. Thank you." She embraced him tightly. "I need you right now," she whispered in his ear.

"Oh, Josie. I'm sorry for not being here. But the more I thought about it, I knew this is where I needed to be. Maybe—maybe I'll get some sort of understanding about all this."

Josie gently eased out of the hug and turned to face everyone. "I'd like you all to meet my husband, Robert."

She moved around the room to make introductions but noticed Linda impatiently tapping her bare foot on the wooden floor. "Josie, please. Tell us your news."

Robert reached for Josie's hand and held it tightly in his, and Josie gazed into Linda's eyes again. "Thank you for letting me share this special day with all of you. This is the happiest day of my life . . ." She turned to Robert, hoping to borrow some of his strength. He nodded for her to go on as tears poured down Josie's face. Linda was already moving toward her, dread on her face.

"What is it? Tell us, Josie."

Josie smiled, and as Linda reached her, she took her free hand and reached for Linda's. "The tumor is gone."

Linda's eyes narrowed. "What does this mean?"

"It means . . ." Josie drew in a breath and blew it out slowly. "I am going to be around for many more of your birthday celebrations." Josie glanced at Mary Ellen who had a hand clamped over her mouth and eyes filled with tears. "If that's okay with your mother and everyone else," Josie added as Mary Ellen moved toward her.

Linda's feet were rooted to the floor, her expression one of disbelief, but Mary Ellen cupped Josie's cheeks with her hands, and whispered, "You are a Daughter of the Promise. Miracles happen to those who believe."

"Yes," Josie whispered as she fell into Mary Ellen's arms. "Thank you. Thank you, Mary Ellen."

The room grew quiet, as if everyone was trying to absorb the magnitude of what was happening, but Josie heard sniffling among the women.

"The cancer is gone," Robert said, his voice cracking. He put a hand over his eyes, shielding his own emotions.

Josie left Mary Ellen's embrace and went to Robert. "It's all right," she whispered as she held him.

"I want to believe, Josie," he whispered, his words caught in his throat. "I really do."

Josie knew what it felt like when you began a spiritual cleansing, when you truly opened your heart to God, and she could see that happening now with Robert as he wept in front of all of them.

Josie recalled Dr. Phillip's explanation of her prognosis two weeks ago in his office.

"There won't be any operation, Josie," he'd said. "There is nothing to operate on."

Dr. Phillips had gone on to explain that doctors from all over the state had been brought in to look at Josie's MRI, and not one of them had a medical or scientific reason why the tumor would have just vanished.

"That's medically impossible," Robert had argued. "Redo the test or something, because you guys have messed up."

But Dr. Phillips, along with Drs. Bissmeyer and Simpson, just shook their heads. "No," Dr. Phillips said. "We did not mess up. The tumor is gone, and we are sure of it."

"But how—how in the world . . . I don't understand."

Josie hadn't spoken when she'd heard the results. Within a few minutes, Robert's and the doctors' words had faded away, and all she heard was, *Live well, My child.*

"Sometimes, there is no medical explanation as to why these things happen," Dr. Phillips had said. "It's a medical mystery."

But it was no mystery to Josie, and all the way home from the doctor's office, she'd cried and laughed, unable to stop doing either. "It's a miracle, Robert, and it's the power of prayer," she'd told him. "It's real, Robert. It's so real. My faith in my heart, the way I feel, it's the most incredible feeling in the world."

Robert had refused to open his mind to the possibility, even though she could tell that his heart kept slipping in that direction. Two weeks later, he remained confused—not just about the results, which of course he said he treasured, but about how he'd lived his life thus far if there was truly a God overseeing things. His befuddled thoughts dragged him further and further down, and only yesterday, he'd said he didn't think he could attend Linda's birthday party.

"What if—what if I've been wrong my entire life? Would I even be worthy to be in a room with all of them?"

Josie had tried to talk to him, to explain that it was never too late to reach out to God and His son, Jesus, but Robert just shook his head.

Now, as he stood before her, Josie knew that life as they knew it had changed. Perhaps a larger miracle than her own healing was her husband's change of heart.

When Linda moved toward her, Mary Ellen pulled back to make room for their daughter.

"God is *gut*," Linda said. "So very, very *gut*." And she wrapped her arms around Josie.

Lillian looked around her and knew that this was not the right time for her and Samuel to share their news, but Samuel disagreed.

"Now is as *gut* a time as any, I reckon."

"Samuel, this is Linda's day, and Josie's. I don't think we should share today. It wouldn't be right." Maybe if they didn't share today, it wouldn't come to pass, and they'd never have to tell anyone that it was ever a consideration. "Besides, what if we change our minds?"

"Lillian, everything is going to be fine," Samuel said, trying to assure her once again. The commotion in the kitchen had settled and folks had broken off into smaller groups. "I promise you." He paused with a sigh. "You know we need to do this."

David walked by them in the den, his eyes blazing in his father's direction.

"Your son is definitely not happy with this news." Lillian held the screen door open and motioned for Samuel to step onto the porch. She waited until the door shut behind him to ask, "Are you sure about this, Samuel?"

"Lillian, it makes the most sense." He lifted her chin and kissed her. "I love you. Please don't look so sad."

Just then, Linda rushed out of the screen door and ran down the porch steps.

"Hey! Where ya going?" Lillian called after her.

Linda edged her way around the volleyball game her cousins were playing. "I have to go do something. I'll be back soon, though!"

"Should we wait until she gets back?" Samuel pushed back the rim of his hat as he watched Linda kick the scooter into motion.

"No, Anna and Elizabeth are tired. I think we should go ahead and talk to everyone else so we can get them home." Lillian let out a deep sigh as she sat down in the rocker on the porch. Samuel sat down in the other chair, and a tense silence formed a gap between them. Samuel wasn't only her husband, but her best friend, so she resolved herself to support his decision and to be happy about it. "I love you."

He turned toward her. "I love you too, Lillian."

She smiled. "Then, let's do it."

Samuel nodded.

Linda was disappointed that she wouldn't be able to share her news about Josie with Stephen until the next day, when she saw him at worship service, but she couldn't wait to see what he might have left for her on the bridge. She pushed her scooter forward and felt a bottomless sense of peace and contentment.

Thank you, God. Thank you, God. Thank you, God.

She recalled a conversation she'd had with Jonas. It seemed like such a long time ago.

"*Mamm and* Daed *will always be* mei *parents," she'd told him. "That will never change.*"

"*Of course not. And I reckon they'd lay themselves on the train track for you and both your brothers," Jonas had said. "But here's where it gets tricky." He squinted in her direction and then pointed a finger at her. "I reckon Josephine would lie down on a train track for ya, too, give her life willingly for you. That puts you in a unique position. All these people that love you. Do you have room in your heart for all of them?*"

Linda stared upward. "I miss you, Jonas. And I have enough love in my heart for all of them. I love Josie, and I thank you, God, for leaving her here for now." She scuffed her foot along the road even faster until the bridge was in sight.

Breathless upon arrival, she inched toward the special spot, then clenched her teeth. "Today's my birthday. And no note!" It had been a more than perfect day up until this moment. She hadn't expected a present, just one of his poems, maybe an extra long one. Something. She reminded herself how blessed she was, but anger and hurt still bubbled to the surface.

"You could have left me something!" She stomped her foot, knowing her behavior was childish. "A note, a poem. Something! If you really cared—"

"If I cared, I'd what?"

Linda spun around, her cheeks wet with sweat, but she could still feel the blush of embarrassment coming on.

"Stephen, where'd you come from?"

He squinted his eyes as he neared. "None of your business."

"Don't you talk that way to me, Stephen Ebersol." She stood taller and folded her hands across her chest. "Today is my birthday."

"Really? I had forgotten." A smile tipped the corner of his mouth on one side as it quivered.

"What you got behind your back?" She inched forward, but he stopped.

"Nothing for you."

"Then let me see."

"No."

Linda got within a couple of feet of him. "You have something behind your back."

Slowly, Stephen produced a bouquet of roses.

Linda gasped. "They're beautiful." She reached for them, only to have him pull them back.

"These are for a very special someone."

Linda raised her chin. "Really. And who might that be?"

Stephen's lip began to quiver in a way that Linda had never seen. "What's wrong with you?"

He dropped to one knee, pushed the flowers forward, and practically yelled, "Linda, will you marry me?"

Her heart sang as she accepted the flowers. "*Ya*, Stephen, I will marry you."

He stood up, wrapped his arms around her, and Linda basked in the feel of his embrace.

"I love you." He kissed her tenderly on the mouth.

"I love you too, Stephen." Then she pushed him away, and he blinked with bafflement.

"What'd you do that for?"

"I almost forgot!" Linda jumped up and down on her toes. "It's Josie! She's cured. She's well, Stephen! She's not going to die."

"But the tumor, what about—"

"Gone! It's a miracle." Her eyes clouded with tears. "Josie is not going to die. And I'm going to be Mrs. Stephen Ebersol. This is truly my most perfect day." Linda threw herself into his arms.

Thank you, God.

Linda was glad that all the family was still there when she and Stephen got back to the house. He'd parked his buggy out of sight a ways from the bridge, so they'd loaded up her scooter and headed to her house to spread the news. This wasn't the typical way to do things. Normally they would keep it rather hush-hush and then publish it a few weeks before the wedding, but Linda couldn't keep her joy to herself.

"Are you sure you don't want to wait?" Stephen secured the horse and buggy.

"No. I can't. This has been a perfect day, and I want to share this with my family today."

"All right, I reckon." He shrugged, but the spark in his eyes warmed her heart. They walked up to the house.

Everyone was gathered in the den. Linda heard a few mumblings, but the room grew quiet when they entered.

"We have some news!" She ran to her mother's side, still holding the flowers. Then she glanced at Josie and smiled. "Stephen asked me to marry him!"

"*Ach,* Linda!" Her mother hugged her as her father found his way to Stephen.

"Congratulations, Stephen. We'd be honored to have you in the family." *Daed* shook Stephen's hand, and then both Linda and Stephen made their way through the den, accepting congratulations from the family.

When she got to Josie, both of them started to cry. "I'll get to see you get married."

Linda threw her arms around Josie. "*Ya*, you will. We're so blessed."

"Yes. We are."

Linda withdrew from the hug and glanced around the room. Everyone was smiling, but Linda sensed an uneasiness. "Is everything all right?"

"*Ya*," several people answered at once.

Her cousin David stood up and folded his arms across his chest. "No, everything is not all right."

"David, that's enough!" Linda had never heard her Uncle Samuel speak with such authority, and she couldn't imagine why.

She felt a hand on her shoulder. "Honey, everything is fine." Lillian gave her a pat on the arm. "We were just telling everyone that we will be leaving for Colorado after the fall harvest."

Linda raised her brows. "How long will you be vacationing there?"

Lillian bit her lip, then turned to Mary Ellen.

"Linda, it's not a vacation. Samuel and his family will be moving there." Her mother glanced toward her right. "And your *Onkel* Ivan and Aunt Katie Ann are moving also."

"Why?" It had been a day filled with so many blessings. Why in the world would they move to Colorado?

"There is a place there called Canaan, a beautiful place there that Jonas bought before he died," her mother said. "And Samuel and Lillian have their reasons for wanting to move." She looked cautiously at Ivan and Katie Ann and smiled. "As I'm sure your *Onkel* Ivan and Katie Ann do, as well."

Aunt Katie Ann nodded, but Uncle Ivan just stared at the floor. Again, Linda recalled the conversation she'd overheard between her aunt and uncle.

"We won't be leaving until after the fall harvest," Samuel said. "And today is a day of celebration. Stephen and Linda are getting married!" He stood up. "I say we all go have another piece of birthday cake to celebrate."

Linda chose not to let this news dampen the blessings of the day, so she followed everyone to the kitchen, her fiancé by her side. She grabbed Josie's hand on the way, glad to see that Josie's husband was better. Poor Robert had been quite a mess earlier.

She couldn't help but wonder why Samuel and his family, along with Aunt Katie Ann and Uncle Ivan, would want to move to Colorado, but God works in mysterious ways, and whatever His plan was, Linda was sure His will would be done.

Life is good. God is good. What a perfect day.

Two months later, Josie pulled up at Linda's house to have lunch with her and Mary Ellen. It had become their weekly thing, lunch together on Wednesdays, just the three of them. Josie walked up the cobblestone steps, glad she'd grabbed a light jacket at the last minute. Cool October winds whipped across the yard, scattering the fall foliage in whirlwinds around her. Rays of sunlight peeked through blue-gray skies, and Josie could smell the comforting aroma of Mary Ellen's cooking wafting through the screen door before she reached the front porch.

"Meatloaf today!" Linda swung the door wide for Josie and gave her a quick hug as she moved over the threshold.

Mary Ellen's meatloaf was no longer just Linda's favorite. Josie breathed in the familiar smell. "Ah, you're making my meatloaf." She edged over to Mary Ellen who was stirring potatoes atop the stove. Josie wrapped an arm around her shoulder.

"I've never seen two people get so excited about a simple meatloaf." Mary Ellen shook her head, placed the long wooden spoon on the counter, then turned to Josie and gave her a hug. "But I'll keep making it as long as you two keep requesting it."

Mary Ellen had given Josie the recipe weeks ago, but Josie just couldn't seem to get it to taste the same way Mary Ellen did—as moist and seasoned to absolute perfection.

Linda spread out sheets of paper across the kitchen table. "*Mamm* and I were going over the guest list for the wedding, and—"

"And I still can't believe we're planning a wedding this quickly." Mary Ellen chuckled, and Josie had never felt more blessed than to be included in all the plans. Both women leaned down to look at Linda's list.

"Josie, these are the people you and Robert said to add, Amanda from his office and a few others." Linda pointed about halfway down the list. "We're up to about two hundred now with Stephen's cousins from Ohio coming." Then Linda frowned. "I'm still sad that *Onkel* Samuel's family won't be here, or *Onkel* Ivan and Aunt Katie Ann."

Mary Ellen sighed. "I know, dear. But they are scheduled to move in mid-November, and it would just be too much for them to travel back here the first of December. I know they're all regretful about it. And you know we already tried to move the wedding up, but the first couple of weekends are already booked for weddings, weddings we'll be attending. You know how it is, everyone gets married in November and December, after the harvest. I'm sorry."

Linda tucked her chin. "They won't be here for Thanksgiving or Christmas either."

"Actually . . ." Josie drew in a deep breath, then blew it out slowly as Linda looked up at her. "I have a few people I'd like to add to that list, if it's all right with you."

Mary Ellen arched her brows. "*Ya*, it's fine with us. Anyone we know?"

"Um, no." Josie folded her arms across her chest and looked down for a moment, then looked up at the two of them and smiled. "It's my parents, and my brother and his family, if that's okay."

Linda's eyes widened. "But I thought you didn't really get along with your parents."

Mary Ellen smiled. "I think that's wonderful, Josephine. Just wonderful." Then she waited, as if knowing Josie had more to say.

"I've been talking to my mother a lot on the phone." Josie clasped her hands together in front of her. "I think I know now how special a relationship between mother and daughter can be, and I'd like to work toward that with my own mother."

Mary Ellen touched Josie's arm. "It's very special, the relationship you and Linda have formed." Then she smiled again.

Josie shook her head, then reached for Mary Ellen's hand. "No, Mary Ellen. I didn't mean *my* relationship with Linda. I meant *your* relationship with Linda. I am Linda's best friend. I hope to always be that, but what you and Linda have is everything that a mother and daughter should be."

Mary Ellen squeezed Josie's hand as her eyes filled with water.

Linda reached for Josie's free hand, then Mary Ellen clasped onto Linda's other one. The three of them stood in a circle, symbolic of the bond the women had formed.

"How blessed we are to all be Daughters of the Promise," Mary Ellen said.

"Yes." Then Josie closed her eyes and looked toward heaven.

Thank you.

Dear Readers,

THANK YOU FOR TRAVELING ON THIS INCREDIBLE journey with me. I bring to life the stories that God and His goodness inspire in me. If this book touches at least one person and helps him or her find a relationship with God through faith, hope, and love, then I've done my job for Him. I'm honored and blessed to be able to do so.

Plain Paradise is particularly close to my heart. It reflects some of God's workings in my own life. Like Linda, I was adopted when I was two-weeks-old, and while nothing about my own true story is like Josie and Linda's, I'm familiar with the emotions that go along with this story line.

When I was twenty-five (many moons ago!), I connected with my own birth mother. We maintained a relationship for a few years, but—like Linda—I already had wonderful parents who had raised me. Over time, my birth mother and I lost touch, and I haven't talked to her in eighteen years. I can't help but wonder if God might lead her to this book and by these words give her comfort in knowing that I am happy, healthy, and blessed. Thank you, MC, for giving me life, and thanks be to God for placing me in the care of my wonderful parents when I was a baby.

My family has also experienced a miracle like Josie's. I suppose her healing could be considered simply a nice way to tie up the story line, but in actuality, Josie's story is my son's reality.

In 2007, my son received two rare diagnoses, one of which was a tumor. Cory spent a lot of time in the hospital and hit prayer lists all over the country. Cory's tumor disappeared, he made a full recovery, and we were told, "Medicine is not always an exact science. We don't know why this happens sometimes." I know why. The power of prayer is stronger than we can imagine.

And lastly, God blessed me with a truly romantic husband. The poems that Stephen writes to Linda and leaves on the bridge are fragments of poems that my husband has written to me. Thank you, Patrick. I love you.

Peace and Blessings to all of you.

In His Name,

Beth

Amish Recipes

Snitz Pie

3	cups dried Snitz*
16	oz. applesauce
¾	c. white sugar
¼	c. brown sugar
	pinch of salt
1	tsp. cinnamon
1	tsp. lemon juice
	pinch of Allspice
2	unbaked pie shells

Cover snitz with water and cook slowly for about two hours. Put through strainer. Add remaining ingredients and put in a pie crust. Crisscross second cross over the top.

Bake at 350 for 50-60 minutes.

*dried apple

High Fiber Balls

1   c. peanut butter
1   c. honey
1   c. raisins
1   c. chocolate chips (mini)
1   c. coconut
3   c. quick oatmeal
½   c. bran
¼   tsp. salt

Stir and make firm one-inch balls.

Barbecued String Beans

6   slices bacon—cooked, drained, and crumbled
¾   c. ketchup
½   c. brown sugar
2   T. mustard
4   14.5 oz. cans green beans, drained
1   large onion (chopped)
     Salt and pepper to taste.

Fry onion in bacon drippings. Add rest of ingredients, except beans, then bring to a boil. Add beans. Put in casserole dish and bake at 350 for 1 hour.

Reading Group Guide

1. When Linda finds out that she is adopted, is her anger at her parents justifiable? Would the situation have been less awkward if Linda already knew that she was adopted? Or would most of her fears and worries still have existed?

2. Is Josie being selfish by wanting to get to know her daughter, especially since she believes she only has a few months to live? What if Josie never went to Lancaster County? Do you think Mary Ellen and Abe would have eventually told Linda about her adoption?

3. Have you ever known an adopted person who reconnected with their birth mother? Did it go well? Was a friendship or bond formed? How did each party react?

4. An unlikely friendship forms between Mary Ellen and Josie. Where do you see God's hand in this, and what did both Mary Ellen and Josie learn?

5. Josie's husband, Robert, is a non-believer, but a good man. What does Scripture tell us about good people who don't believe in God? What is happening to Robert by the end of the book?

6. Josie's healing was a miracle. Have you ever witnessed a miracle—medical or otherwise? Do you believe in miracles?

7. Think of all the lives that Jonas touched just by being himself. Who seemed to benefit the most from his wisdom?

8. Stephen worries that Linda might be tempted by life in the *Englisch* world. What are some examples depicted throughout the story? And why do you think Stephen was never interested in fully exploring his *rumschpringe* (running-around period)?

9. At Jonas's funeral, Katie Ann is upset because a woman named Lucy is there. Do you think this may have to do with Katie Ann and Ivan choosing to move to Colorado?

10. Jonas left letters for the people he loves. Have you ever known anyone who's done this? Why do you think Jonas did it?

11. What would make Samuel uproot his family and move to Colorado? Any speculations? Look for the first Land of Canaan novel—*Seek Me With All Your Heart*—due in stores November 2010.

Acknowledgments

IT'S AN HONOR TO DEDICATE THIS BOOK TO MY FRIEND, Barbie, in Lancaster County. A huge thank you, Barbie, for continuing to read each manuscript prior to publication. I'm so grateful for the time you spend helping me keep the books authentic and for the friendship we share. May God's blessings shine on you always.

Thank you to my friends and family for continuing to support me and understanding about the tight deadlines. Special thanks to my mother-in-law, Pat Mackey, for cooking for us twice a week.

And to my husband, Patrick . . . you're the best, baby. I couldn't travel this road without you by my side. I love you very much.

I'd like to thank Gary Leach, MD, for assisting me with the medical aspects in the book and for reading the manuscript prior to publication. Gary, I know this wouldn't normally be the type of book you would read, so it was extra special when you told me how much you enjoyed it. Much thanks, my friend, for taking the time to help me.

Karen and Tommy Brasher, Gayle Coble, and Bethany and Walter Guthmann—thank you all for hosting book signings each time a new book releases and for your continued support. You've all gone above and beyond, and I appreciate it so much.

Much thanks goes to my editor, Natalie Hanemann. You're so special, Natalie. A bright light in my world! Thanks for all you do to make my books the best they can be and for being my friend. I'm so blessed to have you in my life.

Jenny Baumgartner, I love working with you. Your warmth and kindness shine through in every email you send me, and your editing expertise makes my books shine. And I love hearing about your adventures with the twins. Thank you for everything. Peace and happiness to you and your beautiful family, always.

To my agent, Mary Sue Seymour—what a special friendship we share, and I hope we go shoe shopping again soon! Many blessings to you.

Renee' Bissmeyer, my angel on Earth, thanks for reading each manuscript behind me and for being my life-long best friend. Our friendship is blessed by God, and I'd be lost without you, my kindred spirit.

My fabulous family at Thomas Nelson, you guys and gals are the best! Thank you so much for all that you do.

To My Heavenly Father, you've blessed me way more than I deserve. Thank you for the stories You put in my head, tales that I hope will draw people closer to You.

Seek Me
with All Your Heart

Beth Wiseman is About to Take
Amish Fiction Readers to an Entirely
New Place . . . Literally!

The upcoming Land of Canaan Novels includes many
of the characters you love from Beth's Daughters of the
Promise series—as well as all new friends—in a fresh new
setting: Colorado. As the Amish families relocate to
Colorado for more land, they encounter challenges
that test their faith and their belief in love.

COMING NOVEMBER 2010

Author to Author

THE THOMAS NELSON FICTION TEAM RECENTLY INVITED our authors to interview any other Thomas Nelson Fiction author in an unplugged Q&A session. They could ask any questions about any topic they wanted to know more about. What we love most about these conversations is that it reveals just as much about the one asking the questions as it does the author who is responding. So sit back and enjoy the discussion. Perhaps you'll even be intrigued enough to pick up one of their novels and discover a new favorite writer in the process.

Beth Wiseman Interviews Kathleen Fuller, author of *A Man of His Word*

Beth Wiseman: As a fellow Thomas Nelson author of Amish fiction, what do you think fuels the success of this subgenre? Why do readers seem to have an insatiable appetite for books about Plain People?

Kathleen Fuller: I think part of it is that our lives have become so complicated and hectic. A lot of this has to do with technology and our culture's emphasis on a fast-paced lifestyle. The Amish live life at a slower tempo. They also exemplify that connection to community that the *Englisch* or *Yankee* don't always have. Their dedication to living in this world and not of it, supporting family and neighbor, and living lives that tend to be nostalgic—using a horse and buggy, no electricity, dressing plain—also appeal to Amish fiction fans.

BW: Your Hearts of Middlefield series takes place in Middlefield, Ohio. You have also authored two novellas—in collections with Barbara Cameron and me—that focused on Old Order life in Lancaster County, Pennsylvania. What are some of the differences between Amish life in Middlefield and Lancaster County?

KF: There are quite a few! All Ohio Amish drive the same type of black buggy, which differs from the gray square buggies used in Lancaster. The style of prayer *kapp* is different—Lancaster *kapps* are usually heart-shaped, while women in Middlefield wear rounded ones. Perhaps the biggest difference a visitor will find is that there aren't as many Amish cottage industries or farms in Middlefield, and the Amish and *Yankees* often live side by side. And as you've noticed, the Amish call the non-Amish *Yankees* instead of *Englisch*.

BW: What is the most interesting thing that you discovered in your research about the Old Order Amish, in Ohio or Pennsylvania?

KF: That we share more similarities than differences. The Amish have the same concerns we do about finding work, caring for their families, and serving God. The Amish have a reputation for being a stern people, but that's not the case. They like to have fun and enjoy life, just like we do!

BW: If you had an opportunity to live with the Old Order Amish, how long do you think you could go without all the modern conveniences that we *Englisch* are used to?

KF: I think I could do it, but it would be really hard, and I'd probably be wishing for my conveniences within a month.

BW: What is the one thing you couldn't live without if you were able to live amongst the Amish for an extended amount of time?

KF: I used to say my cell phone, but now I think it would be central air and heat. I don't like being too hot or too cold!

BW: What is most appealing to you about the Amish lifestyle?

KF: Their connection to their family and community, in addition to the slower pace of life.

BW: How does your own faith play a part in what you write? Is writing a spiritual journey for just the reader, or for you as well?

KF: Each book I write takes me on a spiritual journey. I often don't have a theme in mind when I start a book, but by the end God has spoken to me through my characters' trials and conflicts. I hope readers also find God speaking to them in some way through the stories.

BW: Who are some of your favorite authors?

KF: Francine Rivers, Bodie and Brock Thoene, Jenny B. Jones, Liz Curtis Higgs, and Claudia Burney.

For more information about Kathleen Fuller,
visit www.KathleenFuller.com or www.AmishHearts.com.